A SHIFTER VENGEANCE NOVEL

I0690818

NEVER EVER

SILAS REAMES

Copyright © 2023 Silas Reames
Night Loch Publishers LLC
All Rights Reserved

The characters and events portrayed in this book are fictitious. Any similarity to real persons, living or dead, is coincidental and not intended by the author.
No parts of this book may be reproduced, or stored in a retrieval system, or transmitted in any form or by any means, electronical, mechanical, photocopying, recording or otherwise without express written permission of the publisher.
Paperback ISBN: 978-1-961057-11-1
ISBN 13 Ebook: 978-1-961057-10-4
Nightlochpublishers.com

1
Who Else?

"Come again?" I shout in the Bone Reader's ever-changing face, too shocked to even make an inappropriate joke about what I've just said.

"His. Mate." The Bone Reader stresses the words, flipping one hand over to examine it. The fingers have short, rounded nails. They have long, pointed talons. It's impossible to tell, because the Bone Reader never wears any single feature for long, and he doesn't allow you to remember any of them once you leave the icy cave he calls home. "And he's rather put out about it, I should warn you. Thus why the dragon will be waiting and fuming on your couch when you arrive back to Sacramento."

Multiple thoughts hit at once. Memories of a certain steamy cave scene with Nahum, his pixies potentially trashing my house while they wait on me, and the part that stings the most. I let my vanity win out.

"Just what would make Nahum upset about having *me* as a mate? I'm fabulous, you know. He should be so lucky." I toss my head, forgetting for a moment that I'm wearing Were fur and not the silvery hair I have with my skin on.

"He *is* so lucky," the Bone Reader reminds me, multiple laughs echoing over each other as he finishes the statement.

The Bone Reader is never wrong, but even so ...

"How can you be so sure? I just got rid of one half-mate. I don't have time for another! And besides, Weres *choose* our mates. They're not fated. And dragons—" All right, folks, I'm stumped on this one. Dragons aren't big on sharing information about themselves in the supernatural world.

The Bone Reader gives a slow blink, eyes cycling between green, blue, magenta, and even chartreuse.

I sigh.

"Care to enlighten me as to how dragons do work, then, since you're so all knowing?"

"Dragons can have fated mates. It's only rare because *they're* rare. And alone. How often do you think two that are meant to be together just happen to find one another? A true tragedy in the magical world, if you ask me; so many fated dragons out there guarding their hoards and missing out on their mates. Then again, I never was particularly romantic; I'm pragmatic enough to see the benefit of placing the hoard first. It's far better business sense."

"Your bleeding heart is touching. Truly." I roll my eyes. "But still naught to do with me. In case it has escaped your all-powerful notice, I am no dragon. And I'm not even sure I buy that bull hockey." I don't want to buy it.

"Cross-species pairings aren't unheard of. You've been around long enough to know that. And if there aren't dragon mates, then where do you think baby dragons come from, hmmm? Please tell me I'm not going to have to provide a birds-and-the-bees lesson to a centuries-old, hardened enforcer?"

I huff, stamping a furred foot on the snowy ground of his home and beginning to pace. I can feel emotions thanks to my intuition, and I know he has the utmost confidence in everything he's said.

"And you're not *just* a Were, either. You're a vampire lady. An intuitive. The Defeater of the Claw." I roll my eyes at that last part. I had plenty of help from my friends and even the meddling magical government, the Magikai, for that one. And I only led the defeat of the Claw because my ex half-mate was running the organization, and I had vowed to hunt him down.

"Before this is all over you'll rise to be something even greater," the Bone Reader predicts, tone ominous. He pauses, and I wait for the melodic echoes of his voice to die out. Letting the Bone Reader draw me into deals because of my own need to know has cost me plenty. I let his baiting statement slide.

"And Nahum's plenty of things as well. A powerful nightmare dragon. An empath. A fellow survivor of the Isle," I supply, although it's likely the Bone Reader already knows as much. Darned ancient creature seems to know everything. Except my name. Then again, I don't know his, either.

The Bone Reader taps his nose, then points at me.

"Exactly. Some magical laws, traditions, whatever you'd like to call them, are species-based. Some are not. I'd wager that your connection has been forged because of your abilities. If you're worried about how the dragon might treat you, I can assure you he'll be different from your last mating experience. Dragons guard their hoards with the utmost care. Do you really think they wouldn't guard a mate with even more ferocity?"

Guard, he says. That's all well and good for him. But guarding doesn't just mean protecting. It means locking something away to keep it safe. Nahum and I both survived the Isle. And while we were mistreated, the Collectors were guarding us. Keeping us for themselves. Visions of bars, a prison, and chains roll around in my brain.

I clutch my neck, sucking in deep breaths.

"Well, that's just great!" I throw furred arms in the air, claws longing for something to shred. "I just got rid of one overbearing male. I'll not tolerate another!" I point an accusatory claw at the Bone Reader, as if he caused this. For all I know, he could have. Sneaky thing.

"I won't accept! I don't accept! I'm not falling into some male's arms like a helpless damsel. Not me. No sir. I have no need to be part of some Fates' damned power couple."

"You don't like him, then?" the Bone Reader questions as I reach a break in my tirade. I stop in my tracks, turning to stare down the mysterious magical.

"Well, that's. I mean. That's hardly the point. Completely *beside* the point, as a matter of fact. It's neither here nor there whether I *like* the dragon," I sputter.

"Really? And here I was under the impression that mated magicals often placed their immense love for each other over everything else."

Humor hits my intuition. He's toying with me. He finds this whole thing funny. But it's my life. And I just got it back.

I sigh, skin rolling back over me. The magical silver eyepatch the Bone Reader made to cover the wound where the Fates stole my eye shrinks to fit. Talented being, this Bone Reader.

I'm the only one alive who can read him, but sometimes it doesn't feel that way.

"I do like the dragon," I admit. Might as well get that out of the way. Moon knows it won't change things, but I can be honest with myself. "But I can't be his mate. I may have run down the Claw, but the Magikai are anything but thankful. Our sovereign government is one insult away from boxing me."

I shiver to make a point. Getting chained into a box and thrown into the depths of the sea to heal yourself for years and years? Not the way I'd like to go.

The Bone Reader nods along to my pronouncement, agreement rolling off of him.

"You did upset them rather thoroughly. Damien had already made them look foolish, going behind their backs to become leader of the Claw. Then a rogue enforcer bests all their other agents to take him out. They'll want to teach you a lesson." He walks closer. He's tall, short, muscled, and lithe. It's dizzying how fast he rolls through features.

"I'm about to walk into a viper's den here. I'm supposed to go train Ever. I'm already supposed to be there," I admit, even though, technically, that's not entirely true. I promised Amun, head of the Magikai, that I'd train the only other known intuitive Were. My deal stipulated that I would have until Halloween this year, and it's barely into March. When I managed to get rid of Damien early, though, the head representative's patience came to an end as well. He'll be livid that I dodged his forces and came up here instead of reporting straight to him. Well, tough. He can stew.

"I need to find a way around my agreement with our oh-so-magnanimous government; I can't also be fighting a dragon about whether I'm his mate. I'm not letting anyone sock me away like books in a library. Never to be seen in the outside world again. And I'm not taking my eyes off the Magikai. Something shady is going on there, mark my words, and I intend to find out what. And neither a dragon nor all the representatives and enforcers are going to stop me. No indeed, absolutely not, over my dead body," I ramble, back to pacing until I run into the Bone Reader as he steps into my path.

A chill that has nothing to do with my icy surroundings runs over me as I fight the urge to cower. Whatever the Bone Reader is, it's overwhelming.

He holds up a finger. Long and slender, short and callused.

"Funny you should mention 'over my dead body,' because there is one thing you might be interested to know—"

I hold up a hand in front of his mouth, which shifts from soft, plump lips to a thin, stern line. From a square jaw to an angled one, an inch from where my hand hovers.

"Not a word more," I caution him. "I'll figure the Magikai out myself. And Nahum. If that dragon wants to try and stake some kind of mate claim, he can bloody well do it himself, without you as some sort of intermediary. And woe to him the consequences."

The Bone Reader just smiles.

"As you say. Have it your way, then. But you should know you're in for some surprises."

"And that's what they'll remain. Surprises. I'm on to you, B.R." He frowns at the abbreviation. "All this 'free' information I've been handed by you. It all turned out to be pretty costly, if you ask me. So I'll hear whatever I'm going to hear straight from the dragon's snout. Thank you very much."

"If you prefer," is all he says, emotions neutral, as if he truly couldn't care less one way or the other. The only tell is that hint of amusement he lets off whenever I get on a tirade.

"Right. Well then, if that's all, I'll be on my way." I reach a hand up to feel the cooling metal of my new eyepatch. There's nothing more to be gained from staying. If anything, I've just got more to deal with than I did before. Who would've thought? You free yourself from a two-hundred-year-old vow by sending your ex to the Underworld, and that's the easy part. Now I've got an eye lost to the Fates, a dragon mate, friends who are undoubtedly anxious for my return, and a pissed-off magical government I've sworn my service to, even though I fully intend to use it as an investigative opportunity.

Potential Magikai overthrow, party of me.

No wonder I'm not looking forward to my trek home.

"And Never!" the Bone Reader's voice booms after me as I reach the entrance of the icy cave. I don't bother to turn. "Don't forget our deal. I'll send you the details in several months' time, but you owe me a ride. Be available to pick me up. Halloween, let's say ten p.m. Don't be late."

From one deal to another. I *never* learn. Maybe that's how I decided on this name?

2

Homecoming Highs and Lows

I am tired. Bone tired.

No? Not even a chuckle? Bone Reader? Bone tired?

Fine, I'll get on with it. Honestly, why does no one share my sense of humor?

Back to the point. I'm weary, exhausted, more than ready for a week's worth of naps as I make my way up my front steps in Sacramento. Common sense, and all my other senses, tell me that's not going to be an option. After all, I've kept everyone waiting.

In spite of my many to-dos, and to be honest more likely *because* of them, I did a bit of dilly-dallying on my way back from the Bone Reader's lair in Alaska. That is, if one can consider an extended, weeks-long road trip home through the Pacific Northwest along gorgeous coastal Oregon 'dilly-dallying.' I walked along the sand, stared out at the crashing waves, even gave Chrys's scream therapy a few tries. That witch knows her stuff. And only once did I terrify a few unsuspecting beachgoers as I screeched out to the waves. Felt a lot better afterward, though.

My favorite bear shifter and fellow enforcer Todd called a week ago, telling me several of the Magikai's enforcers were circling my block like vultures, but Chrys had kept them off the porch. Useful little defensive-spell witch. Even so, he'd been eager to have me back.

"Stop stalling and get your furred ass back here before the witch breaks herself trying to cover for you!" I believe were his exact words. Always so cryptic, that one, no idea what he was getting at.

I take a deep breath as I turn the doorknob to my own home, readying myself for whatever and whoever waits within.

"She's here! You guys, she's here!" My ears pick up on Aggie's excited squeal and proclamation, followed by the witchling shushing everyone. Perhaps the Bone Reader is right, and there is a dragon on my couch. But it seems he won't be the only one in my welcome party.

I push open the door to my entryway. The lights in the house are off, but sunlight streams across the floor through the open blinds. Smells assault me as my nose picks up on shifter and magic. Time to get this over with.

"Guess I'll make myself some coffee," I say, too loud, "then just sit alone."

Aggie titters from behind the couch, and I hear someone else shush her. Chrys, maybe?

"I sure do miss everyone. You'd have thought they'd have shown up to say hello once I got back," I lament as Aggie's giggles get louder. Terrible at surprises, that one.

And I *did* miss them on my trip to the Bone Reader. I just missed my mattress more, and the idea of entertaining them instead of falling into a deep slumber is draining me.

I walk into my living room, flopping into my soft papasan chair in a dramatic heap.

"Surprise!" Voices explode around me as several supernaturals pop up from behind the furniture. I leap up in faux surprise.

Someone really should tell Todd his big behind was visible from behind the couch. Someone, not me. I *am* shocked to spot his brother, the bear shifter king Rex, jump out from behind the other side of the couch. He's less enthused, mouth set in an uncertain half-grin.

"You guys! You shouldn't have!" I gush, hugging Aggie back as the witchling runs over and wraps her arms around me. Hugging is something I'm getting more and more used to with her around. Darned witchling reeks of affection most of the time. If she weren't a powerful stripper who could suck the magical ability out of supernaturals, I'd worry for her.

Standing off in a corner, even less enthused than Rex, is another familiar face. Full lips set in a flat line, purple eyes, black hair that's faded on the sides. Wingless for the moment. My dragon shifter. At least, 'mine' according to the Bone Reader. And if that's the case, I have my work cut out for me. Nahum scowls, arms crossed over his chest. Around him, some of his blue pixie friends flit and whir, smiling and chittering, in stark contrast to his stony countenance.

But I'll have to deal with him later.

"Never!" I'm enveloped in another hug, albeit a less squishing and squeezing one than the witchling managed. "*¡Sorpresa!*"

Nadia releases me and steps back, her brown eyes watery as she tucks a strand of hair behind her ear. Elated, but also stressed. Just goes to show, my intuitive mentee Were is smart. We're about to walk into the lion's den. Literally, given that the head representative of the Magikai is a barbary lion shifter. She should be stressed. I sure as hell am.

"Ever." I give her a toothy grin as I address her by her new and chosen name. Not sure how much good it's done her at concealing herself from those who would endanger her Colombian pack to get at her intuitive abilities, but I'll use it as asked until and unless she changes her mind.

She looks gaunt. There are circles under her eyes that shouldn't be anywhere near a face that's only nineteen years old.

"Rough homecoming?" I question.

She nods, one hand clutching her other arm.

"You could say that. The Claw stopped chasing me,"—because their leader was bent on dragging me involuntarily to his side as his mate—"but the Magikai kept sending enforcers to Colombia. If I'd known they were going to do that, I might have just agreed to go with them sooner. They kept popping up unannounced, and they've been bothering everyone. We don't do anything against the Magikai's laws, but the enforcers kept following pack members around, questioning them, insinuating that we have something to hide."

I clench a fist. "Bastards."

Ever had already promised to throw away her freedom to let the Magikai train her up as an enforcer. And *I'm* the one who asked for an extension on our start date. So I could chase down Damien and defeat the Claw. Which, if anyone was asking, helped the Magikai out quite a bit. Not that those self-important, moon's damned representatives care.

A palm covers my fist as Ever pushes it down.

"It's all right. I'm here now, so my family should be fine. I'll admit the Magikai were more insistent than I liked when they showed up and told me I needed to 'haul my Were behind' up to Sacramento immediately and wait for their word. That was a couple of weeks ago. I've been staying here with Aggie; I hope you don't mind."

I shake my head. I'd bet serious money the Magikai pulled that trick knowing someone would reach out to me once Ever was here. Would have known that I'd come back for her. I hate being predictable as much as I hate being under their thumb.

"I don't mind your being here in the slightest. I'm sure the Magikai have just been biding their time, waiting for me to make an appearance. Which reminds me, Chrys!"

The defensive-spell witch steps out from behind Ever, purple eyes already flickering with magic. She snaps her fingers.

"Already done. The Magikai representatives are not welcome through your defensive barrier." She blows her fingers like they're a smoking gun.

My mouth gapes.

"Simple as that?" Even with defensive spells being her key, the one set of magic she gets as a 'freebie' that she doesn't have to work for, things aren't that instantaneous.

She just giggles, adjusting her headwrap over her springy white curls.

"Of course not! I re-warded the house the minute you disappeared up to Alaska to see the Bone Reader. Silly Were. Honestly." I should have guessed that. I must be more sleep-deprived than I thought.

Chrys shakes her head as she walks off toward the others. So far, so good. And no one's even mentioned my eye. I reach a hand up and drum my fingers over the silver eyepatch in what is fast becoming a habit. I see Todd over in my kitchen; he dips his chin at me. Interfering bear. He told them not to say anything. I'm sure of it. Lynx is cutting slices of a large cake as Todd hands them out. Chocolate and raspberry? And a large wolf drawn on top of the cake.

"I'm *not* a wolf shifter," I yell over to Lynx. He just laughs.

"Sure, sure, we know that," the feline teases before letting out a howl.

All right, we do make some similar sounds.

Someone clears their throat, and a Were reveals himself, walking out of one of my hallways. In full fur. A gorgeous russet that catches the sun, and jewel-green eyes. Hugh.

My reliable vampire-turned-Were historian and knower of all things paperwork at my vamp mansion in Vegas. He may have been a willing volunteer, but without him I never could have paid back the Bone Reader. Never could have defeated Damien.

"Well?" He raises his arms and spins, tail swishing against my hardwoods. "What do you think?"

I reach a hand up and tap my chin.

"Why don't you tell me?" I counter, determined to settle something sooner rather than later.

Hugh shakes his head, the edges of his ears flopping up and down.

"I can't. Turns out your turning me didn't give me intuition. There's one mystery solved, right?"

He's ... relieved, and yet disappointed at the same time. Emotions are complicated like that.

I reach a hand out and thwack him on his shoulder, which is a good several inches above my head, since he's in his fur and I'm not.

Quick construction tip for all my aspiring Weres and shifters out there: vaulted ceilings and wide hallways. Trust me, kids, it saves so much on home repairs.

"Hugh. Now that you're one of the best kinds of magicals, I was hoping that. I mean, *I'm* a Were, and still lady of the Vegas coven. And I'm guessing you've got your furred hands full." I cast a glance over at Chrys, who stands watching us. "But I'm determined to convince you that—"

"I should remain on staff at the Vegas mansion as your legal advice-giver, vampire organizer, reader of books and knower of many things?" he asks, tilting his massive head and showing his fangs. He'll have to learn that smiling as a Were doesn't come off quite the same.

"Yes. That." I clear my throat. "And I won't take no for an answer! We're all in the cross-hairs now, and we've got to stick toge—"

"Deal." He reaches out a furred hand for me to shake, pleased as punch when I take it. "Now, if you'll excuse me. I haven't quite gotten used to this whole 'naked when shifting' bit."

He heads back toward the guest bedrooms.

"There's a spell for that! If you're willing to drain your savings!" I yell after him.

Ever brings a piece of cake to me, holding the chocolate and raspberry ganache–filled delicacy up like a peace offering. She's staring openly, but even if she weren't, I can feel the mix of awkward emotions.

"I'm sorry. That everything you did to keep the Claw away from me cost you so much. I didn't mean—"

I hold up a hand.

"Not your fault. Damien would have come after me, one way or the other. No stopping crazy." And now he waits in the Underworld, with the powers of a god. I take a deep breath. The Bone Reader promised Damien was no longer a threat to me, and I'm choosing to charge ahead as if I believe it, even if I can't quite manage to do that just yet. Fake it till you make it.

"But you *did* stop it," Ever insists, perhaps playing off my emotions. I'm thinking the same thing. She can pick up on how that makes me feel. There's one intuitive too many in this house.

"I did what was necessary to protect my family," I assure her, reaching to pull the young Were into a hug. I suppose I need practice, but I'm sure it's nothing Aggie can't fix. When I release her, she heads back to the kitchen, where most of the others are chatting around my counter.

I search for Nahum. He's not hard to spot. His pixies have fled to the kitchen, along with everyone else, and he's the lone presence left in my living room. He looks out of place standing there, silent and foreboding. Hard as steel as he refuses to settle on my soft and plush furniture.

I clear my throat and tilt my head to the side, indicating the front door. The dragon picks up on my meaning quickly enough and follows me outside. The sun is beginning to set, brilliant flashes of color lingering over the roofline of my home. I stare at that, instead of the sulking dragon.

"The Bone Reader warned me you'd be here," I say.

"I'd like to meet this mysterious magical," he intones aloud, and then, in my mind.

You realize if you didn't want us overheard I could have spoken to you like this?

I huff, hands on my hips.

"Yes, but I can't answer back that way. You told me once that it's just a generic dragon trick, speaking into minds. But you insisted that unless you're terrorizing people with their nightmares, you don't see what they're thinking."

He sighs. Resignation.

"I pictured starting this conversation quite a few ways, but this wasn't it. I still can't read your mind. But you can speak into mine if you want. Because we're mates."

I stare at him, hard, tensing all my muscles as I strain, willing my thoughts at him.

Well isn't that just peachy! Our own two-way radio. A fate-controlled walkie-talkie system that no one asked for.

"You're angry," he says aloud, dropping the mind-talk. I sigh, letting my muscles relax.

"Yes, and no. Not at you. At a lot of other things. And I can read that you're feeling the same. I know we've got to deal with this, and I know you've been waiting since I left Sacramento. But can you give me this night?"

He's silent, out loud and in his mind, several seconds before he responds. He inclines his head. He's also surprised. It's possible he wasn't expecting such a reasonable reaction. Not that I'm dramatic all the time. Just a lot of the time.

He dips his head.

"Of course. I'll leave you to your friends. If I return tomorrow, can you empty the house so we can have a private discussion on the matter?"

So formal, my mate. Not surprising, given he's a good eight or nine hundred years old. I don't know, and according to him he'd have to do the math to figure it out. Age truly is just a number when you're this old.

"Yes, I can manage that," I promise, relieved for once to not have to argue my way into, well, getting my way.

As I re-enter the house, Todd has abandoned the cake and whipped up a popcorn bar instead. Caramel, three different kinds of cheese, traditional butter and salt, and one covered in chocolate coating and tossed with candy. A connoisseur of snacks.

"I take this to mean I'll be enjoying your company for the remainder of the evening?" I raise a brow at him.

"As if you could ever get sick of me." Todd nudges me with a wink, flopping onto the couch and dragging me down next to him. The bear has grown on me.

"Movie night?" Lynx questions as he joins us, munching on all the types of popcorn thrown into a bowl together.

"And you question *my* tastes?" I demand, sticking my tongue out at his popcorn concoction. He just shrugs.

"What's on the agenda?" I ask, single eye scanning my guests. "Never mind, I'm choosing!" I leap off the couch and run to my DVD—*yes*, D.V.D.—collection, snagging an old favorite.

"*Hello, Dolly,*" I announce as I put in the disc. Confusion buffets me from most of the others. "Don't tell me you haven't seen it?" Only Hugh and Rex's hands raise. I throw my head back. Truly,

I have to do everything in this group. Including educating the youth—along with Todd and Lynx—on classic films.

"An old musical—really, Never?" Lynx groans as the credits start up.

"Hey!" I lean over Todd from where I've taken my place back on the couch and smack his hand. "Show this film some respect!" He rolls his eyes, and I'm about to dive into the history of each and every actor.

Hugh may not have intuition, but perhaps he can sense the onset of a tirade.

"I've seen it. And I agree, it's quite good," he says. No one else argues, and we settle in.

A reasonably normal evening, after everything I've been through.

But I've got a dragon waiting, and the Magikai aren't patient.

My clock is ticking.

3

Unwanted Escorts

"You've reached Never. Lady of the Vegas coven, defeater of the Claw, unrivaled intuitive Were and owner of a fabulous set of hips and lips. Now, kindly explain who you are and why in all the circles of hell you're waking me up this early in the moon's forsaken morning!" I let my tone slip from flirtatious to fiery as I snap into my cell.

Indignation. Whoever is on the other end has their feathers up. Good. I was up until after two in the morning, and I had every intention of sleeping in until lunch, not rising before the sun.

"This sort of behavior is exactly why you need this retraining. Get yourself up and presentable. And let your enforcer escort in. Now." Amun's words are tense, like he's clenching his jaw on the other side of the line. The head representative of the Magikai gets angrier and angrier with each syllable.

Is he going to be at the Magikai's headquarters when we arrive? This just gets better and better. I'd like to tear him a new one, but I've got Ever to consider as well. And at the moment, everyone packed into my house. Lynx and Hugh are sacked out in one guest room. Chrys, Aggie, and Ever squeezed into the other.

I throw off my covers with a scowl, ignoring the request to make myself presentable and padding down the hall in grey sleep shorts and a cream tank top that would be translucent in the right lighting.

"If you had called ahead, I could have removed my defensive spell and let your enforcer find their own way in," I hiss into the phone, settling on something between annoyance and all-out hostility.

"The head of the Magikai does not have to explain himself to underlings," Amun snaps. I just manage to hit the mute button as I snarl into the phone. It vents my frustration, and he doesn't need to know. I click it again when I'm done having an outburst.

"I'll let them in," I respond, my voice syrupy sweet and false.

"Good. And don't think this rebellious behavior can continue. It stops now, Never."

I end the call before he can. I grumble as I pass the couch, where Todd has an arm thrown over his face and is snoozing away. His brother is nowhere to be seen. Left early? My home is a mess. Not my usual M.O. I actually prefer a calm environment to balance the chaos that lives in my mind, but Amun wanted fast, the prickly old lion.

I tug open the front door and stalk across the lawn to the end of Chrys's boundary. I can't see anyone.

"Hey!" I yell into the not-quite-light sky. "This way, genius. Follow the voice." I turn and walk back to the house without stopping to see if anyone's following. By the time I reach my own steps I can hear someone behind me. I spin and find myself face to face with a familiar enforcer.

"Oh, they sent *you*." I frown at Brutus, the Magikai's head enforcer and general jerk.

"You lost an eye!" the wolf shifter blurts, pointing at my face.

"Well, score one for observation. At least there's something you're good at!" I snark, walking into my house and slamming the door in Brutus's freckled face.

"Never!" he yells through the solid wood. "Never, be reasonable!" He's giving off an odd mix of annoyance and humility. Perhaps because the last time we came in contact I saved the over-important head enforcer's behind. Chrys did the majority of the work, to be fair. Still, I'd warned him he was woefully underprepared to take on the Claw. I'd been right.

He could have cost us the whole battle. And Brutus? A betrayer? Come on now, that name alone says it all.

"Never! Come on, please," he pleads as he starts banging on the door. I can tell by the hesitance that niceties aren't something he's good at. I put a hand to my forehead and squeeze. Haven't had to do that since the last time I was around the Magikai. Brutus is going to wake the house, if he hasn't already. I glance behind me, but either Todd's asleep or he's an excellent faker. I can't tell whether I catch him peeking out from under his arm or if he's just adjusting his position.

"Fine!" I hiss as I open the door and bare my teeth at Brutus. "Fine. Just shhh and come in."

"Hi." He lifts a hand in a wave, a small blush running over his freckled cheeks and across his nose as he gives a sheepish half-smile.

The wolf shifter is tall. Broad-shouldered with a squared jawline, and fair skin. The freckles would make him look sweeter if he weren't such a pompous ass. Although, now that he's been admitted to the house, he's all relief and awkward uncertainty. Perhaps there's room for improvement?

The beginnings of a plan start to form.

"Have a seat, won't you, Brutus?" I sweep an arm out, indicating the loveseat that sits kitty-corner to where Todd is resting. Suspicion washes over me as he frowns but walks over to it. He flops down, spreading his arms along the back of the piece of furniture.

"Coffee?" I offer, giving him a smile that I hope looks welcoming and not feral.

"No. I don't drink the stuff. A magical's body is an elite weapon. It shouldn't rely on substances like caffeine to function."

Deep breaths, Never, deep breaths. Don't hit him with the coffee pot.

"Is that so? I'll have to keep that in mind," I respond, before ignoring the advice and heading straight to my coffee grinder. I let out a sigh of pure bliss at the smell of fresh grounds. One positive about house guests; someone thought to run the grinder last night. It's a loud contraption.

I'm convinced Amun sent Brutus on purpose just to piss me off. The lion's lashing out like a child with a stolen toy. I did intend to come straight home from the Bone Reader's. At first. Every time I felt the urgency to get back sooner, I envisioned Amun demanding my immediate presence. That normally bought me a few more days of dawdling just to shove it in his furry face.

Maturity; it's practically my middle name.

"Coffee? Already?" Ever stumbles down the hall, rubbing her eyes. The dark circles are faded, but still there.

"Of course. Only the best for my favorite Were." I hand over the cup I intended for myself. Am I the most selfless being I know? Not hardly. But this *is* a huge sacrifice which someone should note. "Moon knows it's understandable you'd need the rest and caffeine after being harried and harassed by the Magikai's little stooges for months." I level a glare at Brutus, who blushes again.

"It wasn't me! I was busy preparing for the battle against the Claw and then cleaning up the aftermath. And don't think I've forgotten how you called me *unprepared*," he accuses, scowling at me.

"You *were* unprepared! Had you even seen any real battles prior to that?" I throw my arms up as I stalk toward him. Todd's sitting upright on the couch now, the silent observer to this whole spat. Without a word, he pushes himself up and walks behind the wolf's back and down the hall. For reinforcements, or to hold off the impending flood of magicals?

"I've been on assignments."

"But have you seen actual battles. Between two large groups?" I demand again.

"Training drills," Brutus mutters.

"Not the same as real experience. Lucky for you, I will soon be at the Magikai headquarters to offer my expertise. And I'd be more than happy to offer you some lessons—"

"I don't need lessons!" Brutus protests. I wave a finger at him.

"You and I both know that's a lie. You know how I know?" I tally the points on my fingers. "One, I've seen you fight. Two, the Magikai must have had a reason for setting you up to blunder so spectacularly, so you have to know *they* don't have your best interests at heart. And three, I can *feel* that you're aware you need lessons, because I. Am. An. Intuitive. Let's cut the back and forth and skip to the part where you agree to my magnanimous offer."

I reach over and rap him on his forehead with my fist a few times before leaning back and folding my arms over my chest. He rubs at the spot, even though there was no force behind it and I'm well aware wolf shifters are more durable than that.

"Yeah," he puffs out a sigh, "all right. For the good of the other enforcers, I'll work with you." The response has cost him. I can feel it. And he also means it when he says he'll do it for the good of those under him. It's that sentiment that has me reaching toward his offered hand to close this deal.

I pull it back at the last moment and a growl escapes him.

"As soon as you promise to have all the enforcers who tailed Ever and her pack apologize," I amend.

"Apologize?" Brutus yells, cheeks pinking.

"And send my family a fruit basket or something to make amends." A voice pipes up behind me from where Ever has just sidled into the kitchen. The Wereling is gleeful as she sips her coffee and stares down the head enforcer.

"Stubborn, exasperating Weres," Brutus grumbles, but he holds his hand back out. "Fine. Fine. It's a deal."

"Marvelous!" I take his hand and shake before he can rethink things. It's not a magically binding deal by any means, but intuition gives me the benefit of knowing that he takes it seriously. He's not intending to renege on his side. At least not now.

He sighs.

"Now can we get on to business?"

I nod. "Certainly."

"Good. I need you two to pack your bags, and we'll head out. I'll have transportation ready and waiting for us, and then this evening we can—"

I hold a hand out, stopping my palm less than an inch from his nose. He stares, wide-eyed, over my fingertips.

"Sorry, Brutus old chum, but I must be misunderstanding. Seems you think we're leaving today. And that's *not* happening. Now, here's how this is going to go down. Ever and I will take the rest of the day to settle things. Pack, relax, sort things out for our absence. We'll get a good night's sleep, which we were robbed of thanks to your arrival this morning. Then, and *only* then, will I give *you* a call when we're up tomorrow, at which time you can tell us where to meet you for this transport." I drop my hand, grinning at him.

"What she said," Ever quips from behind me, leaning over my shoulder and smiling at the wolf shifter.

Brutus is flabbergasted. And folks, I *love* whenever my intuition picks up this particular emotion, just because it's so fun to say. Flabbergasted. Flabber-gasted. Flabb-er-gasted. Try it.

Go on, I'll wait.

See? Fun. Some words are just like that. *Discombobulated* is another one. Anyway ...

Back to Brutus, if we must.

"And what am *I* supposed to do? Call Amun and tell him you're refusing to come?" the shifter demands. He's more than a little nervous at the idea. I really do think there's something to the Magikai setting him up. Amun's a pain in my tail, but he's not stupid. He wouldn't have sent an inept leader unless he wanted that leader to fail.

"No, not refusing. Just delayed. And don't call him. If I were you, I'd set myself up in a nice hotel for the night. Maybe one with a spa? I can make a few recommendations. Schedule a massage or something. Perhaps a facial? Enjoy yourself for once. I'd imagine being around the representatives, you don't get the opportunity often. And you're free to relay to Amun that I'm being as difficult as always. He'll be expecting that. Hell's moon, if I didn't refuse your first offer I think he'd be mightily suspicious. Really best for us all if we do it my way," I reason.

"It's not a negotiation!" Brutus sputters, even as I move around the kitchen counter and nudge him out of his seat, guiding him toward the door with an arm over his shoulder.

Now, I want to clarify something here, people. No means no. Yes means yes. Consent.

But in the case of shoving a shifter out your door, who's in sore need of a vacation but reluctant to piss off his boss? He just needs a little push.

"Never. Do not shut this door on me!" Brutus bellows.

"You'll have an excellent time! I'll call ahead to the Moon's Moore hotel for you and reserve you a room. Personal favorite of mine."

"No. Never—"

"Toodaloo, then!" I sing-song, waving as I shut the door in his face.

Flabbergasted, folks.

But he doesn't try to get back in.

"Guess that sorts him out." Lynx grins, sliding into the head enforcer's empty seat and snagging a pancake from across the counter. Todd's managed to slip into the kitchen and start breakfast while I've been handling our uninvited guest.

"Now all that remains is to sort you lot out. As in, out of my house. *After* breakfast—I'm not a monster. But once that's through, pack it up and pack it in here, people." I snag the next pancake before it can even settle on the plate, eating it out of my hand.

Lynx stares, aghast.

"What is wrong with you?" he demands.

"Don't get me wrong, kitty cat. I'm thrilled to see all of you, but I've got some dragon business to settle before I deal with the Magikai."

"Not that! You didn't even use syrup!" he moans, gesturing at the pancake hanging from my fingers.

"Say no more, Never. You need privacy. We get that," Chrys states as she and Hugh join the meal. She snags a chocolate chip pancake. Hugh follows suit.

Chrys waves her hand, blue bubbles flashing and popping as they float around the perimeter of my rooms.

I wave a hand as one passes by my face, shooing the magic away.

"Just what did you do to my house witch?" I demand.

"Soundproofing. For you and the dragon. You. Are. Welcome." She winks as she takes a bite out of her pancake. When she's finished, she grabs for Hugh's hand.

Her fingers are intertwined with his as she saunters out of the house. Now, there's a female who's certain. I've seen a lot of magical relationships, both mates and messes. Including my own. And I'm here to tell you, you'd be shocked how often resistance is the first response to feelings. Mine is much more typical than hers.

When the meal is finished and my kitchen spotless, thanks to Todd, we go through the parade of goodbye hugs at my door. Me, a hugger. Who knew?

"So, you can stay with the bears for tonight and Todd will drop you back off tomorrow," I clarify to Ever.

"When will we see you again?" Aggie questions, the last to leave. She sniffles, poor emotional witchling. She's been by my side since I first took the case to find Ever.

I start to give her a wink, then settle on a grin when I remember my eye patch.

"Don't worry about that, witchling. I've got something up my sleeve." Because Amun needs me more than I need him, and I have the perfect demand to remind him of that fact. "You're welcome to stay here while I'm gone, or you can hang at the vamp mansion."

"Actually, I had something I wanted to ask her about while we're near my brother's territory," Todd states. I shrug.

"Fine by me. But, if you're available, plan to be at the vamp mansion in Vegas. Shall we say, a month from now?"

"What exactly do you have planned?" Todd presses, curiosity growing. "You're up to something."

"Todd, darling, friend, pal. I am *always* up to something. Call this a hunch. I think we'll need a place away from prying eyes to do some plotting. I just don't know what the plotting is for yet. Or who we're after. Or what they're doing wrong. Or how we'll fix it."

"Of course you don't. Some hunch," Todd mutters as he exits the porch.

"But I intend to find out!" I call after them as they make their way across the lawn.

Amun *is* up to something, and I *will* find out what.

But first, I'm going to call a dragon.

4

Timing is Everything

I can feel his presence on the property the moment he lands. I step out the front door to see Nahum zipping up a pair of pants, wings tucking behind him.

"Where'd you stash those?" I gesture toward the jeans as the wings disappear and he pulls a fitted black tee over his head.

"Stashed them," he mutters, with his head halfway inside the shirt. "Next to a tree in your yard. Figured my arriving naked might send the wrong message."

Or the right message.

Not the time, Never, I chastise myself.

I shake my head, clearing away the lustful thoughts. Business first. Because if that doesn't get settled, there might not be anything else to address.

Now, one might think that two mature magical beings would be able to get straight to the heart of the matter. And if that one is you, then you'd be wrong. After I show Nahum in, we stand an awkward distance apart in the entry. No hugs or handshakes, just off-putting unease. After he declines my successive offers of a beer, a coffee, and tea, I've run out of things to say.

"So." *Oh yeah, great start. If I keep going at this rate we'll get everything cleared up by next Christmas.*

"So," he responds, not doing any better than I am. He moves to the couch and sits, and something about the motion puts me more at ease. Even though I can feel the tension coming off him in waves, he at least *looks* the tiniest bit more relaxed. In spite of him declining my earlier offer, I grab each of us a water, just to have something to do with my hands. I walk the cups over to him, and he grabs one and takes a long sip. As he does, I go across the room and plop myself down in my papasan chair.

He clears his throat, and I bite my tongue and wait for him to start things. Maybe this doesn't have to be so awkward after all.

"Almost a thousand years of existence and I get a mate. This is terrible timing," he sighs.

Or, maybe it does.

"Well, excuse me for existing!" I snap. "You're not the only one inconvenienced by this, you know? I just got rid of one almost-mate. Who says I wanted another one so soon? Moon knows the last one was overbearing enough for a lifetime." My affrontedness is getting the better of me, but can we all agree he's being less than charming right now? I mean, hell's bells, is it too much to ask for a little enthusiasm on the dragon's part?

He growls, the sound reverberating from deep in his chest. I can feel the vibrations from my seat. Or maybe that's his sharp increase of denial in the face of my words.

"Make no mistake, Never, I don't think to control you. You're your own Were, and have been for centuries. That being said ... you have only *one* mate. Me. No other. No matter what you've done or who you've been with. It doesn't matter. You are the only one."

I press a hand against my chest, trying to pass off my very real swoon as faux shock and drama.

"Really? A big, bad, possessive male speech? You think that's going to work on me?" I demand, pushing down the part of me that finds said speech rather enticing when it's coming from an attractive dragon. A dragon without whose help I would never have defeated the Claw.

"This is all coming out wrong. I'm no good at this." Nahum moves towards me, wrapping my hands in his larger ones, his claws tracing across the back of my hands. "I didn't expect this. It's not that I don't want it; it just complicates things. And, truth be told, I don't have any better idea how to be a mate than you. Dragon mates don't come around every day."

"Yes, yes. The magic of fated mates." I just manage to bite back a *spare me*. It's not his fault his species has fated mates. It's just another magical quirk, like my intuition or his empathy. And I can't deny a strong pull toward him in spite of the fact Weres don't have an equivalent. We may get to choose our mates, but boy, did I pick a doozy last time. My own judgment counts for nil.

"Do you know why dragons are dying out?" he asks, distracting me from the topic at hand. I let myself be pulled up from the chair and down onto my own couch, sitting next to him and leaning into his chest. He's comfortable, in spite of our circumstances.

"Because you're too busy hoarding to have se—"

"Because there are so few mates," he interrupts, "and yes. Dragons are consumed by their hoards, and their own company. It takes something very strong to pull us out into the open. In truth, I suspected as much when you convinced me so easily to leave my island and go after the Magikai. I should have known, but as I said, I wasn't anticipating this. I haven't heard of another dragon mating in decades. And there's so few of us; they're certainly needed."

I shoot him a glare, poking a finger into his chest.

"Listen here, dragon. Let's set something straight right now. I'm willing to consider you and me. To be open to some kind of relationship, but I am not going to sit at home on some dragon's hoard, popping out baby dragonlings for the good of the species. That's not me."

He shakes his head.

"I know that. I'm just surprised. Weres have a low population count because of their fights with witches and being hunted down during the witch trials." I already know this. And the USA even less, which I only recently discovered was thanks to my last half-mate warning others away from settling here. All so I'd stand out and be easier to hunt down.

Crud, the dragon's still talking. This is what happens when you let your mind wander, friends. You miss things.

"And I've heard rumors that many of them left for Fae with some of the other species," Nahum finishes.

That's new. Fae? Like a place? I give an internal shrug. If the Underworld is real, why not some fairy realm. But I deal with what's in front of me. And right now, the dragon is here.

"Listen, what's done is done. Fate, the moon, spirits … whatever. It's been decided. But that doesn't mean we don't have a say. There's no secret dragon ritual that has to be completed immediately, right?" I realize as the words roll off my tongue that there damned well could be. Turning a Were operates on a schedule. Why not this?

"No. There's no time limit attached to dragon mates." Vague but sincere. I breathe out a sigh of relief. Finally, I catch a break.

"Good. Then why don't we table this for now? Circle back, as corporate humans are wont to say?"

He taps a clawed finger against his chin, but he needn't bother. I can feel he's made up his mind.

"All right. But I *would* like to make a deal with you."

"What kind of deal?" I scrunch my face up at him. After what happened to my eye, I'm more than a bit wary of deals.

"I would like to date you," Nahum responds, the arm around my waist tightening as he hauls me all the way onto his lap. The statement is free of conceit or complications, as far as my intuition can tell. I'm getting something else, though. A feeling I haven't encountered in ages. Is this, chivalry? Consider me surprised. I thought it had all but disappeared in this century.

"What's in it for you?" I press.

"I should think that would be obvious. Time with you. I'm open-minded, and I would never press you into something, not even this. That being said, I'd be a fool to not at least try to court my mate. Get to know me; you might like what you find."

I already like him plenty, but I've made that mistake before. Still ...

"How many dates?" I demand, determined not to be tricked this time.

"How long are you working on this deal with the Magikai?" he counters.

"Hard to say. My original deal stated a year. I assume they'll try to find a way around that, but I have no intention of renegotiating."

"Then give me twelve dates. Even with my plans to infiltrate them and yours to undermine them, surely two accomplished magicals can manage one monthly item added to their social calendars?"

He's being so reasonable. So charmingly, beguilingly, unproblematically reasonable, and yet ...

"I didn't think dragons kept social calendars," I counter.

"We don't, but it seems I have multiple priorities now."

He puts a claw under my chin, tipping my face up to look at him. With my eye.

My one eye.

I cringe as I remember, twisting my face away. Self-confidence is not an area where I'm used to finding myself lacking.

"You are beautiful. You. For who you are. You are physically stunning, it's true. But it was your spirit that pulled me out of that cave. Your bravery and determination to take down your foes, to protect those close to you. Not your face."

"It was a nice face," I grouse, even as the compliments warm me. Once I hit Magikai headquarters I'll need to drop my pity party and put on a strong front, but I can allow myself another day.

"It *is* a nice face," Nahum growls, voice rumbling so close to mine I can feel the vibration across my lips.

"Twelve dates," I agree, and then press my lips on his to seal the deal.

When I do, his growl deepens, and I hear shredding as his wings rips his shirt to tatters.

Now, a lady doesn't kiss and tell.

But I think we've all established that I'm no lady.

So I *will* tell you that I'm very lucky I emptied out my house and have a witchy-barrier to keep the neighbors from overhearing what we get up to for the remainder of the afternoon.

Hours later, we've made the rounds from the couch, to the shower, and back out again. We're wrapped under a blanket on the papasan, and I've made us both espressos.

"Where will you be, during this year with Ever and the Magikai?" Nahum asks, taking a sip. The small cup and dainty movements look almost as ridiculous in his large hands as they do in Todd's.

I shrug. Details evade me. I'm prolonging the few moments where I can pretend we're some average couple content to relax on the couch. It's not the life I'd really want, but it's nice to escape every so often.

34

SILAS REAMES

"I assume they'll be taking me to their headquarters. The location's secret, but I've got it on good authority it's somewhere in Europe. I'm fairly certain it's Italy." *Good authority* being clues and snippets I've picked up during my many years working for them as an enforcer.

He nods his head, claw tapping against his face again. A nervous tell, or just a thoughtful one?

Thoughtful, my intuition decides.

"I already reached out to a representative that lives closer to my island. I'm waiting to hear back from them about an invitation to meet with the head representative."

"And just how will you manage that?" I ask, tapping him on the nose. The dragon works fast.

"Offering them some of my rare texts. And if that doesn't work, charm." He flashes me a smile, tone seductive.

A brief flare of anger rises in my chest at the thought of him charming those smarmy Magikai secretaries. I shove it down. Weres are possessive by nature, but I haven't even agreed to this mate thing.

"You'd give up your books?" I ask instead.

"A small sacrifice to find out what's really going on. Dig into what they did with the rest of the Claw after you finished with them. Ask around about how they managed to hunt down all the Collectors." He rattles the information off as if it's nothing, but I can feel how much it costs him. He's in real agony at the thought of giving away those books, but he's doing it. For me. For a path I set him on.

"You know. You do bring up a good point. Enforcers, me, random magicals, me again. We always seem to do the work digging up these villainous groups and managing things. And yet, the Magikai are the ones who swoop in and clear up the aftermath. Along with any spoils, and any knowledge of what happens to the evil-doers. Doesn't seem right, does it?"

"And you're just now picking up on this?"

I slap him, not hard, on the chest.

"I've been just a bit busy these last couple centuries. Collectors, Claw, Damien, new intuitive Were, and countless regular enforcer contracts. But the Magikai now have my undivided attention." Well, they're on my radar. *Undivided* might be stretching it. I'm still juggling a few different things here. Which reminds me.

"Any chance you could pop by the Isle on the way back to your island?" I know he hates the place; we both do, after what we suffered there. But I have a purpose. "I have a gift for Meeri and Ardus that I need delivered." The two humans, and their ancestors before them, have guarded the Isle since I destroyed the place. And without them we never would have found the information needed to defeat the Claw. Nor would I have met the dragon I can't decide what to do with.

"Already done." Nahum grins. "When I first arrived here, you were off in Alaska. I got a bit restless waiting, and your bear shifter friend indicated I could make myself useful instead of 'darkening the hall with my foul mood.'" I grin. That does sound like Todd.

"You should know they sent back pastries for you. But since you were gone, the others ate them all."

I nearly weep at the loss of Meeri's delectable baked goods. My own fault for taking so long to get back.

We linger a little longer, but ultimately even I run out of excuses.

Brutus may get under my skin, but a promise is a promise. I told him today. When the light coming into my living room gets low enough to signal that sunset isn't far off, I throw myself off the couch and walk to my bedroom to toss a few things into a bag.

"There's one other thing I wanted to ask. To test. Before I go," Nahum says behind me. I turn to find him leaning against the doorframe, and he still hasn't donned a replacement shirt.

"Mmmhmm."

"When you ... when Damien ... during your fight. I flew here after waking on my island. My eye felt like it was on fire. Glowed purple for hours." It's what his body does when he inflicts pain. He feels the same amount himself. A terrible, unique magical trait that also happens to make him invincible.

"You're saying, you felt *my* pain? Even though you didn't inflict it?"

He puts one hand up, rubbing the back of his neck. Uncomfortable.

"I think so. And before you head off to some training facility where you may be putting yourself in danger, I'd like to know what we're dealing with. But I don't want you to have to hurt yoursel—"

I walk over to the first door in my hall, leading to a bathroom. I put my hand up on the doorframe and slam the door shut on my fingers, yowling as they're struck by the wood.

"Well?" I hiss, my teeth clenched against the discomfort as my fingers start to heal themselves. I register only the tiniest discomfort from him, but he's used to this kind of pain.

He holds up his hand.

Purple veins all through his fingers.

"Damn. I guess that answers that." I hold my healed hand up, flexing my fingers as the purple fades from his. "I only hope it doesn't happen when *I* hurt people. 'Cause I have to tell you, dragon, that might be a problem. And it's not a theory I'm testing until I find someone who deserves to take the hit."

"Fair enough," Nahum concedes. "Just. And I know this is a big ask for you. But try. Try not to put yourself in too much danger."

No promises this time.

5
You've Got To Be
Kidding Me

Brutus may have blustered about my shipping him off to a hotel, but I think I'm winning him over. When I get around to calling him, he's full of excuses. I think the wolf shifter is secretly enjoying his short vacation.

"Too late in the day to get ahold of my pilot. We'll have to go first thing in the morning." The dishonesty leaks out of him like he's a sieve. But I'm not going to say no to one more night's sleep in my own comfy bed.

Bright and early the following morning, he calls with a location.

I have my duffels thrown over one shoulder and Ever's over the other as we trudge across the tarmac to a waiting plane. Private charter. Very nice. I wouldn't imagine the Magikai representatives sending themselves in anything less, but I'd rather thought they were put out enough at my rebellion that they might just tell me to walk my way to their headquarters.

It appears that, for once, I was mistaken. I follow Brutus onto the plane, sniffing and clearing the cabin before waving Ever onboard.

Can't be too careful. As we settle in, my thoughts drift to Nahum and when he'll hear back from his own Magikai contact. Wonder where he's at. Dragon might be halfway across the country by now. He's a fast flier.

After the duffels are stowed and I'm leaned back in an acceptably cushy chair, popping open a bottle of champagne that's been left in the plane, I turn back to the head enforcer.

"So then. Where are we headed? Come on, Brutus old pal, you can tell me. Greece? Rome? I've always suspected a European stronghold." I pepper him with questions as we ascend.

"No," is all I get back. A truthful no.

"Cairo? Perth? Greenland? Canada?"

He shakes his head to every single one.

"Not quite."

"South America?" Ever puts forth once we've reached cruising altitude.

"Wrong again," he states, quashing her hopes.

"Glass of champagne, Brutus?" I ask, trying another tack. Direct questioning is clearly not the way to go.

"No. Thank you. A wolf shifter's mind needs to stay sharp and alert. And—"

"Yes. Yes. I get it," I retort as I pour myself another flute of the stuff. This is going to be a *long* plane ride.

"Prepare for descent." The captain's voice crackles from the cockpit.

"Is something wrong with the plane?" Ever all but screams, hands clamping down on her armrests. I take a deep breath. It's possible she's feeding off the unease that's engulfed me with the announcement.

"What gives, Brutus? We've hardly been in the air an hour."

"Looks like the training grounds weren't as far as you thought," the wolf replies, smug. I set the champagne down and scramble across the empty seat next to me, pulling up the window shade.

"Oh, hell no," I mutter as we descend. Landing at a small private airport. It's surrounded by red dirt, rocks, and cacti. They've dropped us in the middle of a desert.

"Now what?" I demand once we've deboarded and snagged our bags.

"Now? We walk," Brutus responds, throwing his shoulders back and taking a long drink from a water bottle.

I already regret agreeing to this plan.

"Why in all of hell's damned moon is it so hot here?" I fling my head back, loath to even shake out my hair because the bottom layer is stuck in a sweaty mat against my neck. The three of us are trudging across the Arizona terrain. In the middle of moon's forsaken nowhere. We left the airport behind what feels like forever ago and have been walking through the wilderness since we lost sight of it.

"Haven't you said before, Weres can handle extreme temperatures? Weres can handle the outdoors? Weres are rugged? Something like that?" Ever intones from next to me, grunting as she lugs along a suitcase. It can't be heavy for her, just cumbersome. Her duffel is stuffed to the brim, whatever's inside poking out at odd angles. I grab the handle and throw it over my shoulder.

"Yes. I may have said those things. But hell's bells, it is April!" I moan, glancing up at the unforgiving sun and giving it a glare. Underworld's real. Who knows what else? If there really is a sun deity up there, I hope they can feel my wrath. We would not be friends if this is how they insist on treating people.

"May starts next week. And not that I blame you, but if you'd come back from Alaska sooner, we'd have been here sooner," Ever reminds me, cheery now that I've got her pack. She pulls her long brown hair up into a ponytail.

"Even so! Who in their right mind is happy about ninety-plus Fahrenheit in the spring? Hmm?"

"And this whiny Were is supposed to be the one who's going to teach me how to improve my fighting? Moon preserve us," Brutus mutters as he marches along in front of us. Bothersome male hasn't even broken a real sweat. He's just got a thin sheen glistening on his skin.

"I assume you're used to this rotten environment." I throw the comment at him with all the sass of an insult.

He looks over his shoulder with a smile.

"It would seem there are some situations I *am* better prepared for than you."

I let out a low growl.

Ever rolls her eyes but doesn't say anything further. There's no need. She can read my discomfort, just as I can read that I'm alternately annoying and amusing her. The curse and benefit of both being intuitives.

When we reach the compound, it's obvious that it's nothing to write home about. Cabins and canvas buildings are thrown up in the middle of the desert heat. The cabins are covered in dust, weathered and worn enough that they could be repurposed one-room schoolhouses from a hundred years ago, for all I know. The canvas structures are little more than tents with cement floors. There's only one modern building, glinting at the far end of the property from where Brutus has us drop our duffels.

"They didn't care much for scenery when choosing this place, huh?" I ask.

"There's not very much water to speak of out here, and we're conveniently located near the only good source. I think that's a good thing."

Brutus and I have very different definitions of 'good'. I've handled tougher situations before, but sunburns, dehydration, sandy lodgings full of who knows what desert critters? Not high on my list of desired traits in my accommodation.

"May as well show us the training grounds. Unless there's somewhere air-conditioned we could stop for a drink?" What I wouldn't give for Elios and his cocktails. I cast my gaze toward the one modern building, but Brutus dashes those hopes quick enough.

"Nope. Three meals a day. Set times. And limited drinking. They turn one of the tents into a bar on the weekends." He disapproves.

"We've entered hell," I mutter as we follow him across the grounds. I don't even dream of throwing my fur on. Too. Hot.

Ever is hesitant as Brutus points out all the main attractions—which include the aforementioned dining-tent-slash-weekend-bar, and cabins where new enforcers sleep. She's eager, though. In spite of the setting, I know she's wanted to learn. Before meeting me, the Were had been very sheltered. She's done some work, but her fighting skills aren't anything to write home about.

"The fight rings." Brutus sweeps an arm out as we come up to a series of interlocking circles swept into the landscape. They're still covered in reddish dirt, but it looks like someone's raked them clear of at least the larger rocks. The one in front of us is ringed with tall cacti.

"Extra motivation to stand your ground in the circle," Brutus informs us both. Ever sticks close by as we walk into that circle and on to the others.

"Yeah I'll bet. One prick in the ass would be enough of a reminder for me." As soon as I've said it, I lament Aggie's absence. There would be a thousand ways to make her blush about the lasciviousness of such a phrase.

We walk by training stations in different circles as we get further from the cactus-covered entrance. Brutus says a few are for hand-to-hand bouts. One has a spelled, wood-planked border for warlocks to practice inside. Another has a series of obstacles set up for climbing and scaling various materials.

"I have the fastest time on the course. Set it my second year here," Brutus shares, proud. I stop listening when I pick up the sound of gushing water. I follow my ears and turn a canyon rock corner to come face to face with a massive waterfall emptying over the side of some rocks and into a pond in front of us.

"Moon be praised!" If anyone was wondering, it's a lack of AC that has me suddenly putting my faith into a, so far as I know, fictional moon-goddess. I'm willing to set my distaste for swimming aside if it means I can cool off. I'm sprinting for the water before Brutus can try to stop me, determined to get at least a quick dip and stave off the worst of the heat.

I skid to a halt as I pass another of the endless training rings, but this one's got a rather notable individual inside, boxing a wooden dummy. A Were. With black and white spots.

"You!" I snarl as fur rips down my back and across my nose, muzzle growing. My claws are out as I lunge toward him.

The Were in front of me looks up, eyes going so wide I can see the whites. His fear washes over my intuition. I let his terror soothe me.

"I'm going to rip you in two," I promise.

Not a nice greeting? Let me explain. When I finally faced off against my Claw-leading ex Damien after a two-hundred-year vendetta, he had a final surprise waiting for me. A gantlet of his toughest and most talented minions, which I had to fight my way through to reach him. I ended nine of the ten, but the last one tucked tail and ran. A Were. A very unique one with black and white spotted patterning that made him look more like a dairy cow than a fearsome magical in his fur.

"No, no, no! I can explain!" My soon-to-be victim has his furred palms up, but it's not stopping me.

"Never! Cut it out." Brutus is between us before I can blink, doing a decent job of looking intimidating even without fur. Blasted shifter. I shove him aside.

"This Were and I have unfinished business. Seems at least one Claw agent slipped through the Magikai's fingers."

"I don't work for the Claw!" the spotted Were whines. "I didn't. I never—"

"Never is *my* thing," I snap, grabbing ahold of his furred arms and shoving him back against a rock wall. "Now, how did you manage to infiltrate the Magikai?"

He doesn't look at me. He looks over my shoulder.

"Help! Brutus, you said she was smart! Isn't her intuition thing telling her I'm being sincere?"

I tilt my head, realizing as he says it that, yes, as a matter of fact I can sense sincerity.

"Never," Ever slides in beside me. "He means what he says."

"Then why were you there with Damien?" I snap.

The Were squirms in my grip as I haul him higher so his feet don't touch the ground. What they're saying makes sense, but fury is a powerful motivator. And I'm consumed with the desire to rip him limb from limb.

"Confirmation! The Magikai wanted to know if you managed to best Damien. I was supposed to see if he defeated you and get word back to the representatives to prepare for open war with the Claw if that happened. But you got through the gauntlet." He's still holding his palms out, cringing away from me as I stare him down.

"So, you ran?"

"Hey, I'm a lover. Not a fighter." He manages an awkward shrug.

I roll my eyes, but I let go and back off. He takes a few steps forward.

"No, really. Watch."

He shifts his stance a bit, puffing out his chest and bringing himself up to his full Were height. I wait several seconds, until my annoyance and impatience hit a peak.

"And? Nothing's happening!" I complain. Nadia stumbles past me and throws her arms around one of the Were's biceps.

"Wow, these are really, *really* toned." She giggles. Something's wrong with her emotions, though. It's interest, but also fright. I shove myself between them, prying her off as the black and white spotted Were backs away, wide-eyed.

"Get away from her!" I snarl, snapping my muzzle at him.

"Oh dear. That didn't go as planned at all."

"Who are you, anyway?" I demand. Enough of this nameless conversation. I want to know who I'm dealing with.

He holds up a finger as he goes back to the fighting dummy and snags something from the ground. He throws his skin on, and I realize it's a robe that he wraps around himself. As he turns back to us, I can see that without his fur he's just under my height, with a long, straight nose, full lips, and hooded eyes. His hair is a black wave off his face, hanging just long enough on the sides that some foolish female might be tempted to brush the end behind his ear.

"Kim Ji-hwan," he says, holding a hand out for me to shake. I glare down without taking it. He frowns for a moment, then flashes that vibrant smile again.

"Ah, yes. Name meanings. Brutus told me. I see where I went wrong. Wisdom. Brightness." He offers the explanation like an olive branch. It's a start. I'll admit Korean names can baffle me a bit. Different hanjas can have different meanings, so a single name said aloud could mean any number of things. You have to see them in writing to really be sure.

I let his hand continue to hang at an awkward angle as I scrutinize him.

"Explain yourself. You said you're not a fighter."

He pulls his hand back and runs it over his hair.

"I do have basic training, of course; hence what I'm doing here." He waves a hand at the training dummy. "But it's mostly for toning and aesthetics. My real talent is seduction. It's a particular skill of mine. A gift I've had for years. I was trying to show you before and seem to have caught the other intuitive instead. My apologies. Typically it works on the closest magical, unless they're mated."

Just great—another damned magical ability to contend with.

I look over my shoulder and see Brutus, one brow up and one down as he thinks. I can feel his suspicion. Lucky for me he's not the quickest tool in the enforcer arsenal.

"That's ridiculous!" I laugh. "I'm *not* mated. You know that well enough. If you stuck around in the shadows, you saw me end the last half-mate I had."

Ji-hwan's loud gulp and the feelings of terror washing off him let me know he saw plenty of the fight between Damien and me.

"I can assure you I didn't go shopping for males the minute Damien bit it." True. I'd gone shopping before. Sort of. Not that I plucked Nahum off a shelf.

Sexy male dragon shifters with trauma similar to mine. Aisle one?

"As an intuitive I can feel your real intentions." He opens his mouth, but I raise a hand. "And, unlike my mentee, I have centuries of experience looking past what people say and do to the truth of what they feel. *And* I have the benefit of already disliking you, thanks to our last encounter. I'd chalk it up to that more than some mythical mate." I scoff for good measure.

I feel my tension fall as the belief hits me from Brutus and Ji-hwan. There's one lie successfully sold. I imagine I'll need lots more in my tenure here. Maybe I should keep a journal.

"Anyway," I steer the conversation away from myself. "Wisdom? Really?"

He flashes that same dazzling smile and winks.

"Was wise enough to tuck tail and hide before you ripped the sky open with that magical river, wasn't I?"

Touché.

"Since we'll be here together, perhaps we can bury the hatchet. What do you say, Seonbae?"

"Never," I correct. It's a respectful term, but I don't need any reminders that I'm older. "And I reserve my judgment on the matter."

"If it isn't the prodigal enforcer herself. Finally deigning to grace us with her presence." A voice rumbles behind me. Authoritative. Self-assured. Pissed off.

Seems we've found Amun.

6

When It Rains It Pours But Not in the Desert

"Head Representative!" I croon, flashing what I hope is a winning smile at the old lion even as I step in front of Ever. "I never imagined you'd be here in person to greet us. What an honor." I fan myself, but it's for the heat, not his over-inflated ego.

"To ensure you actually made it here and did as you were told. And to make sure the other Were made it as well. There'll be no stashing her away; you can't keep her from her place in our ranks, Never." He shakes a finger at me, and I fight the urge to bite it off. What could the Bone Reader do with the information from that appendage, I wonder? The thought has me giddy.

"About that, Head Representative. There was a key detail I needed to clear up with you, at your convenience, of course." Always have to let these controlling types think things are their idea. He's all curiosity and annoyance before he even knows what I'm asking for.

"As it so happens, I was headed over here to retrieve you, anyway. You can discuss it while we walk." He gives me a slow look, head to toe. Creep. But he's just disapproving, not lustful. I'm not winning the lion over that way. "I had rather hoped you'd look more presentable, but I'm guessing this is par for the course. More's the pity."

He turns to walk away, and I scowl at him. Ever reaches up and grabs me. I've got a fist in the air, aimed at the lion shifter's head, but I drop it.

Deep breaths, Never.

I have a feeling I'm going to need to repeat that mantra quite frequently, along with using Chrys's scream therapy, if I can find anywhere around here to yell into the void. I throw on my skin and follow after the insulting male.

"Here's the thing," I start as I jog to catch up to the head representative. "Location, location, location. Have you ever heard that? Well, it's true. And this location isn't going to work for me. I'm sure, as head of the Magikai, you can understand the responsibility leadership can be."

"More than you would," he snaps, arms clasped behind him as he continues to walk. I've upset the male even more than I would have anticipated by keeping him waiting, and I'm not about to make him any happier.

"I'll agree to train Ever here. At this ... lovely compound you've set up. But I'll be needing weekends off."

He stops in his tracks, eyes wide and mouth opening and closing like a fish.

"Weekends off? Listen here!" He starts waving his fist. "I don't know who you think you are, but *I* am in charge here. *You* listen to me. I say sit, you sit. I say kill, you kill. And I say, you're staying here. We had a binding agreement, and you're already toeing the line, Missy."

It's the *Missy* that does it. I really was planning to hold it together, folks. Truly. It was my sincerest intention, second only to giving the old lion a good swift kick to the nethers.

"*You* listen." In spite of the heat, I throw my fur back on, towering over the older shifter. "You may be in charge here, but I am freelance. I have never. Never. That's right, say my name, *Never*, been on the regular payroll. I take the jobs I want. And I took this job via a binding contract. Magically binding. And you may recall that said contract had a start date of fall, which *you* moved, and I allowed. And you may also recall it said zilch, nada, nothing, about *where* my training of Ever had to take place. That's your oversight, not mine. I'm being mighty generous, offering to sit my happy ass in the desert part-time. That's the best you're going to get. If not, I'm happy to turn right back around and not return until the last second that contract says I'm allowed. Or, you can give me weekends off." I flash my teeth as I finish the tirade.

Amun's taken aback, but he recovers quickly enough. He may not be into fighting himself anymore, but I can tell he's ruthless. I feel the cunning ooze over me.

"And what do I get out of it?" he demands.

You get my foot not planting itself in your backside.

"To hold to your word. Which I would think is quite important for someone trying to maintain control of the magical world," I remind him. "If you have any doubts about what's in that contract, I'd be happy to have my historian look over it."

Hugh would wipe the floor with that thing. No clauses, no loopholes. I had him run over it already before I arrived, and he laughed out loud at how poorly the thing's written. As long as I train Ever, with skills that *could* be useful to an enforcer, I hold up my end. The rest is just fluff to get me closer to whatever's going on here. But to review whatever I find, I'll need privacy. And to have that, I need another location.

And now that I know where we're at? Why not the Vegas mansion? The Magikai shouldn't have tempted me by putting me mere hours from the place if they didn't want me to take advantage. It's their own fault, really.

"I am taking you to meet some very powerful and important individuals," Amun starts back in. "It would be of great assistance to me if these guests, did *not* see us as a divided front. While I think it's nonsensical hero worship, the tales of your feats against the Claw have spread." He sighs, as though it's the worst outcome that I might have a fan club. I'm sure that to him, it is.

"And you capitalized on it by putting out the story that I'm working *for* you, on *your* orders," I guess. I can feel I'm right before he confirms it.

"Of course we did. We sent you backup. You never would have succeeded without us." I'm less sure of that than I was when I asked for the assistance, but I'll play ball.

I hold out a hand.

"Fine. I agree to play nice with the guests. Not bite the hand that's feeding me. I act like we get along, and you act like I'm a favored enforcer. Win-win."

"You act like the subordinate you are, and I act like we supported and ordered your actions," he corrects.

"And I get paid," I add, unable to help one last dig. "Whatever the going rate for an enforcer contract is these days. For the year."

He's so mad that he's turning red. But he shakes my hand.

"Pleasure doing business with you, Amun." I attempt a wink, before I can think better of it.

"You look ridiculous with that patch, you know. What even happened that it didn't regenerate, or are you just making an attempt to appear more edgy?" he demands.

The anger that bubbles up is a physical thing. I go hotter inside than out; quite a feat in this desert climate. I only barely manage to contain it. I really hope he's doing something truly foul around here, just so I have an excuse to take him out. I have a year to find out, and good things come to those who wait.

"All the world, magic of epic proportions at your fingertips. You could have settled anywhere, and you chose this?" I sweep an arm out across the reddish desert dirt, then give a snort just for good measure. I'm not dignifying the eye comment with a response, but I can hold a grudge with the best of them.

Amun picks a speck of dust off his shirt, scowls down as though it offends him, and flicks it away.

"Precisely. *We* have the resources. And now that you're officially with us, I can tell you we *do* have headquarters in other places. Surely you can't have thought we'd put all our eggs in one basket? All our combined power in one area?"

"Well, as a matter of fact—" That's exactly what I thought. More fool me.

He laughs, deep and harsh. Amused at my expense. He pretends to wipe away a tear, but I'm not sure whose benefit that's for, since I can spot a faker a mile away.

"You do amuse me, Never, if nothing else. And perhaps now that you're under our control, where you belong, things will improve. You do have a number of talents that could be put to use if you utilized your skills appropriately."

I'm biding my time, but Amun's topping my list right now for pompous ass-hats that need to be taken down a peg or three.

"We have spots all over the globe and even in other realms." I hadn't even known the Underworld was real until I sent Damien off. Who knows what other realities that leaves space for? Nahum did mention Fae. "I reside in our hidden compound underneath the Colosseum. But this desert serves as adequate training grounds for our US-based enforcers. Vast, easy to hide within, extreme terrain, and temperatures to fortify recruits. Yes, it does nicely."

Miserably, more like.

He walks us the rest of the way across the desert compound and over to the one building that has, of course, not escaped my notice. It's the only one that truly looks like any sort of permanent or modern structure. Stucco and stone. It would be spherical, were it not for an outcropping on opposite edges. Two stories in the middle, the upper floor glinting with windows. That's got to be a fun air-conditioning bill. He leads us through a set of sliding doors that whoosh as cool air escapes and we enter.

It's not lost on me that, in spite of the more modern appearance, the Collectors had a castle with a rounded, double-doored entrance. I can't decide if I'm *seeing* similarities or *making* similarities, simply because of my distaste for authority. Guess we'll see.

Amun leads us to the right, toward one of the two, single-story rectangular outcroppings of the building. It turns out this one is some sort of giant boardroom. Also sleek and modern, save for the massive fireplace built into one wall. I'd ask about the necessity of such a thing, if it weren't for the other notable details in the room.

Four—scratch that—five magicals. I initially miss a lutin in the far end of the room. And who wouldn't? They're small. Deadly useful in certain situations, given they can go through solid objects and make themselves all but invisible. They like to cause inconveniences and upsets. Particularly domestic ones. Pebble in your shoe? A lutin. Keep losing socks you could swear up and down you checked went in the dryer? A lutin. They're one of several smaller, fairy-like folk. Unable to take a taller, human form. Although some of the more skilled ones can look like house pets.

And, now that this magical species lesson is out of the way, on to the most shocking item in the room.

Drumroll, please.

What are you doing here?

Nahum's eyes are wide as he spots me at the entrance to the conference room.

7

Roughing It

You're supposed to be in Europe, Nahum reminds me.

And you're supposed to be on your island!

He schools his face into a more unreadable expression, even though I can feel his sense of unease. Are we already found out?

My contact reached out as I was leaving California. Offered me a meeting with Amun. I thought it was fortuitous, but now I'm suspecting it's something more devious.

"Shall we?" Amun grins, gesturing to the table and inviting us all to sit. He's satisfied with himself, but he's not anticipatory. Not the way he might be if he were about to spring a trap. I sit, keeping myself tense and ready to jump right back up again in case I'm wrong.

Intuition is a great tool, but it's not the only tool. And I've been around long enough to know better than to relax just because he's not giving away his plan through his emotions.

"Welcome," Amun starts, gesturing around the mostly empty table. "Thank you all for taking time from your busy schedules to attend. As you all know, we have the conclave coming up later this year, when we'll see all the representatives, but given the events of late, I thought several of our local representatives should meet sooner."

Another individual slips into the room. I recognize his scent. Human. I met him when Amun drew up our contract for me to train Ever. The head representative's version of Hugh, I believe. Without a word, the human sits and shakes out an old-school parchment. He's got a pot of glowing ink and a quill. I stare openly at one of the rare exceptions to the 'don't let them know about us' rule. What must he have done to integrate into the supernatural community and into the Magikai?

"Now that we have someone to record minutes, we may begin."

Wily old lion. Anything on spelled paper is going to hold some sort of power. And I've no idea what. Could anything we say here be misconstrued as some form of contract? Will it try to imitate my abilities and check the responses for falsehoods? I'm not the only one frowning at the paper. The lutin in particular looks put out, scowling at the human over his beard.

"First. Introductions. Amun. Head Representative of the Magikai, barbary lion shifter."

Amun gestures to the individual to his left.

"Unkai. A Main Representative of the Magikai. Raiju," states the one representative I have a less than contemptuous relationship with.

"Scrub. Representative from the Louisiana region. Lutin." The Magikai have a whole cascading system. Amun. His main representatives. Then any others under that, serving to represent different regions and species across the globe. I've never paid it much attention except to find out who's paying me, but maybe I should start.

"Sky." The third magical introduces herself. She's got moon-pale skin and icy blue eyes. Silvery hair a few shades lighter than mine. "Wind elf. Representative of the US plains region."

A tornado-maker, perhaps? As she announces her species, she flicks her arm, and feathers extend from elbow to wrist. Wind elves don't have traditional wings, but they have feathers that come out along their ankles and forearms. They float and flit more than coast when flying. But they're wicked useful in creating a wind storm.

I turn my attention from her to the next individual, doing all I can to appear nonchalant.

"Nahum. Dragon. Merely a guest at these proceedings."

Amun clears his throat, and Nahum raises a brow, then dips his chin to the representative.

"I thought it best, after our events with the Claw, and their dragon leader, that we recruit another dragon representative. It's been ages since we've had one." Liar. Well, partial liar. He means what he says about wanting a dragon representative, but it was his good luck Nahum fell into his lap. "As you can see, we also have another ... guest ... with us. Her purpose is twofold."

I open my mouth to speak, but he holds a hand up in my direction.

"After the Claw's dragon leader was deposed, a Were took over. Having Never here gives us some insight into the ways of Weres. She has also been an enforcer of ours for years, and under our direct supervision assisted with eliminating the remains of the Claw."

Way to give partial credit there, Amun.

"While the heroics surrounding her actions have been greatly exaggerated, she is a valuable tool in our arsenal. Her *intuition* in particular is something which I plan to make better use of in the future." Amun grins as he announces my ability to the room.

The lutin is nonplussed, too shocked to decide whether he should be angry. The raiju has no real reaction, since he's already well aware of what I can do. The wind elf is livid. I see her click her jaw, but then she gives a noncommittal smile. Won't work on me, dear. Nahum is still all concern.

What's his game here? I question.

No idea, but be on your guard.

I give a small snort. As if I'm ever *not* on guard. Such is the life of an enforcer. Especially when you're one like me who has a knack for pissing off the people around her. What can I say, I'm not for everyone.

The last representative clears his throat, a rumbling Scottish accent that matches his chiseled features echoing in the boardroom.

"Calder. Kelpie. Highlands and Islands Scottish region representative. Pleasure to meet you both." He looks first at Nahum, then me. Green eyes lock onto mine, assessing. His name means *rough waters*, and I snort a laugh at that. I'll just bet. His dark brown hair is just long enough that I can see the beginnings of a curl. This mate thing must act as some kind of attractiveness dampener around others, because I'd rather be staring at the dragon. That being said, we are talking devastating charm here, folks. Utterly. Devastating. And I do mean that, since kelpies can lure you down to a watery grave in their horse forms.

The room's gone silent, and I look back to the head representative to see him frowning at me, impatient.

What? *Now* he wants me to talk? How in hell's moon was I to know?

Hell's bells, this lion.

"Charmed, I'm sure." I dip my chin to the kelpie, then the rest of the representatives, not lingering on Nahum longer than any of the others. The wind elf snorts, hiding a giggle with her hand. The lutin continues his bearded scowl. Unkai rolls his eyes when I bat my lashes at him. Perhaps it doesn't have the same impact with only one good eye.

Once we've gotten the introductions out of the way, Amun settles into his seat and begins droning on and on about the Magikai's relationships with the various supernaturals across the globe. Most of it's mind-numbingly dull, but he keeps mentioning the conclave coming up. All the representatives in the world descending on one location. I know they hold one every decade, but I've never been invited or bothered to crash the event. Given his tone and the anticipation buffeting me from the head representative's direction when he speaks of it, I gather this will be an extra-special occasion. Which means I have every intention of learning all the juicy details.

Is he onto us? Nahum's voice echoes in my mind.

I don't think so. The only feeling he has about you is greed. A dragon representative is a powerful ally. You might have more of a chance of finding out what he's up to than I will, I admit.

If he's up to anything. You do still have to consider the possibility that Amun and the Magikai as a whole are on the up and up. Not likable perhaps, but not devious.

We'll see.

I'm fantasizing about my mattress back in Sac by the time Amun calls the meeting to a close. He personally escorts me out, alongside Unkai. I admit to some level of devastation when the air outside is only marginally cooler than before, even though the sun has set.

The representatives come to a stop in front of some canvas-walled monstrosity of a tent with what appears to be a cement foundation.

"I'm sorry. *This* is where you expect us to sleep?" I stare down my nose at the cement floor, the rows of cots, with derision as the raiju pulls a flap open. "Absolutely not."

Amun frowns as Unkai fidgets behind him, flowy fur waving even though there's no breeze to speak of in the moon-forsaken heat.

"That's not optional. You agreed to be here."

"And you agreed I had until Halloween," I retort.

I can hear the click of his teeth as Amun's jaw snaps shut and just catch the glint of a lengthening fang. I've never seen him in his lion form. I never trust a shifter that won't show their non-human side. It's as if they've tried to remove themselves from the rest of us.

"We're not having this argument again!" He's tense enough to snap, but I don't want to push him over the edge. Not yet. I want to keep him right on the line.

"So, it's to be torture, then? Stuffing me in here like some college kid with a bunch of pubescent shifters. The smell alone could drop a centaur." I sniff to make a point. I'm not wrong. This tent is chock-full of what must be recent recruits. And teenaged magicals aren't any less smelly than humans. More, in fact.

"You really don't have a choice. You dramatic, bothersome, insane—"

"Why don't we stop there, before you get to my *really* great qualities?" I smirk at Amun and he glowers back. Unkai hides a grin. He finds me entertaining. One of several reasons he's not on my take-down list. For now.

"Just get in the barracks!" Amun yells, temper breaking. Who put this guy in charge? I certainly didn't get a vote. How did the representatives get decided, anyway? After all, they're offering Nahum a seat up on a silver platter. Now, I can vouch for the dragon, but he could be the devil himself, for all Amun knows. This is what I get for having no interest in politics. It's high time I got involved.

"This building is for all the wolves. We group by species here," Unkai explains.

"Not a wolf," I correct as I enter the tent. Under great duress, I'd like to have noted.

There's only one thing that keeps me inside overnight as opposed to sleeping out under the stars. Scratch that. Two things. The first is air. It may only be a standing fan at each end of the tent, but it's a step up from the oven-like heat that lingers outdoors well after sunset.

Two. Stubbornness. I'm a big enough Were to admit it, and not big enough to take the high road. Amun thinks he can trip me up this easily? He's got another think coming. Wolf barracks. Ha. It'll take more than this to get under my skin.

I toss myself onto a lumpy mattress with a scratchy blanket and send myself to sleep using sheer will.

The moon hasn't even set yet when a blaring, discordant alarm goes off across the room.

"Would you shut that thing off?" I nail Brutus in the head with a pillow even as he clicks the alarm to silent. I may have already been awake, but it's the principle. I've been up and sweating for at least an hour, if I had to guess.

"Do you *ever*, ever solve things in a civil manner?" he demands before throwing the offending pillow back at me.

"Never." I smirk. I'm lying, of course; I *would* consider a pillow civil.

"All right! You heard the wolf. Up and at 'em!" I yell gleefully into the bunk. A few groans meet me in response. With the sun rising I can see that, in addition to Brutus, Ever, and Ji-hwan, I'm sharing the space with a good half-dozen wolf shifters. All closer to Ever's age in appearance.

"So then, fearless leader,"—I look back to Brutus in spite of what I'm sure will be many objections—"where's the chow tent? Point me to the coffee."

"We eat after the first block of training. Builds character to fight under less than ideal circumstances, like hunger." He crosses his arms, full of himself and his supposed abilities once again.

"It also builds annoyance," I snap.

"It has the added bonus of getting a training session out of the way before the heat really hits," Ji-hwan calls from across the room. He gives me a tentative smile, and I scowl in his direction. It'll take more than that to worm his way into my good graces. But, still.

"All right." I tap a finger on my chin. "I've been partially convinced. Coffee, training, then breakfast."

"That's not what—"

"To the dining hall!" I yell, pumping a fist in the air. I don't bother with clothes. I just throw on my fur. Ever grins at a slack-jawed Brutus as she follows me out of the bunks. Ji-hwan trails behind her, giving his head enforcer a shrug.

"Her idea is better," the little brown-noser states. Still, smart male. The poor wolf teens are in utter confusion. In the end, two are rebellious enough to join us for coffee. Or they're just that addicted to caffeine. Who knows.

One thing I do know is I'm in a battle for control, and I don't intend to lose.

8

Making Friends, Making Enemies, or Just Making Everyone Suspicious

I make it through the pre-breakfast training block well enough. For all Brutus's blustering, it's just a lot of stretching, followed by a rousing trek across the desert terrain. Uncomfortable due to the heat more than anything else. And for all my outward whining, I can assure you, I've endured far worse.

After some very sad, runny eggs that would make Todd weep, we're in the cactus-lined ring, taking turns practicing against one another. I see a few things right off the bat. On the compound, they keep the training separated by species a good portion of the time. And everything here is very structured. Too structured. No wonder Brutus wasn't ready for the real deal. Also, the seducer, Ji-hwan. He's off on his own, boxing dummies the whole time.

I wave him over.

"What gives? No one's so much as thrown a punch at you. Which I find hard to believe, given I'd certainly love the opportunity." I stick my hands on my hips as I stare him down.

"They don't want me to mar my perfect features," he states with a grin before heading back to his isolated area. Still, I can feel how frustrated he is. Are the Magikai really this dense? Surely they're smart enough to realize these methods aren't going to produce well-rounded enforcers. Just one-note wonders who can't think for themselves. Then again, maybe that's the idea.

Speaking of the Magikai, I'm mid-fight with one of the young wolf shifters when I smell lion and the intoxicating scent of a certain dragon shifter. Petrichor, with a hint of sea salt. It reminds me of his island. I can't quite make out what they're saying as their steps turn away from the rings.

Curiosity may have killed the cat, but it's about to benefit a nosy Were. I have a whole year here, but I want answers sooner rather than later. And even faster than that if possible.

"How about a break?" I offer to the wolf shifter in front of me, whom I've been holding off one-armed while I focus on Amun. The poor enforcer candidate is panting, and he plops down into the dirt at my offer.

"What? No, no breaks! We continue through the afternoon! That's what our instructions are!" Brutus charges into the circle, arms waving. Any other time, I'd happily engage in a battle of banter and wits he'd be bound to lose. But I'm in a hurry, so I go with an excuse I just *know* will get the annoying shifter off my back.

"Brutus, my dear, I need to tend to some lady issues, if you get my drift. You wouldn't happen to have any feminine hygiene products in the training circle, would you?" I glance around as though I'm expecting a package of tampons to pop out of a cactus.

As predicted, Brutus goes red as a cherry tomato, and awkward embarrassment oozes off of him.

"Well. No. I mean. I didn't think. And. Yes, well." The poor thing clears his throat, getting his bearings back. "You may leave. Everyone else stays."

He's so flustered he doesn't even warn me to hurry.

It doesn't take me long to locate Amun and Nahum's voices again, once I've exited the circle. Luck's on my side today. They're headed into the building with the board room. Blessed air conditioning.

Once inside, they turn the opposite direction of where Amun led me before, heading toward the west side of the building. It occurs to me, as I begin to follow them, that Amun is likely to have a monitoring system on this place. Which begs the question, to snoop or not to snoop? The choice is taken from me as two bickering figures emerge from a side hall.

"I'm telling you, he's—" Sky pulls up short, her hair lifted by some nonexistent breeze. The wind elf's forearm feathers flutter. Calder stops beside her, letting out a very horse-like snort. Their curiosity smacks me in the face, but they're not upset. Not with me, anyway.

"Looking for something?" Sky questions, finding my presence intriguing more than anything else.

"The bathroom." Why not stick to the same lie? "I refuse to believe in this century that 'go behind a bush' is my only option. No matter what the enforcers say."

Sky titters and Calder snorts again.

"I quite agree. A most useful modern-century invention. And you've already passed it. That way." She holds out a slender, moon-pale finger. Her eyes are locked on me, and I can feel the challenge. I've got no good option but to turn around. She follows me in, and when I emerge from a stall and stand at a sink, she's waiting, staring into a mirror.

"You know, I was rather pleased Amun brought you in," she starts.

"You were?" I am pretty great, but the head representative doesn't think so. And I've no clue what most of the rest of them think. I've been content to be the hired hit-Were they needed. I wasn't interested in getting to know any of them personally.

"Oh yes," she insists. Her voice is melodic and breathy. "The Defeater of the Claw. Had to meet you for myself. We've needed someone to shake things up around here. I do hope you'll keep things interesting, Never. I wouldn't mind seeing the status quo upset a bit."

And with that, she's gone, blowing out of the room like a breeze on her ankle feathers. I follow her out, but she's disappeared. I'm in the hall mere seconds before I turn around and duck into the nearest doorway. I can hear Amun and Nahum's voices somewhere nearby.

"Snooping?" I turn to see Calder leaning up against the wall. His body may say he's relaxed, but I can sense the conniving and cunning. We're not near any bodies of water, but I have no intention of turning my back on a kelpie.

"Just keeping a low profile. I'm here to train, not relax in the air conditioning. I'd hate to give Amun the wrong impression."

Calder pushes off the wall and walks forward until we're chest to chest.

"And what impression would you be afraid he might get, hmm?"

"That I'm a lazy enforcer who prefers lounging inside to beating people up in the harsh outdoors," I quip before flashing the kelpie a smile.

His mood goes a bit sour.

"Ah, yes. We'd certainly hate for him to think that. The head representative does so value his prized and best weapon."

A low growl rumbles in my throat.

"You disagree?" Calder asks, one dark eyebrow raising.

"I don't like being referred to as an object of any kind. No matter whose or what for," I offer, "but I follow the head representative's orders."

He nods.

"So you do. And yet, I wonder if you've taken the time to consider why. And whether that's your best option."

"What do you—"

"Nice to see you again." He reaches his fingers up as though he's going to tip his hat to me, but he isn't wearing one. Then he leaves.

Now, is it just me, or have these interactions been weird as hell? I can't quite tell if the two representatives were trying to feel me out, warn me off, or win me over.

I follow Calder out, but go after my original prey. I catch up to Amun and Nahum near the lobby.

"-which is why it would be a benefit to us all if you were to join the highest rung of representatives. I'll be hosting several of the others this weekend, ahead of the upcoming conclave. A little property I run called Lusca Palms. I insist you make time for a visit before you leave the States. Better yet, you could agree to my offer of having you attend the conclave." Amun throws an arm around Nahum, and I can read the dragon's discomfort, but he's got a good poker face. The lion is scheming.

Tell him yes. You're going to Lusca Palms. And so am I.

Nahum jumps, and I pull my head back into the alcove.

"Something wrong?" Amun questions.

"Stepped on something. Perhaps a stray bit of cactus," Nahum mutters.

Don't do that! Warn a dragon first. He chides in my mind, but he's happy in spite of his thoughts.

He's invited you to the conclave. Which means he's invited us. Without realizing it, I insist.

You really want me to go?

Absolutely. My instincts are still telling me there's something off about this whole operation. You know they separate the trainees by species a good portion of the time? And some don't train in combat at all. It's like Amun is purposefully preventing his enforcers from living up to their full potential.

I can feel Nahum giving my statement consideration.

It is odd, he relents.

"Amun, if the reception at Lusca Palms is as kind as it's been here, I'd be happy to attend. And if that goes well, why not stay for the conclave?"

"Excellent! I knew you'd come around." Amun claps Nahum on the back. "I'll win you over, just wait and see. Once you've visited the property, you'll be only too happy to stay there for the conclave as well. I'll call ahead and ensure you've got the finest rooms."

The two of them exit out the front doors, warm air seeping in behind them.

I wait a good five minutes after their voices have faded before I go back to the ring.

9
Take Me Home, Desert Roads

"*Se le soltó una teja.*" Ever throws her arms up as I slide across the wide, curved drive of the vamp mansion and stop the car. She's not a fan of my driving. I, for one, am thrilled we ended up so close to Vegas. I'd planned on having to fly back and forth, but thanks to the location I was able to take one of the mansion's many sports cars, which Hugh was kind enough to have dropped off just outside the training grounds for me. True to my deal with Amun, I've taken the weekend off. Nahum's planning to go to the Lusca Palms tomorrow to meet him. And thanks to a quick phone call to Hugh, I happen to know exactly where it's at. The newly-minted Were is working overtime.

"Can't believe the head representative is running some magical casino and resort," Ever mutters as she all but throws herself from the vehicle. "You're sure it's a good idea to go after him? Seems like a trap, inviting Nahum along, with him practically in your backyard."

"A trap. A good bit of luck. Or both," I return with a grin. Truthfully, it doesn't matter if it's meant to be a trap. I just have to outsmart it. Because I'm sick of being out of the loop of Amun's motivations.

The front doors of the vamp mansion swing open wide. The vamps themselves are nowhere to be found, quite possibly because of the rays of sunlight that are currently shining across my entrance floors. Hugh steps out from one door, Chrys the other. A witchling hurtles between them both, launching herself at me.

"We got you a surprise! Actually, two surprises!" Aggie gushes, giddy and dancing on her tiptoes as she backs into the front hall. Her wine-red hair is braided down one side of her face. A new look for her.

She shoves something into my hands. I unfold it to find a t-shirt emblazoned with a vibrant, metallic wolf's head and the phrase *'Will Howl For Hugs'*.

I stare at it for a moment, biting down my commentary as Aggie beams.

"It's, um, really something," I manage. Aggie bursts into laughter and Lynx steps out, waving at me.

"My idea," he says, pointing to himself. I let out a sigh of relief. I can't crush the witchling's feelings, but I can pummel him. I ball the shirt up, throwing it at his face. He peels it off, grinning.

"You only have to wear it on special occasions. Ready to see your second surprise?"

I give Todd a side-eyed glance as he steps out from behind one of the doors.

"Trust me," he whispers as I walk past him, "you'll like this one."

I follow the witchling through the main hall, the dining room, and into the kitchens.

"And don't drop those—I need 'em for the pre-dinner drinks!" An angry, cursed satyr who looks like an elderly human man is waving a dishrag at several of my vamps. They skitter in the face of his soppy-ragged fury, following orders.

"Elios! You old goat! Couldn't stay away from me, huh?" I beam at him, and then at Aggie. She was right. I do like this surprise. I like it even more when Elios shoves a cocktail into my hands. It's blue, luminescent, and swirling. I stare at him over the rim.

"This looks suspiciously like the magical river the Bone Reader's vial summoned. Not going to cost me a second eye, is it? Because I have to warn you, I'm out of spares."

His cheeks puff up and go red and he blusters at me.

"Ungrateful, of all the cheek! If you don't want it, I'll take it back and toss it to one of the vamps! But if you'd take a moment to try it, I think you'd change your mind."

This. *This* is why I love Elios. I can feel his reaction when I mention my eye, but he responds like his same old gruff self. Doesn't even miss a beat. He's the last magical to treat someone differently because of their appearance.

"I didn't say *that*, you cranky old man! I'll drink it!" I give it a sip, and heaven washes over my tongue. Okay, maybe an exaggeration. But only the teeniest, tiniest, slightest one. It's got a berry flavor on the front, not overly sweet. And just a hint of sharp and sour at the edges. A dangerous beverage. The likes of which I could down a dozen without a thought.

"I've missed you," I croon, staring at the glass. Behind it, Elios rolls his eyes and mutters something about 'crazy Weres thanking the drink after all my hard work.'

"That hell's awful compound only slings cheap beer. And only once a week!" I inform the satyr.

"Blasphemy!" he declares, slapping his damp towel down on a silver cart in my kitchen. Droplets go flying. *That* accessory he could have left at home. But beggars, choosers, all that.

"Have to admit, I'm a bit surprised this is the first time I'm seeing you," Elios informs me, hunched over his towel and swiping at the already pristine surface of the tray. I can feel the upset, and I realize I should have stopped by his bar. The Lusty Lute is one of my regular haunts, after all. In spite of his demeanor, and our banter, Elios is one of the magicals on my 'protect and don't kill' list.

I'd been a bit focused on the dragon and my other friends when I got back. Not the bar. Priorities, right? Little Miss Never is growing up.

But still. An apology isn't how to get this goat's goat.

"So, you break into my mansion, huh? If you wanted an invitation, all you had to do was ask."

"Break in! Break in!" He turns a charming shade of vermilion. "More like kidnapped! Coerced! Drug here against my will is what it was, you daft Were."

"Well, either way. I'm glad to see you." I lean down and plant a kiss right on the satyr's nose. He goes from vermilion to scarlet and walks away, cleaning and muttering.

I turn to see Todd.

"We paid him. Out of your mansion's coffers, I might add. You should know, he didn't come cheap."

I down the remains of my blue drink and start after the satyr for more.

"Worth it!" I throw over my shoulder.

A second drink and a short shower to rinse off the desert dirt later, I've got everyone gathered around the laughably large banquet table in the dining room. Utterly useless before I got here. Vampires live off alcohol and blood. Not that I'm getting rid of it; the thing's inlaid with marble and gold.

"Something very fishy is going on with the Magikai," I state, tapping a finger against my chin.

"And to think, they don't even have a sea monster," Aggie quips. She giggles.

"Not your best work," I inform her. "Then again, I could be saying that because I can't think of a way to turn it into an innuendo."

"You're losing your touch." Chrys starts tallying. "I'll let you see my monster, for one."

"All right. All right. Losing sight of the goal here." I cut her off, but Hugh high-fives her. She gives him a wicked grin.

"Actually," Hugh points out, "sea monster's not far off the mark. Lusca Palms casino and resort uses a lusca as its emblem. It's a magically kept secret; you've got to be invited in by someone. Lucky for all of us, I've been digging through Costas's old files since coming back to the mansion."

I'll admit to having little interest in the paperwork of my vamp predecessor, whom I flambéed.

"Whatever Amun's into, Costas was somehow involved. He invested quite a large sum of the mansion's money into this business endeavor, and unbeknownst to me had sent some of the vampires for staff at the resort. As such, we've still got some identification cards and employment forms I could complete for some of you. And a few invitations he must have received as a perk. Very fortunate for us, but all the more concerning when you consider that—"

"That your former vampire lord was in league with the Claw? The very organization the Magikai claims to be against?" I finish for the vamp.

"It could just be a coincidence," Hugh clarifies, "but either way, it does raise one's concern."

I look around the group. Lynx is falling asleep in his chair, no doubt exhausted from the continued care of his triplets. Aggie and Ever are alternating between listening and gossiping between themselves.

"Got anything to add, Daddy Bear?" I ask Todd. He rolls his eyes, shaking his head at me.

"I have repeatedly asked you not to call me that."

"No you haven't!"

"Well, consider this me asking you repeatedly in advance, and then I won't have to repeat myself. But as a matter of fact, I do have an idea. We need to take the initiative here and go on the offensive. What you found so far is great, but we can't keep waiting for more information to fall in our lap. We use the paperwork Hugh found. Perhaps Chrys's family, or some other witches, can help us with disguises. Get a few of us in as workers and a few as guests. And we go now while Nahum's drawing the head representative's focus. You seem to think Amun is up to something, and I trust your judgment. It's our duty as enforcers to find out, if nothing else."

Todd slams a fist on the table, eyes blazing. I keep telling and telling you, ladies. He cooks, he cleans, he lifts, he protects, he attacks, and he has a sense of duty. Snag him up. He's affronted at the very idea of Amun's possible abuse of power. But I'm gleeful, if I'm being honest.

I've always had a healthy disrespect for authority. And I've never cared for the head representative. This is my chance.

Hopefully violent justice, here we come.

10

Bring On the Slots

It says *slots*, not *sluts*. Yes I saw you look up to check. No, for all my potty-mouthing I wouldn't refer to my fellow females in such a way. Hell's bells, I'm inappropriate, not an asshole.

Back to business.

I crane my neck to stare up at the sign at the entrance of the head representative's casino. We're clustered in an alleyway across the street.

"Lusca Palms," Ever reads. "*¡Que mamera!*" She tugs on the collar of her floor staff uniform. It's abysmal. High white neckline, black bowtie, and a buttoned up sleeveless black vest over top of a long-sleeved button up shirt.

The sign that hangs over the casino's entrance isn't much better. A larger-than-life Lusca, shark head bearing a massive, toothy grin. Each tentacle of the creature painted on the sign is reaching for something. A slot machine, dice, pushing chips in for roulette, grabbing a cocktail, even one tentacle pinching the buttocks of a blushing waitress. Very cheesy.

At least we didn't have to throw Ever into what passes for a waitress outfit around here. If the sign is to be believed. I'd have ripped the head off the first magical to lay a hand on her, if she didn't get to it first. Lynx is standing in a floor staff uniform as well.

Aggie and Chrys *are* dressed up as cocktail waitresses. Tied tops that are more bra than shirt. Fishnet stockings and heels. And short skirts that are going to give someone an eyeful if they need to bend or lean to reach anything. They both volunteered, and I'm not going to tell them no. But one wrong grab from a patron and I may well blow our cover.

"Not a word," Aggie grumbles as she tugs on the skirt for the thirteenth time.

Hugh and Todd are both wearing black-on-black suits. Hugh's going to be our limo driver, and Todd my bodyguard. Inside our "limo," borrowed from the vamp mansion, Hugh's set up a lovely surveillance system.

While the others look like themselves, Chrys provided some glamour potions for us Weres, courtesy of her family. Jaw-droppingly expensive, but effective. Ever is now even shorter, with chin-length sandy hair and blue eyes.

I am currently sporting thick, wavy black hair that cascades over my shoulders, and an emerald green eye. I've filled out a bit, and if I make it through the evening without bumping into something with my ridiculous cleavage it'll be a miracle. The only small issue is my missing eye. Whatever the power of the Fates is to have prevented it regenerating, it must apply to concealment magic as well. I've got my thick locks pinned in front of that side of my face, covering my eyepatch.

Ever and Hugh go in first, through the employee entrance. I wait several minutes until I see a sleek purple sports car pull up.

"Shiny." I hold my hands out and pretend to grab at it. Nahum steps out and onto the carpeted walkway that leads into the casino. He glances around, purple eyes landing on our hiding place.

"Time to go," Todd murmurs out the side of his mouth as he ushers me toward the limo.

I don't like this. Too many variables.

Nahum echoes in my mind from across the street. Grouchy dragon.

Maybe not. But we need to find out what he's up to, I shoot back.

And I'm already in Amun's inner circle. You can leave this up to me. You can trust me, Never.

I let that thought linger without a response. I *should* be able to. I *want* to. But every time I consider taking that leap, the urge is followed by a wave of self-loathing. Haven't I made this mistake? What did trusting Damien cost me? Years of my life with the Collectors, and a couple hundred more of being a lonely enforcer who didn't let anyone else in. I'm not ready.

If you want something done right ...

Hugh circles the street and pulls us up to the entrance. I take a deep breath as Todd gets out and walks around the side of the car. He opens the door and offers me a hand.

Now or Never.

Never.

I guess it's now *and* Never.

Man, I crack myself up sometimes. And sometimes *only* myself, judging by the reaction of the bear when I voice my 'now or never' pun out loud. Todd just rolls his eyes.

I throw on a dazzling smile and kick one leg out of the car, highlighting the slit in my shimmering, curve-hugging emerald gown. My features may look different than normal, but I know how to put on a flirtatious show.

"Thank you Fox," I intone, smiling at Todd. He rolls his eyes again. It's like he's got them set on a spin cycle around me. His name's meaning is a testament to the fact that some magicals really don't think before they name.

I hold my breath and walk through the entrance. No alarms sound, so I think we're in the clear. Chrys told me her family's appearance glamour would get through any detection devices. Then again, trust but verify. Now I just have to contend with the fact that the effects are temporary. We've got until maybe midnight before the spell could fail.

"I feel like Cinderella," I mutter as Todd follows me in, doing an excellent job of looking the silent and lethal bodyguard type.

We're sitting down to poker, Nahum informs me as we enter.

Todd and I make our way past the main lobby. There are several large fountains, some of which are sitting in between slot machines.

I let out a whistle.

"Fancy."

"Cluttered," Todd counters.

We pass the poker table, but I don't so much as glance at the dragon as I make my way over to a roulette table. Close enough that I can see him, and far enough to avoid suspicion. A silent Todd follows in my wake. Amun doesn't so much as give the bear a second glance. Todd's met him before, but not spent much time around the head representative, and I doubt Amun deigns to notice anyone he considers beneath him.

I glance over my shoulder once as I place my first bet, and see Todd shooting glares at anyone who happens to glance in my direction. I can tell most of the gazes are lustful, or curious. New guests are always interesting, after all. But one or two rounds of suspicion hit my intuition. We need to be careful. After all, we're playing a very dangerous game.

I've been at the roulette table long enough to suffer through one very lackluster cocktail, Elios would weep, when someone is bold enough to sit next to me.

"You seem to be doing well." I snap my head up at the Scottish accent and find myself face to face with Calder. The kelpie leans close, examining my growing pile of chips. In my current disguise, our features aren't all that dissimilar. Both dark wavy hair, both green eyes.

I will my heart rate to slow down. No doubt he can sense it.

I flash him a dazzling smile and kick one leg over the other, revealing a toned calf and black stiletto heel.

"Would you believe it's all beginner's luck? I've never even played before." I stare down at my chips and bite at my bottom lip. They're fuller than normal right now, and I've got a shade of "you wish you could kiss me" red lipstick on them.

"Actually, I would. I thought I knew everyone who was a regular here. I've been staying at the resort the past couple of months. And I would certainly have remembered seeing you."

The kelpie is throwing me off my game. His words are flirtatious and forward, which one might expect in this setting. His emotions, though. He's almost worried to find me here. Maybe that's too big a word for it. *Concerned*, and also put-out. Like I've interrupted something. But he's the one who sat next to me, so he'll have to deal.

"Place your bets," the reptilian shifter running the table instructs.

"Ladies first," Calder insists, green eyes shimmering. Shows what he knows. I throw a couple smaller chips onto a random number. Calder picks the same one. I tilt my head, making sure to keep my hair over my missing eye as I look at him.

"That's risky."

"I like to live on the edge. And I've found gorgeous females such as yourself are worth the trouble." He smiles, perfect white teeth in his human form. Oh boy, is he laying it on thick. I bite back a laugh as Todd's disdain rolls over my shoulders.

I lose the first bet; no surprise there. I continue making other small ones while I try to home in on Nahum and Amun's conversation over at their poker table. A few more magicals have joined them.

What's he saying? I demand.

He's introduced me to a few other representatives. A bunch of them are currently staying at the resort on the floors above this. Here early for the conclave.

I'm definitely going to that, I insist.

He did also invite me to 'make use' of some of the females who work here. Although he presented them as formal employees, so it's at least above-board.

I scowl. Not because I'm jealous, you understand. Just because it's loathsome to talk about 'making use' of another being.

It goes without saying I turned that offer down. Dragons do not betray their mates. Nahum is adamant.

Well, that would be a change of pace for my relationships. Although as far as I know Damien didn't cheat on me. Just dumped me with the Collectors and then hunted me across the globe once I got loose.

Nahum doesn't find it funny. In truth, I don't either. And I don't buy "above board" for a single second. Amun is slimy; I'm sure of it.

"Are you placing a bet this round?" Calder questions from my side. He's apathetic about the game, but I do sense an undercurrent of impatience. If not for the gambling, then what?

"My drink must be going to my head!" I state, feigning a small swoon as I push a tall pile of chips onto seventeen black. He follows suit again. After this round, I'm headed to that poker table, invite or no.

"Seventeen black," the reptile shifter calls out. His voice is as flat as his emotions. Not nearly as exciting when it's someone else winning the money, I suppose.

"I think I'll take that as a sign to quit while I'm ahead," I state, signaling to Todd to gather up my chips as I scan the room for where I can cash out. I spot the cage over on a far wall. Some human casinos do have their tellers behind bars, like it's a bank. Not here. What's the point? I'm sure they've staffed security with some very heavy hitters, given the wealth no doubt held in this building.

He's invited our group to see some of the inventory we'll be discussing at the conclave. Nahum's voice echoes in my mind as Calder speaks next to me.

"How about just one more round, darling?" Green eyes beseech me, but I've no interest in them. I flash him a regretful smile.

Probably showing off his hoard of magical money and trinkets. It could be this is where the Magikai pays people from, when enforcers are paid out of their personal stores.

Hoard, Nahum scoffs, *a dragon would never use its hoard that way.*

The Magikai only offer the payment option rarely. Magical artifacts, objects, and even spells. They're rumored to have an unparalleled collection, but they're very miserly about it. Most of the time we get paid the boring way—jewels, coins, and cold hard cash. Not that it ever bothered me before.

You should go with him. See just what they're working with. I stand up to move toward the poker table. Maybe if I play my cards right—cards, ha, no, not the moment? All right, then—I can pretend to flirt with my own dragon mate in this form and get myself an invite as well. I am trying to trust the male, but I prefer what I can see with my own one eye.

"I'm afraid I really must insist." Calder reaches out and wraps a hand around my wrist, tugging me back down into my chair.

"Hands. Off," Todd snarls. He's staring Calder down and growling over lengthening fangs. Calder blanches a bit, but he doesn't release me.

"Listen. If you knew what—"

Nahum's group has already stood up and is almost off the casino floor when an alarm starts blaring.

Several of the patrons stand, shoving back chairs and toppling tables. A few move toward the front doors as they burst open and dozens of supernaturals force their way inside. The human-formed ones are clad top to toe in black clothing, including masks and caps to conceal their identities. A few, though, seem less deterred at the prospect of being outed.

Right off the bat, I see a pattern. There are several boobries, which are always easy to spot. Think flamingo meets dinosaur and you'll be on the right track. If I'm not very much mistaken, there's a water bull charging through the casino, upturning slot machines. Not that I've encountered many of those. There are also several horses with seaweed and shells woven into their manes. Even in the desert, they're dripping water onto the floor. More kelpies.

"All Scottish creatures. Friends of yours? A robbery, perhaps?" I level the questions at Calder with a glare. Whatever he's up to, he's ruining my recon mission. Although I must admit, the sight of several of the representatives hauling ass away from the gaming floor instead of standing to fight lightens my mood considerably.

Dammit, I've lost track of Amun.

Over here! Nahum's voice hits my mind at the same time as Calder's response.

"We have higher aims than robbery," Calder sneers. "And I'm no mere kelpie." The last word is garbled as he transforms. He grows until he's larger than any kelpie I've ever seen. His coat is the same dark, almost-black of his hair. His mane is interwoven with kelp and seaweed. His teeth become sharp, dagger-like points. A long tongue flits out that's forked at the end. Instead of hooves, his front legs end in long green talons that could easily be mistaken for reeds in the water if he were in a dark loch. He lifts his head and lets out an echoing screech, and the floors shake.

"Amun!" Calder yells. "Where is she? Where. Is. She?" He stamps his hind hooves into the floor, forming dents.

I shove at Todd.

"No idea who *she* is, but *we're* getting out of here right now!"

"What—" Todd tilts his head at the demonic-looking horse-like creature in front of us, perplexed.

"Each-uisge!" I yell at him, and a few of the fleeing magicals must overhear me, because several echo it in fear.

"Each-uisge!" they yell, scampering away from us.

A kelpie on crack. A kelpie on steroids. A kelpie on a very intense exercise regimen. Take your pick. Both species will lure you to your watery grave, but each-uisge are far more vicious, calculating, and dangerous. Far more powerful as well, which is why I'm not even that surprised when the fountains on the rims of the playing floors start overflowing and flooding the carpeted area.

Todd and I make our way across the floor, wading, but the representatives, or whatever muscle they've hired, are beginning to fight back. The floor is a mess of machines, Scottish creatures, and casino staff. Calder dives into the rising waves and swims toward what I imagine must be the vault. I really hope he doesn't hurt Amun.

Because that old lion is mine.

"To the exit!" I yell at Todd. He grunts, throwing on his fur. I'm not too proud to admit it: I hop on and cling to him as he swims us through the unnaturally high waters. Weres and water don't mix under the best of circumstances, and I'm still not keen on showing myself. We're getting close to the doors when I hear a familiar yell.

"Hold on, we'll cut a path!" Chrys. I see the purple glow of her magic as she begins weaving it into the water. Aggie is back to back with her fellow witch, stripping the magic from anyone who gets close, whether they're Magikai or Scottish supernatural.

"Lynx and Ever are getting the limo!" the witchling yells.

Todd surges forward, and we're almost through the path Chrys has cut for us when something collides with me, sending me tumbling into the waves.

"Never!" I hear the others scream as the water carries me away.

11

Casinos and Calling Cards

I let my claws lengthen, but whatever or whoever pummeled me doesn't strike again. I push against the sloshing water, but it's no use. I put my energy into keeping my head above the waves. The edge of my sequined green dress catches on something, and for a few terrifying moments I'm tugged back under. I rip the material, frantic, and kick to the surface. As I do, my leg catches on something sharp, slicing into my calf.

I gasp as my head breaks through the water, sucking in air and cursing the leg wound that's already stitching itself up. Plus side? My bangs are in place. Great to know that if some representatives are pulled past me on the waves, my cover isn't blown.

You're hurt! Where are you?

The dragon. Oh, thank the moon!

I'm stuck in the water. I can't swim against it.

Hold on!

He's terrified and furious all at once.

I float by a slot machine. Its glinting neon lights are unsettling under the water as I hear the flap of wings over the current. Nahum dives and pulls me from the waves.

"The water is blocking the front doors!" I warn him. I can't see the witches anymore. I can't see anything in the front anymore, over the wall of water barricading the exits.

"I have an idea!" he yells. He tucks his wings back and dives over the counter of the cage where the casino workers help people cash out. The water is lapping at the counter's edges, but the floor here is only soggy, not flooded.

"The workers must have run the first chance they got," I observe as I catch my breath and look around the empty cage. I lean against a stack of boxes that jingle with the sound of coins as I press against them.

"Amun's got personal security on the way down from the resort floors. Whatever the Scottish representative's aims, I don't think he'll get what he hoped from this visit," Nahum informs me, back in his skin except for his wings.

"He asked Amun, 'Where is she?' But I have no idea who he could mean," I tell him, giving up the only information I have. Beyond the cage I hear shouting and a crash. Feel the waves of anger coming from two different contingents as the Scottish forces and Amun's security and enforcers meet on the water.

"Should we help them?" Nahum tilts his head, wings flexing behind him as he asks the question.

"Which side?" I dislike Amun, but I'm not letting it bias me in something of this magnitude. For all I know, Calder's an even bigger villain. He could be the only villain. It's still possible that Amun is one of the 'good' guys, even if he is an asshole.

I shake my head.

"We'll let them settle it and see what information can be gleaned from the results," I decide. Waiting and watching isn't what I'd call my strong suit, but I have had to flex the skill from time to time as an enforcer. My 'rush in and figure it out as I go' strategy works on most occasions, but every now and again exercising restraint is the better option.

Particularly when one is in a disguise that's due to fade any moment, and one doesn't even know who the enemies are. Or their motivations. Or their numbers. Or how to stop them. You know, all those pesky details.

"Well then, as long as we're waiting ..." Nahum walks over to me, arms grabbing at the shelves above my head as he stares, towering over me.

I glance down. The dragon's naked since he doesn't shift back with clothes.

"What do you plan on doing about your attire when you leave?"

"I'll put my scales back on," he responds, but his eyes drop to my lips.

Nahum presses us up against the shelves and coins clatter, cold metal hitting my back as they cascade to the floor.

I reach behind me and snatch one, holding it out to him.

"What do you think? Take the money and run?" I tease. As if I ever would. I have a lot of flaws. But I can't be bought. I stay where the action is. Where I'm needed. Nahum grabs the coin and tosses it.

"You're very attractive when you're plotting, but even more when you're throwing away riches and endangering yourself for other magicals."

A clawed hand reaches up to cup my face. He tilts my chin.

"There you are." He sighs. He wraps his other hand in my hair, and as he pulls it forward I see the edges are beginning to transition back to silver.

"You do realize this will make my leaving the facilities that much harder?"

He scoffs.

"I'll throw a few attendants into a nightmare long enough to sneak you through the hall. Easier done than said."

And here he said *I'm* plotting. It's easy to forget how dangerous Nahum can be. I almost wouldn't believe it myself. Almost. But I've been on the receiving end of those nightmares, and they're nothing to snort at.

"You would do that to help me?" I press, needing the reassurance. Needing more than that to feel the affirmative emotions that come alongside it, confirming I can trust the dragon.

"I'm still hoping we're wrong about the Magikai; that at worst they're disorganized or inept, not villainous. And I know we're still figuring things out; I don't want to threaten your independence. That being said, if the Magikai mean you harm, I will decimate them all without a second thought."

Ladies, gents, shifters and succubi, there are a few moments where someone has said something so moon's-darned seductive to me I really couldn't be held responsible for my reaction. And threatening to destroy an entire corrupt government for an anti-authoritarian like myself is one of those times.

I wrap my legs around the dragon, balancing against the shelves as I pull him in. Our tongues intertwine as my mouth slits open against his, and I start a different kind of plotting. After all, we're stuck in this cage for who knows how long.

Nahum is biting a trail down my neck that's leaving a delicious, electric feel when the general cacophony of yells and bangs outside is replaced by a singular voice.

"That's it! Drive them back! Bring them down! We've got them now!" Amun. And the cock-blocking lion is gleeful and vengeful at once. That means he's winning. I find myself disappointed at the notion, even without knowing who the villain actually is here.

I press against Nahum, pushing him off.

"I can get you out now, before they see you," Nahum says. "My offer still stands. I can hide you from the Magikai and Scots alike."

"No. That would be a waste of your cover. I have a better idea. If you go out now and join the end of the fight, you could get even closer to the head representative."

He frowns.

"I'd have to put some of the Scots into a nightmare."

"You can let them out again once they're in custody, right?"

He nods his head.

"Correct. I won't kill them. Not until we have the answers we're looking for."

I think for another moment, and outside the cage Amun yells again.

"That's it! We've got them now!"

"The Scots are falling anyway. Throw one or two into a nightmare, just temporarily. And go with the lion. I'll slip out while they're distracted and find a back way out."

He hesitates, but I push at him again.

"It's all right. I've been in worse spots before. Now go, before you miss your chance."

Nahum begins to put on his scales and readies to leap over the counter of the cage.

"And Nahum?" He glances back at me. "I'm afraid this will have to count as our date this month." The dragon snarls, frustration fueling him as he leaps into the fray. I hear screams and feel terror. I assume he's found his first mark.

I make my way to a door at the back end of the cage and let myself out. It opens into a hallway. It's not carpeted or fancy, so it must be employees only. Following a series of confusing halls with no useful signage whatsoever—honestly, Amun, put up a map—I'm able to find a stairwell with carpeting that leads up. At least I'm getting somewhere.

It lets out into a lobby with vaulted ceilings and marble floors. I must be at the resort entrance over the casino. And it's emptier than a tomb.

I take a few steps in the lobby, and while my features are halfway back to normal, my outfit isn't. The black stilettos I'm wearing click and echo against the marble floors. I cringe and bend down to rip them off, but I'm too late.

"Hey! What are you doing up here?" My hair has fallen over my face, so at least I've got that going for me. They haven't seen my features yet. I kick off the shoes and run as fast as my feet will carry me across the lobby and into a darkened hall beyond. No sense blowing my cover now.

"Stop!" I hear the enforcers behind me, but I ignore them and push myself faster, my feet pounding the floor. I'm dying to shift, but I'm saving it for the most dire circumstances.

"Grab her!" another person yells. If I don't miss my mark, there's a good four sets of feet running behind me now.

"Stop her. At all costs! Amun said they've all got to be caught!" Do they think I'm a Scottish supernatural?

I round a corner, realizing when I see the dead end in front of me the mistake I've made. Trapped. I'm in some dark alcove, with nothing more than a giant mirror on the wall and a cushy bench for seating. A nice little secluded place for a tête-a-tête, but useless in an escape. The footsteps are getting closer.

I am screwed. I have every confidence in my ability to fight my way out, but that means blowing my cover, and possibly everyone else's if they get suspicious about the others here tonight. Amun is sharp enough to guess anyone connected to me was involved.

I let my claws rip loose, and as I do a hand clamps over mine. The corner next to me is shadowed. And, I should have realized, *more* shadowed than is normal.

"Come with me," a familiar voice says before wrapping me in darkness.

When the hand releases me, I shake the shadows loose. They're soft, like being wrapped in silk. Not exactly a bad feeling, but off-putting to say the least.

"What in hell's moon?" I demand, kicking away the last of the pesky things as Visitor sucks the shadows back into himself. I give our surroundings a quick once-over. The Bone Reader's messenger has transported us to an alley somewhere on the strip. Bright lights abound, but we're safely hidden from prying eyes. Behind a dumpster loaded to the brim with garbage. I raise my lip at a rotting banana on top of one refuse pile. Gotta love the city.

Visitor adjusts the cufflinks of his pristine slate suit.

"You were careless," he accuses, not glancing up at me.

"And just what were you doing there?" The Bone Reader is mysterious enough on his own, but this particular entity is someone he's sent for me a few times now. Always bringing word from the Bone Reader. And always complicating things, even when he appears to help.

He looks at me now, raising one dark brow. Disapproving. His shadowed form is gone and in its place is a pale-skinned man. Clothing immaculately pressed, chiseled jaw clenched. Eyes bluer than any human could naturally have. Species? A mystery.

"You're welcome. Thankless Were," he scoffs, put out at my lack of gratitude.

"I—" All right, point taken. "Thanks for the save. But that doesn't answer my question. What were you doing in a magical casino around some very shady characters?"

"Shade." He gives a half-chuckle. The closest I've ever seen him to cracking a real, warm smile. "Not half bad. I was there, and am here, for the same reason as always. Representing the interests of the Bone Reader."

"And he's interested in what? Slot machines, debauchery, representative intrigue, and some sort of European overthrow of the Magikai?"

"As a matter of fact, yes. To some of the above." Sincere, and amused. We're back to our typical territory, then. "But most of all, he's invested in you." Visitor stabs a slender finger out to my chest. This male is maddening. He's cold and refined. As he stares me down, it's not lost on me that he could get people to toss their hearts to him with those eyes if his gaze weren't so harsh. I've seen his control of shadows before, but I'd never realized he could transport others inside them.

"I've got to tell you. You show up at the moon's damnedest times, but I'm not complaining. I don't suppose there's a way to summon you if I need a quick escape again?" I mean it in jest, but his upper lip raises into a sneer, offense clear as it slaps my intuition.

"Cheeky. And impertinent. Still, I do think you're on the right track. I'm sure the Bone Reader wouldn't mind offering his assistance. For a fee, of course."

"Naturally."

"Although in this case, I think you'll find getting myself to you will be simple enough. Just tap your eyepatch. Twice."

I reach up, feeling the always cold silver under my fingertips. There's an etching on it that I can't decipher, courtesy of the Bone Reader.

"Is that how you found me? It's some kind of tracking patch?"

He laughs, the sound hollow and chilling.

"I was here already, as fate would have it." I growl, and he laughs again in response.

"Come now, Were, if you can dish it out, surely you can take a jest." Given the Fates are currently using my missing eye for their own purposes, it's not a topic I find funny. He clears his throat, impassive expression falling back into place. "But tap twice if you need something again. Just remember, everything has a price."

"I don't intend to pay the Bone Reader again."

He smirks, one side of his lip turning up.

"Oh, I wouldn't be so sure about that. And I wouldn't be so certain you'll regret it, either. The Bone Reader can be a powerful ally."

I've no doubt. I've got a soft spot for the ancient magical being. But power doesn't equal right.

"Where did you take us, anyway? I need to get back to my friends. Who knows how long it'll take to find them in a city the size of Vegas?"

I look out into the streets, then back at Visitor. He's never given me a real name. His form has gone unsolid as he shifts back into shadows. They roll over my skin, a silken caress as he disappears.

"I think you'll find you're just where you need to be. Remember, two taps."

The shadows fade, and the lights and sounds of Vegas rush back in.

12
Of All the Luck

"We've got to go back for her!" The unmistakable sound of a familiar witchling's voice finds me in the alley. Decisive, determined, and self-assured. It's nice to feel these emotions from the once-timid stripper.

"Is it possible you're referring to me?" I step out of the alley and onto the sidewalk, spreading my arms to gesture at myself.

"*¿Donde andaba, que le pasó?*" Ever demands, scowling as her shock fades into relief. "And stop feeling so cocky. We were worried."

"Thank goodness!" Aggie has already wrapped her arms around my middle and is staring up at me as she squeezes me into a tight hug.

"We've got her. Back alley," Lynx rattles off what I assume are the nearest street names into a cell phone. His dirty-blond hair is always a bit disheveled, but even more so now. He looks like a drowned cat.

"Calling our getaway car?" I question, glancing over the others to look for Chrys, Todd, and Hugh.

"Yes. Amun's got enforcers, casino employees, and his personal security scouring the area for any lingering Scottish magicals. They're

rounding up everyone who was in the casino, so be ready to move."
Lynx is a pretty carefree kitty most of the time, but he's on edge now.
Jaw clenched and grinding.

Tires squeal as an SUV careens onto our street. It screeches to a
halt next to us, and I drop into a defensive stance, ready for whatever
comes out.

"Put your claws away and get in! Now!" Todd's voice sounds
from the driver's seat. The side door pops open and a grinning Chrys
greets us as we pile in. She slams it shut before I've even sat down and
Todd guns it, speeding away from the area.

"I take this to mean things did *not* go according to plan?" I tease,
attempting to lighten the mood a bit. After all, the others may not
realize it, but this much negativity in an enclosed space is suffocating
to an intuitive. Compounded by the fact that Ever and I can feel each
other's discomfort.

"Since when do things ever go according to plan around you?"
Todd grumbles. "Certainly not any time we've worked together."

"Hey! My plans are works of art," I snark back, poking a finger in
Todd's face as he drives.

"Never, I think you got your name because you *never* have a plan.
Except to win," he fires back, but in spite of his words his bad mood
is seeping away. Sweet relief.

"Wrong. I run a two-step process. Number one, identify a target.
Number two, hunt them down. Number three, collect the money
and celebrate."

"Never, that's three, maybe even three and a half—oh, never
mind." Ever huffs as she pulls off the bowtie from her casino uniform.

The car falls into relative quiet as Todd drives us out of the
strip and up into the canyons that surround the vamp mansion and
grounds.

"Don't suppose anyone wants to tell me what happened to my
limo? Hugh, perhaps?"

The vamp-turned-Were gives me a sheepish smile.

"Valet parked in a random hotel lot. Too many of the Magikai's guests had arrived in one, so we were forced to find alternate transportation."

He squirms, and I can feel the guilt. I give him a wide grin.

"Hugh, my law-following, paperwork-interpreting, legal-eagle Were. Am I to understand that you *stole* this car?"

Confirmation slams into me from his direction. Hugh opens his mouth to respond, but Chrys cuts him off.

"*I* stole it. Technically. Hugh doesn't know how to hotwire. And I disabled the GPS, so if someone decides they're missing it, they can't track us. Pretty sure it's an airport rental."

I give a sniff. Underneath all of our scents, I can smell the numerous layers of past passengers and half-hearted attempts at cleaner to cover up the fact that someone smoked in here. She's probably right.

"Good thinking, witch." A personal car, I would have felt the need to pay back. A company car? These rental agencies are large enough to stomach the loss.

We pull onto vampire property, and my mansion appears as we pass the gates. It's invisible beyond that, thanks to Chrys's defensive spell skills. When we exit the car and walk through the double doors, it's like a cue to everyone to relax. Weariness batters me as the others slump into the chairs and chaise-lounges that litter the front hall. I still haven't gotten around to redecorating. Maybe someday.

I clap my hands hard enough that the sound echoes in the cavernous entrance. Lynx jumps, already half asleep in his chair. Todd frowns.

"All right, crew. First, sleep. Then, breakfast. And at breakfast, we plot."

Ever groans.

"I hate to even suggest this, but shouldn't you and I head back? All this happened at the casino while we were off training grounds. Won't Amun be suspicious?" She shakes her dark hair loose.

"No. That's just what *would* make him suspicious, if we come sneaking back right after this fiasco. I'm going to act normal. Which means we linger here tomorrow and go flouncing back to the training grounds at the last possible moment. Unbothered by anything except the fact that we'll be bunking in the desert," I inform her. Her emotions are at war. She's uncertain about the idea, but she's bone-tired.

"All right. Fine. *Estoy redindida pero vamos.*"

"Praise the moon!" I exclaim as I walk into the dining hall just after first light to find the table already laden with food. One of the many vamps sets down a silver serving tray full of bacon slices and gives me an uncertain smile as he sniffs at the food.

"Thank you." He dips his chin and skitters away. The vamps haven't given me any issues, but I still wouldn't say they know what to make of me. They like me better than their previous ruler, Costas, because I'm not forcing any of them into a harem or mercenary service for the Claw. Still, I know I'm not boss of the year. I'm no vamp, and I don't have much in common with the shopping-addicted, blood-guzzling supernaturals.

I reach for the tray and grab a fistful of bacon to stuff into my mouth.

"Get your grubby paws off that!" Todd's voice booms. He sets another silver container down, this one holding cheesy eggs. "You can sit down with everyone else. I'll ask the vamps to go wake them."

I gaze longingly at the tray and swipe one more piece as I walk past.

"I hate waiting," I grumble as I follow Todd back to the kitchens. If I can't eat, I'd better engage in one of my other favorite pastimes:

making a nuisance of myself. Or so I think, until I spot someone I'm even happier to see than Todd.

"Elios, my sunshine-dispositioned satyr. Old friend, old pal." I'd forgotten he was here.

"It's too early, you daft Were. Get out of my kitchen!" His watery eyes glare at me, but I can tell he's comfortable here. Probably a nice break from the Lusty Lute and its rowdy crowd.

"Who's running the bar while you're gone?" I ask, popping my last slice of bacon into my mouth and licking my lips.

"Are you completely mad? I'm not letting anyone touch that bar without me there! I've shut it down for the week." I cringe, mostly because that must have taken some doing, to pry him away from his home and business. Todd wasn't kidding; I've no doubt it cost me. Better make it count.

"Elios, I will agree to get out and stay out of this kitchen"—I hold up a finger as he moves to interrupt—"if you can whip me up some mimosas. Perhaps a whole flight of them?"

"Oversimplified nonsense. Not even a challenge," he mutters as he makes his way back to the liquor shelves.

"Can some of them glow and have bubbles that float out of the glass?" I yell after him, throwing out the first two suggestions that come to my head.

"Crazed, demanding female!" he shouts back at me, but I feel the interest and happiness as I set the challenge.

"He was going to show Nahum a vault? Containing what? Are they using the magical world's wealth to give out goodie bags to all the representatives at the conclave or something?" Chrys demands as I fill the group in on my admittedly limited intel over breakfast. I take a sip of a mango-pineapple mimosa, smacking my lips in appreciation.

"Or could he be adding to it? Maybe he meant to show it as an incentive? You know—'Look at all this stuff, if you want any favors from me you'll have to give me something even more impressive'—like he was trying to get Nahum to bribe him?" Todd guesses, but he's uncertain of the answer.

"No one laugh," Aggie insists, nose scrunched up as she scowls at us. "But why does it matter what he does with the Magikai's stores? Doesn't the stuff belong to him, anyway?"

"Actually—" I start, then feel the positively giddy emotions floating at my intuition from Hugh's direction. Stuff like this is his Christmas. "Go ahead," I say instead, sticking my tongue out to catch a floating blueberry champagne bubble.

"Thank you, Lady Never," he says, then turns back to Aggie.

"When the Magikai were first formed, years and years ago, they set down the few binding rules we all live by today."

"Binding!" Chrys sputters, letting out a harsh laugh. "We all know that's bogus. What are they again? No harming innocents—but we all know everyone works around that by claiming their enemies aren't any such thing. Settling conflict through pre-approved means, which just means going to the Magikai. And if they and some of the enforcers end up being corrupt, that one's out the window—"

"And no exposing ourselves on a large scale to the humans. Yes," Hugh finishes, side-eyeing the witch even though I can feel his affection for her.

Discomfort hits me from Lynx and Todd. I'm not the only one becoming more bothered by the not-so-ironclad nature of our laws. Not that I like following the rules, but it'd be nice if those who set them could.

"Anyway." Hugh snaps his fingers, bringing everyone's eyes back to him. "Yes. Rules. Flawed as they may be. But that's not all. Naturally, this new government would need funding. How else were they going to pay to train and employ enforcers to keep the peace? Provide aid to magical factions impacted by violence? And so on and so forth. So they set up a way to get funds. Not unlike taxes for the humans, although I don't think any supernatural appreciates the similarities being pointed out. All official covens, herds, sleuths, or however species name their groups, provided the Magikai an initial sum. And continue to provide them every decade, when the conclave convenes. It's what keeps everything running."

Nadia and Aggie are nodding along. My only interest has been that the Magikai pays me, but I never stopped to consider how and where they got it.

"Most of the time, they pay enforcers in some form of cash. One country's currency or another. From those funds. But some of the tributes come in the form of spells, trinkets, artifacts. When they really want a job done, they offer this as payment."

"Like they did when you tracked me down!" Ever volunteers. "Did you ever get any artifacts for that?"

I scowl, setting the champagne flute in my hand down gently on the tabletop. No sense wasting good bubbles.

"No. The Magikai were so furious that I won you over before they could get their grubby claws into you, that they wired us cash and were done with it. Even though we did, in fact, request to be paid via artifacts or spells as promised."

At the time I'd been mad, but I'd also been hunting down a way to turn Hugh into a Were so I could defeat my ex half-mate. Priorities.

Hugh nods.

"So the idea that they might be using the funds for things outside their professional guidelines, or even funneling it back to magical leaders at the conclave, is concerning, to say the least."

"Embezzlement, misuse of funds, bribes. All white-collar crimes," I grouse, scowling into my strawberry mimosa before taking a sip. Elios gave me eight flavors. Each tastier than the last. "Boring."

Hugh gasps, eyes wide and truly affronted. My silly paperwork-handling second in vamp command.

"Public corruption is *boring* to you? This could be a huge crime! What did you think you'd find?"

I shrug.

"Knowing her, she was hoping for something more violent, so she could respond in kind," Todd supplies, gesturing toward me.

"Todd, it's like you know me." I flash the bear a smile.

I should be happy that at worst we're likely dealing with a money-funneling scheme.

But I find myself disappointed.

What does that say about my violent appetites?

"Regardless of what the crime is, we'll take him down," I promise.

That lion is on my list.

13
Help Not Heroics

I've been able to find out nothing new or useful since returning to the Arizona training grounds. Amun hasn't made another appearance, and for that matter neither has Nahum. Which means no progress on the Magikai's money-handling front. But I am learning a lot about my fellow enforcers.

Namely, that most of them stink in comparison to me. And I'm not even being conceited.

Well, maybe a little.

I make my way down from the breakfast tent to the training grounds alongside Ever. After a few weeks, I've settled into a routine. The same one as when I first arrived, as a matter of fact. Go along with the charade, dig for information I have no idea how to find, and count down the days until I sleep in my beloved vamp mansion and not on a cot that I have not once, but twice, found things both creepy and crawly on top of. I have magnanimously decided to stay here until my next date with Nahum, forgoing my weekends at the mansion for more opportunities to poke around. Truly, no sacrifice is too great. I'm enduring not only shared living quarters and a lack of air conditioning, but also suffering through a brown sludge each morning that the kitchen staff have the nerve to call coffee.

"Not bad." Brutus is begrudging but impressed as I knock out one of the young wolf shifters. The head enforcer is beginning to soften toward me.

One training circle over, Ever is stretching with Ji-hwan. I still don't trust the Were, but he's kept whatever seductive abilities he has to himself around the Wereling, so I've let him keep all his appendages. In truth, he's fond of her, in what can be confirmed intuitively is a platonic way. To my disappointment, I'll admit, it might be because she also isn't much of a fighter. She can scrap with the rest of us, but the more we're here, the more I can feel her coming to the realization that deadly enforcer is perhaps not the life for her.

I go over to the edge of the circle, taking a break to pour water down the back of my neck. As much as it pains me, there's no decent bartender here. Their weekend bar is just some shifter slinging cheap beer. No elegance. Not like Elios and his cocktails. So I've traded taste for hydration.

A group of other shifters, mainly a mix of feline and reptile, walk over to Ever's circle. I take a sip but watch out the side of my eye, senses on high alert.

"Hey, Cookies and Cream. Toss over that spear, since you wouldn't know how to use it anyway," a drake sneers, addressing Ji-hwan.

I pause, waiting to see what the black and white spotted Were will do as I feel his annoyance rankle and hit me like a soft breeze.

"I have told you many times before that I prefer to go by my given name," Ji-hwan snaps, for once a snarl instead of a smile on his flawless face.

"We prefer the one we gave you. Spotty, dotty, and too soft and sweet inside to be a real enforcer." The drake spits on the ground in front of Ji-hwan's feet.

I've got to give them that one. The Were has no fighting skills to speak of. Granted, our species used to *need* combat skills as part of day-to-day life, and we don't now. Still. I shake my head, prepared to let him lose his own battles.

Ji-hwan moves to hand over the spear. The drake snatches it with a sneer.

"And who can pronounce that mess of a name, anyway? We're in Arizona. Pick something appropriate."

I did *not* just hear what I know I did. The water bottle in my hand is one of those stainless steel things that's meant to keep drinks cold. I snap it in half as I stalk across the yard, sweaty and cross.

"Hey!" I yell at the drake. He looks at me, then rolls his eyes and turns back toward his group. Big mistake. The two feline shifters and a centaur at his side leak worry. The other reptilian shifter is concerned. At least they've got some brains.

"I was talking to you!" I whap the drake across his thick-skinned lizard-head with one half of the bottle. Hard enough to make a cracking sound that echoes along the valley. He rubs his head with one hand while spinning and swiping at me with the spear in his other.

"Gorgon's hell! What was that for, you mad witch!"

"Well!" I huff. "Consider me unsurprised. You can't figure out species any better than you can figure out languages, you dull reptile. *I* am a renowned enforcer. Were princess. Vampire lady. And while I know several whose abilities you'll never come near, I'm *not* a witch. And you are going to apologize."

He snorts.

"Like hell. I wouldn't apologize to you. Everyone knows you're only here as a show pony after your work with the Claw. Killing your mate? That's cold. But I doubt it required any real talent. Backstabbing isn't a hard thing to do. Treacherous female."

Keep it together, Never. Don't rip his face off. Mustn't kill the other enforcers. Perhaps just a light maiming?

It's more than tempting. Darned reptilian magical isn't even sweating in this heat. He's more comfortable than us all combined, I'm sure. Which only adds to my temper.

"Not to me. To Ji-Hwan." I point. The Were in question stares at me, shock and surprise hitting my intuition like a slap.

"Sweetheart, there's not a soul in this circle who could make me. So why don't you go back to your little training session with the wolves before we decide to teach you a lesson as well, hmm?"

All right. He's officially gone one condescending nickname too far.

I feel the rain of emotions from those around me. Ever is anticipatory. Brutus is curious. Ji-hwan is beyond uncomfortable with the whole thing. The drake's compatriots are on edge, eager but nervous. And the drake himself? Over-confident. Someone should fix that for him.

I smile. Batting my eyelashes.

"Thank you," I simper at him.

"For what?" he scoffs.

"Giving me an excuse to do this."

I go with a classic. Hauling one furred arm back and throwing a punch straight into his jaw. He reels, stumbling into a few of his buddies as he spits out a fang. He's not fully shifted yet, and he drops to a knee.

Beautiful. I live for the simple things. Like retributive violence.

"Bitch!" He spits the word, along with a little bit of blood, onto the training circle. Behind him, his posse shifts as well. They're not as thirsty for the fight as he is, but I've seen this dynamic before. They're not backing down while he's watching.

I plant my feet, crossing furred arms as I wait for the drake to shift fully. I'm nothing if not sporting. After several seconds, I pull one hand up and examine my claws.

"By all means, go at a snail's pace. I will have to leave at lunch, you understand, but I've got some time to spare. Happy to extend a courtesy to those who never mastered the quick shift."

The drake flips his head up, final scales falling into place. He growls, snapping fangs. Seems he also hasn't mastered speaking in this form.

"Ready?" I ask, leaning in close. He lunges, and I pull back just far enough for his fangs to snap shut on empty air.

"Oh, a feisty drake. How fun." And it *is* fun. I haven't felt this free in a while. Sometimes you just need to pummel someone.

I back up, the shifters following me into the cactus-lined circle. I've learned already that they're spelled somehow, durable enough to have a magical slam right into them and stay standing.

I duck, weave, and kick past two felines and a reptile shifter from the drake's crew. The centaur turns and kicks out with his back hooves, and I drop to the ground to avoid having my skull cracked open. Life hack: never walk behind a centaur, friends. Their kicks are no joke. I roll and come up on the side of him, jumping up and using his back as a springboard. He lets out a whinny as I leap off him and through the air at the drake.

My claws just manage to graze him as two cats slam into my side. For a few moments, we're a pile of snarling fur and fangs, but I've got them yowling and retreating out of the circle quick enough.

I'm realizing it's a little bit harder to handle people if you aren't willing to just rip them open.

The reptile shifter runs at me as the centaur readies for another kick.

I sidestep, and I'm shocked to my furred feet that the move works. The centaur's hooves slam into the reptile's chest and he goes flying into the cacti. It pierces even the thick reptile's skin and he yelps, tucking his leathery tail as he exits.

"Ever?" I toss the words to my protégé. "Care to join, or am I having all the fun today?"

She sighs, exasperation present. I love many things about the Wereling: her sense of family and loyalty, the easy way she connects to others. But she's got a total lack of interest in brawling that I can't quite wrap my mind around.

I step back and watch her handle the centaur, but it's clear it's more of a chore for her. Still, she *is* handling it.

"Shall we?" I hold out a hand to the drake and curtsy. He lets out an odd sound that's half hiss and half roar.

I weave us around the circle, dodging his talons and striking him when the mood strikes me. Drawing things out. I haven't had this much fun in ages. No sense in cutting it short.

When are you finished training today? Can you meet me east of the Magikai's grounds?

My cheek throbs as the drake lands a hit. That's going to bruise, dammit.

Do you need help? Panic consumes Nahum. I can feel it from here. That's just what I need. For the dragon to swoop in and totally blow the cover off our secret connection.

All handled here, thanks. But I'm a bit busy at the moment. Beating a foul-mouthed drake into the ground.

Have fun. But I have some information to share with you. And you owe me a date.

Is it the lure of a date with the dragon or the promise of information that has me deciding to end the fight now?

I yawn, ignoring the ache in my jaw and appreciating the fury that comes off the drake in waves.

"This has been mildly entertaining, but my ride is here," I state just before launching at him full-force.

In only a few blows, I've got an unconscious drake at my feet and the rest of his group running for their tents.

"Wow!"

"Awesome!"

"You really showed them!"

The teen wolf shifters crowd Ever and me, oozing admiration.

Brutus approaches and holds out a hand to shake.

"Not bad. But don't play with your food," he teases.

"Brutus, are you demonstrating a sense of humor? Is it possible we are becoming besties?" I do my best imitation of Aggie and throw my arms around him.

"We are no such thing!" he huffs as he shoves me off, but he smiles. "Although I have to admit you can fight. Having you here has been a good model for the others."

Ji-hwan steps past the head enforcer.

"Thank you," he says, staring at the ground. All this time trying to win me over, and he's frustrated now that I've actually done something to help. I take a guess at the issue.

"Hey," I snap, "I have no intention of adding 'savior complex' to my ever growing list of traits. That was a one-time event in the name of Were pride. But you're going to learn to handle yourself. I've no intention of fighting your battles for you."

He looks up, anticipatory but forlorn.

"I can't. I don't know how."

"Which is just the problem with all the enforcers here. And it ends now. You're going to learn. Starting tomorrow, you come to the training circle with Ever. And I teach you to fight. *Really* fight."

Joy spreads and envelopes me as the Were gives a dazzling smile.

"You won't regret it!" he promises, all eagerness.

And I land on the real problem here. Brutus is a good fighter, but he hasn't studied any kind of strategy. Ji-hwan can sneak and seduce all kinds of information out of people, but he can't fight to save his own hide. And they've divided everyone up and pitted them against one another, even though the enforcers would be much more effective working as a unit.

They're given uncomfortable lodgings, little sleep, and crap food. And while learning to tolerate challenging environments can help endurance, there's no reason these enforcers couldn't be given access to a wider variety of experiences to better prepare them for missions.

The possibility that this is all accidental due to a poorly managed system is getting smaller and smaller. And I'm not a big believer in coincidences like this. They're not poorly trained because the Magikai made a mistake. My bet is, Amun doesn't want independent-thinking enforcers who can adapt and conquer. He wants single-purposed supernaturals he can use like tools to achieve his agenda.

That lion is going to wish he never brought me here.

14

Date With a Dragon

I run by the sad, wooden-walled outdoor stalls that pass for showers out here before heading off to meet Nahum. I ignore the way my heart rate speeds up as I near the area he asked us to meet.

Listen, I don't have to like certain aspects of the magical world to believe in them. A moon goddess who created wolf shifters and Weres? Never met her, but she could be out there. Mates, though? I've seen plenty of them firsthand. Their dedication to each other that supersedes all other bonds. And the unspeakable and irreparable devastation wrought if one of them dies. It's not infrequent for it to drive the surviving mate mad, if they don't just perish together.

And that kind of commitment? For someone who just got out of an almost-mating? Terrifying. Now, in fairness, Damien and I hadn't been anything to each other for a couple hundred years. In theory, I had plenty of time to get over him. Trust me when I say I got over and under plenty of other magicals while I tried. But there's no ignoring a mating bond. Even the self-imposed half-measure Damien and I had. And it doesn't hold a candle to the real thing.

I haven't even given the dragon a real 'yes'; haven't spent much time around him. But as I head to meet him, I think of all the ways this plan could go wrong. I really let myself envision the consequences. Amun finding out. Hurting the dragon.

The moment I picture it, I'm overcome by rage so suffocating I have to stop and take a breath. Even imagining it makes me want to burn down the world. Mate bonds. Powerful stuff.

And that leads to another emotion I can't stand. Guilt.

The Bone Reader told me that Damien made some kind of deal, although not with my favorite chaotic ancient magical, to help me defeat the Claw. Not that the Were bothered to tell me about it. According to the Bone Reader, Damien traded time. He gave away the years and years it would have taken for our almost-bond to actually madden him, and descended into mate madness rapidly so he could help. It led to him doing horrible things. Endangering my friends. Attacking me.

But I did send him to the Underworld. Is there a good greeting card for that?

"Sorry I condemned you to an afterlife of ushering around the supernatural dead, but you had it coming."

I shake out my damp hair, and with it the lingering thoughts. Even if I wanted to apologize, and I'm not sure I do, there's no way to accomplish it.

You appear deep in thought. Nahum's rumbling voice materializes in my mind as he steps out of the shadows. I hadn't even noticed how dark it had gotten during my walk. The sky overhead is filled with stars. You can see a lot more of them when you're not in downtown Sacramento. My heart clenches, and I wouldn't have to be intuitive to recognize nostalgia.

"Beautiful, isn't it?" Nahum asks, coming up beside me and taking my hand. I let him. I watch the dragon, and he watches the stars. He's wearing his skin and has on dark jeans and a grey shirt. His purple eyes stand out in the dark.

"Stargazing. Not a bad date idea," I inform the dragon as I turn my attention back to the night sky. He laughs.

"This is just where I pick you up for the weekend. I have somewhere else in mind."

He flashes me a seductive smile, and I bat at him half-heartedly.

"Just what kind of Were do you think I am?" I ask, halfway to winking before I remember how useless that would be. He picks up my meaning without it.

"I wouldn't say no to that, but I'd like to fly you somewhere. Did you know there's quite a few concealed magical areas across the globe? Teeming with all kinds of species right next to humans?"

"I know of a few." I've had occasion to visit some for jobs, although most of my time is spent strictly in the human-visible areas, since that's where supernaturals would cause the most trouble if they revealed themselves. "You're taking me to a centaur city, perhaps? A favorite elven hideaway?"

He shakes his head, hair replaced by scales as he does so.

"Not at all. I have a more secluded spot in mind. But it will take a couple hours to reach. I'll fly us."

He holds out a clawed and scaled hand. I hesitate for only a moment before accepting. I don't trust my heart or the dragon yet, but I do trust his abilities. He won't drop me.

"You can tell me about Amun and the conclave on the way," I instruct as he scoops me into his arms. He hands me a small pack to hold, and when I peek inside I see clothes. Maybe I should get him the same spell I got myself, so he can shift back with pants. Some dragons are as big as a bus, or several times larger. Nahum in dragon form is smaller than some, although he still towers over my Were form. I have to admit, though, in this case, I think I like being held in his muscled arms far more than I would riding atop the back of a massive reptile.

As soon as I'm settled, he launches us into the sky.

"I do think he's misusing the Magikai's funds and artifacts," Nahum agrees as I finish telling him our group's theories. "I also think I've won him over. Even though it did cost me a few more books."

A sense of true loss sweeps over me. They're part of his hoard. It's a sorrow so deep I could choke on it. Despite all my swearing off of deals and owing, I vow to myself right here and now that I will get him back those tomes.

"He indicated that it would be a small sacrifice compared to what I could receive in return. I think the Magikai pool the resources they gain from the magical factions, and then the representatives use the items themselves. I doubt very much that things are distributed to any supernaturals in need."

"Despicable. But not all I believed he was capable of," I state, clutching at Nahum as he catches a wind current and we go shooting up further into the clouds. "Warn a Were, why don't you!" I hiss.

He just smirks.

"My fearless mate, scared of heights?" he teases.

"You know what I'm scared of," I mutter back before I can bite my stupid tongue. Within seconds I can feel his regret.

"I'm sorry that you had to endure the Isle. And I'm sorry I threw you back into the nightmare of that experience when we first met."

I give his arm a squeeze.

"It's all right. I don't hold grudges." He chuckles, chest reverberating against me. "Okay, I *love* to hold a grudge. But I *won't* against you. Not for that."

He hadn't meant to throw me into the nightmare. I'd shown up to his home smelling like the Isle. The horrible place that haunted us both following our captivity and the abuse we suffered there under the Collectors. A lovely and long-destroyed group of magicals who collected and traded other beings for all sorts of nefarious purposes.

After I burned the Isle, hunting down the rest of the Collectors was one of the few truly useful things the Magikai have ever done.

"The conclave is next month," Nahum reminds me, getting us back on track. "The Scottish rebels threw a wrench in things, but Amun's had his employees working hard to fix up Lusca Palms. During the conclave it'll be closed, except for representatives, employees, and a select group of enforcers running security."

"Who wants to bet I won't be making the guest list?" I joke, well aware the head representative would sooner fillet me than grant me that kind of opportunity.

"You would be correct. Your name has come up a few times, actually."

"Oh?"

"Yes." Nahum clears his throat. "He finds you, um, rather bothersome."

I scowl up at the withholding dragon.

"I can feel when you're hiding something. Nice try. Now tell me again. What did he say?"

Nahum lets out a deep sigh.

"Very well. He loathes you. He admitted you're a very valuable asset—his words, not mine—when it comes to hunting down rogue magicals. That aside, he referred to you as a wild, out-of-control, violent, vile she-devil of a Were who had all the self-control of a juvenile prank-pulling pixie. And he indicated that he has every intention of finding a way to make your stay at the training grounds permanent so he can be sure to 'bring that bitch to heel,' as he put it."

I rub my hands together, grinning.

"Oh, this is excellent."

"Excuse me? Did you not hear what he said? It took everything in me not to toss him into an endless nightmare the whole time he was speaking. He's vile, Never."

Nahum takes his eyes off the sky to glance down at me, and I give him a wicked grin.

"Exactly. This is just the kind of thing I was hoping for. All the evidence I need that it's not just my imagination that he's got an unfounded vendetta. He'll answer to me when this is all through, and he'll deserve anything he gets."

"I cannot decide if I find your love affair with vengeance alluring or frightening."

"Both," I suggest.

We start to descend. When we land, Nahum sets me on the ground.

"Where are w—" I spin in a circle, staring at the scenery. "Oh."

I'm dumbfounded. Silenced. Stunned. You're all shocked, I know. Mouthy Never with nothing to say. But I wasn't expecting this.

You say *dragon date* and I think dinner and a movie. Perhaps some hanky-panky. Maybe slaying a rogue, villainous magical together. But I have to admit, none of my dates has ever brought me somewhere like this.

"It's absolutely beautiful," I manage.

We're in a garden. A massive one. I can't see the boundaries of it from where we've landed. It's almost like a hedge-maze. And the whole place is filled with magic. Small, floating orbs of light dance down different paths in the greenery. Some of the plants around us could be found in the human world, but I can tell many are magical in nature. Some glowing and some glimmering and glittery.

I reach a hand out and touch a shimmering cerulean leaf. Glitter dust showers down when I do, and I feel an inexplicable burst of happiness.

"Careful with that one. It grows around the mountain hot springs where I used to live." I blush as I recall a different hot spring, the one on his island. "It causes temporary joy, but it can leave you a bit giggly."

I walk past it to the other stunning inhabitants of the garden: the sculptures. Down each path I can see fountains and sculptures, stone and metal alike, all depicting various supernatural species.

"The Gargoyle Garden, it's called. Magically warded. It's tended by a cooperative group of different species, to grow and harvest the plants within it for various spells and potions. But it's also a beautiful spot in its own right."

He's certainly correct there.

I let him lead me down a few of the paths, holding hands like a couple of lovesick teens. It's nice. But nice makes me all kinds of itchy. Like my skin is too tight and I need to run. Because nice always gives way to bad eventually.

I try to distract myself with the scenery. The dragon did hit the nail on the head with this date. Back on the Isle, there were fountains in the back garden. For all the evil that place housed, the fountains and statues in the garden when I walked to and from my cage and the castle were my only glimpses of beauty. It was the one part of it I felt any ounce of regret for having destroyed.

We come to a circular clearing with a large fountain in the center. Stone gargoyles in flight, or grotesques, I suppose; they're not spouting water. Several hover in the air. I can't help reaching out to run my hands over the wing of one.

"They look almost real."

"Enchanted by witches to float. I read up on the history of all the statues before we came."

I turn to the sheepish dragon. Of course he did. Anything for an excuse to seek out a new book.

"You know, I didn't get out of my confines as often as I suspect you did on the Isle. I was inside with my books, save the few times I was sent off the Isle at the behest of the Collectors' customers, but I liked the statues, too." He runs one hand along the back of his head.

"How did you kn—"

"I saw it in your nightmare. The one I put you in when you arrived on the island. The statues were the only things you didn't react to with fear. Never, I don't know exactly what happened to you. And you don't know what happened to me. But it doesn't matter. I like who you *are,* and for who you inspired me to become again."

"A meddling, self-righteous vigilante who may very well overthrow the government?" I'm making only a half-hearted attempt at teasing. I can't put my usual oomph into the statement. Not with the dragon baring his heart like this.

"Thank you," I say instead, "for seeing some of the worst parts of my life and finding something beautiful."

"*You* are beautiful," he assures me, stepping forward and cradling my cheeks in his hands.

Listen, if you're out there rolling your eyes and making some comment about how cheesy he is: I know. I get it. Normally I'd be right there with you.

But right now? This time?

I throw myself against Nahum, knocking him back onto the grass.

15

A Brief Dragon
Interlude

I pull back from the kiss. Our breath is coming short and ragged. My senses are overwhelmed. As a Were, I can scent lust, but I can feel Nahum's desire enveloping my intuition as well. He reaches up with one hand that's grown talons and raises an eyebrow at me. I nod and he slices through my shirt.

I'll shift and shift back, and my clothing options will be taken care of. He grabs my sides, pulling my mouth back down to his again. His kisses are those of a starved male. Hungry and demanding. The only kind of demands from a male I'll allow. At least this male.

As we find a rhythm he moves his hands down my sides again, rolling us over on the grass and staring down at me.

I smile at him.

"Your moves aren't bad for an old man," I tease. Is he eight hundred, nine hundred? Who knows? Who cares? "Any other tricks I should know about?"

The grin he shoots back at me could make a frozen heart melt and swoon.

"I'd be happy to show you."

His talons tangle in my hair as he tilts my head to the side and bares my neck. A vulnerable position for a predator. I relax under him, and he leans down to kiss the curve of my neck. Then he bites. I gasp, a delicious shudder rolling through me.

I reach around him and trace my claws down his back, pulling him closer as he shreds the remainder of my clothes. I wrap my legs around him. Emotionally, I'm still at war with myself. Physically? I want the dragon closer.

As we move together he puts one hand up to my cheek, tilting my face to stare up at him. His eyes glow brighter, and for one brief moment I have the world's most sickeningly sweet thought. That I'd rather look at them than all the stars in the night sky.

We lie next to each other in the garden, staring up past the flowers that wind their way up the hedge walls and to the sky. I enjoy the silence for a while. Nahum is contemplative, and while I often feel bombarded enough by others' emotions that I'd like to block them out, this time I want to know what's got him feeling this way.

"What are you thinking about?" I blurt. I am immediately aware that I sound like a walking, talking, teenage romance. But what can I say? I'm genuinely curious. My intuition tells me the what, not the why. Often enough, it's easy to figure out, but this is not a scenario where I want to guess. I need to *know*.

Nahum rolls to his side, staring me in the eye. It's only when he's this close that I can see the gold flecks dancing inside his purple irises.

"Only that," he begins in a serious tone, "I should have bargained for a lot more dates." He smirks when I laugh.

"If they were all like this, I wouldn't deny you."

I'm lucky he's not the intuitive, because I know when I say it that the words are a lie. I like the dragon. I'm drawn to him. I don't know whether that's his upstanding personality or the mate bond, but I can't deny it. That being said, I've set myself a goal, and I intend to see it through. Sadly, toppling a very likely corrupt government doesn't leave one much time for a social calendar. What a drag, right?

Maybe when this is finished.

"I'll work on training the other enforcers. I'll get as many as I can to pull together," I say as Nahum sets me back down in the desert at the end of our weekend.

"And you really think that's wise? There's a good chance plenty of those enforcers will side with Amun and not you, if it comes down to it."

I nod my head, already lamenting the loss of the garden as I feel sweat beading at the back of my neck.

"I'd rather have well-rounded enforcers who could potentially help us if they turn out to be allies. And if they don't, that's fine as well. I'm a much better fighter than them, regardless of what tricks I teach." I shrug.

"You are fierce," agrees Nahum.

I'll have to stop by the waterfall and take a dip in the pool before I go back to the bunks. Otherwise the pack of wolf trainees will scent Nahum for sure. And that's just what I don't need. To have a bunch of teen shifters nosing into my sex life while simultaneously blowing the lid off this whole operation.

"And while I'm working on uniting the enforcers?"

"I will be sticking to Amun like glue. Gaining his trust and being his friend. And all the while looking for any cracks in his story," Nahum confirms.

The world's best plan? Far from it. But for now, the only one we've got.

16
And Then There Were None

"Right! Now duck under her arm. And strike!" I yell instructions at Ji-hwan and he lashes out, punching Ever in the nose.

"*¿Que le pasa estupido?*" she yelps, clutching at it, but it begins to heal itself within seconds. Ji-hwan grimaces as she insults him.

"Sorry!" He's getting better and better at fighting, but has no idea how to pull his punches for practice. After how long he's gone without this training, I don't really want him to, anyway.

"And you two, stop slithering around one another and make a move. No, not like that! You're tensing your tail just before you strike. Breathe, and relax. Don't give your enemy any tells of what you're about to do," I shout to two dueling reptilian shifters.

I wouldn't say I'm a compound favorite by any means, but over the last week or so we've been gaining new enforcer trainees. I've had to do something to take my mind off the anticipation of the conclave and the relentless summer heat. And telling other shifters what to do? If it involves fighting? I'm all over that.

"They're doing well," Brutus observes, walking up to me and placing his hands on his hips. He's smiling, and between that and the freckles, it softens his harsh exterior. The wolf still has his flaws, but he's making great progress.

I raise an eyebrow at him.

"Should we give them a lesson on how it's done?"

He has pointed teeth as he grins.

"Absolutely."

I stretch as we enter the cactus-lined circle, rolling my neck as I let my fur flow over me. Hell's bells but it does feel good to be a Were.

"Ready when you are," I say to the massive grey wolf in front of me. He snorts back, and the fight is on.

I'm just getting into a rhythm, hauling Brutus over my head and preparing for what I am certain is going to be an epic body slam, when Amun strides into the ring.

"Stop!" He holds out a hand. "We have an assignment for you all. This is of the utmost importance. Brutus!" He stares at the wolf twisting to get out of my grip. "Put together a team. There was a recent attempt on my life and that of some other representatives. We managed to subdue many of our attackers, but learned that several made off with a priceless artifact the Magikai have guarded for centuries. It is paramount that it is retrieved and returned to us for safekeeping."

Why do I feel like that whole baloney story was just his way of saying, 'Scottish magicals ransacked my casino and took an item I probably had no right to in the first place'? But I'm not supposed to know anything about that, so I put the wolf down.

For Amun's part, he certainly has a good poker face and a way with words. He believes everything he's just said. That he's the victim here. He's found a way to lie through his teeth, even while telling the truth. If I weren't so furious he's found a way around my intuition, I'd have to give him credit.

"I volunteer!" Ji-hwan yells, throwing his hand in the air before the head representative has exited the circle. Amun pauses and turns around.

"No, we won't be needing your particular set of skills for this, Were. And what is everyone doing in this training area together? Get back to your assigned exercises."

People begin to shuffle, but no one goes anywhere. Instead, I feel attentiveness, loyalty, and respect as their gazes turn to me. A fact that is not lost on Amun. The old lion puffs out his chest, cheeks going red.

"What are you looking at her for? She's not the head enforcer or head representative. She has no power here! She is here under *my* authority only. By *my* good graces. To rectify the mistakes she made handling the Claw. Now, move."

I pause for a moment, relishing the stillness that's settled over the others. Several are thinking about it. I can feel their indecision. I incline my head, and as soon as I do so the magicals disperse.

I really shouldn't, but I can't help the smirk I give Amun. If I were one percent more childish I'd stick my tongue out at him. His fury is mounting, but to his credit he sometimes has more self-control than I. He turns and storms out of the circle without another word.

Brutus blows out a breath behind me, back in his skin and zipping up a tattered pair of jeans.

"That was interesting. I doubt he'd want you along on this mission."

"Listen here, wolf. I've been thinking about—"

"But I'm going to take you anyway."

My face splits into a grin as I throw an arm around the shifter's shoulders.

"Brutus old pal, I knew you'd see things my way. Good for you, spitting in the face of authority." He cringes at that.

"I'm bringing you because you're skilled. Not to upset the representatives. That's the last thing I need."

But he *is* bringing me. Progress. He lists several other people, including a wolf shifter trainee named Lowell. I kid you not, it means young wolf. Told you people have no originality these days. Also a couple of feline shifters, a warlock, a couple of reptile shifters, one drake, and a centaur. I really feel like there's an 'eight magicals walk into a bar' joke in there somewhere.

"Also Ever, and Ji-hwan."

Their reactions are night and day. Ji-hwan is giddy. Over the moon, one might say.

Moon pun? Weres? Shifters? Honestly, I'm waiting for someone to appreciate me in my own time here.

Ever is hesitant.

"Don't worry. We probably won't even get to kill anyone," I tell her, at the cost of my own disappointment.

And if right about now you're thinking: *Geez, Never, do you have to solve everything with your fists? What about diplomacy?* Then, who are you and when did you get here? Also, I will remind you that as an enforcer, and before that a regular Were princess hundreds of years ago, that was kind of the way of things. Even now, as a matter of fact.

I wasn't surprised Amun had the Scots detained, given he's still mid-investigation. But I won't be any more shocked if, once he's to the bottom of things, he has them eliminated.

Brutus is throwing supplies into the overhead bins of the plane the Magikai are allowing us to take. We get to travel in style when it benefits Amun. Speaking of whom ...

"Champagne for everyone!" I announce, holding out a few bottles as several of the others whoop. Brutus slaps a hand to his forehead.

"Tell me you didn't."

I just grin.

"You did. Of course you did. I know you did, because I personally had alcohol removed from the enforcers' transport after our arrival. Which means you got it from the only other aircraft in this hangar. And I'm assuming you already know—"

"It's Amun's personal jet? That he'd skin me for a Were rug if he knew? Which is why, Brutus and fellow enforcers, we shall tell no one!"

Ever giggles as I pass her a glass of sparkling water. She's technically not old enough to drink in the USA, but even if she were, she doesn't care for the stuff.

"Thanks, Never," she whispers as she sips a sparkling mango pineapple water from the flute.

I wink. I think I'm beginning to get the hang of it, too.

"All right, team." Brutus stands up front once we reach cruising altitude, facing everyone with his hands on his hips. He's not quite scowling, but he looks stern as he addresses everyone. I've done my best here, people, but old-dog-new-tricks and all that. Some habits die hard. "I've been told we're going in for this." He holds up a tablet with a photo of an orb. "That is our objective. Retrieve it and eliminate anyone who attempts to stop us."

Seems I might have spoken too soon when I told Ever we wouldn't need to kill anyone.

"What is it exactly, sir?" Lowell questions. The wolf teen is all anticipation and respect.

"A relic of high value. The head representative didn't feel it pertinent to include details. Suffice to say it is a matter of great importance. Of safety. Amun indicated there could be dire and deadly consequences if it remains in the wrong hands. If you retrieve it, handle it with the utmost care until we can return it to the safekeeping of the representatives."

I just manage to hold back a chortle at that speech, but I do roll my eye. *Safekeeping*, my furry ass. Even *hoarding* is too nice a word for it. Stealing. Piling up wealth. Most likely. And if this whole thing turns out as rotten as I anticipate at the conclave, I'll find the rightful owners and return it myself.

Let no one say I never do charity jobs.

After just a couple of hours, the plane touches down in a barren stretch of field.

"Where *are* we?" The drake gives a derisive snort as we all exit onto a flat extension of red dirt.

"Nowhere anyone with sense would inhabit," our grumpy warlock responds. These two are downing my vibe significantly. As if the desert was better. At least it's cooler here.

I can't deny the area has a certain dead and desolate motif. I spin a circle, able to see for miles across the flat expanse, save a few scattered hills and rocky outcroppings that break up the horizon.

"We're in the Oklahoma panhandle," Brutus supplies, holding his tablet and looking very official in cargo pants with some sort of utility belt. What is he going to do with it? If he shifts, he loses everything anyway.

"Kap, which way?" Brutus turns to the warlock, who holds out his hands and closes both eyes tight. I can see a glow shining beneath his eyelids.

"Cap? Like, captain?" I question. A new name. I must collect. Maybe I do fit as a dragon mate. I just hoard intangible things. Names, emotions, anything that can get me closer to the meaning of others.

"Short for Kapaneus," Brutus answers.

"Ha!" I bark out a laugh. "Just great," I grunt, crossing my arms over my chest. Ever walks over, and I can feel the question without her voicing it.

"Greek. It means arrogance," I inform her, looking down at the petite Wereling. She'll always be small, but she's no longer haggard-looking, now that she's working with the enforcers and not having them chase her around her pack's territory.

"I have located the object," Kap announces, sweeping an arm out and pointing east. "This way." He strides across the ground, looking down his nose at us as he passes by. His key must be locating magic.

"Maybe there's something to your name thing, Never. In this case, it's fitting at least," Ever states as the warlock leads us all away from the plane.

For a while we weave a zig-zagging path through the flat fields. After a while, the warlock leads us to one of the rocky outcroppings. As we get close I see that what at first appeared to be a bit of rock a darker dirt-red than the rest of the structure is, in fact, an entrance.

Kap comes to a stop just in front of it.

"We're here."

"Oh yes, a creepy silent cave in the one tall environmental structure in the area, not at all suspicious," I mutter.

His tone is haughty when he responds, his emotions just as off-putting.

"And your opinion on the matter is important why? We were tasked with retrieving the orb. It's in there."

"That's right, so make like a good doggy and go fetch," one of the reptilian shifters says with a smirk.

I've got the reptile slammed into the ground with my hands around his neck before he can even start to shift. I'm in my skin, but I can feel my canines growing and would bet any amount of money my eye is going black. He squirms under me.

"Now's not the time! You two can bicker once we get the orb. We're *all* going inside." Brutus steps up behind me, waiting. He doesn't pull me off. I can feel both sides of him. The exasperated leader babysitting two argumentative enforcers, and the wolf who approves of me thrashing the reptile for his insulting words.

"We can go," I say, "as soon as he apologizes."

"Fat chance," the reptile gasps as I squeeze harder.

"All right," he wheezes, and I let up on the pressure just a bit. "Sorry."

I take my hands from around his throat and haul him up. As soon as my back's turned, he starts up again.

"Oversensitive female. This is why there's no point in having you all on these missions. You take everything personally, and once a month you all lose your minds."

I don't look back as I draw one leg up and kick out behind me. The grunt and sound of his knees hitting the dirt tell me I've hit my mark.

"Whoopsie! My poor female mind must be getting the vapors. I declare! I *am* glad we have all you strong males here to help me if I swoon."

Ever chortles, and Brutus keeps his head forward, back ramrod straight as he ignores my antics.

"We go in. We get the orb. We get out," he says as he leads us into the dark.

17

Don't Count Your Chickens, or Anything Else With Wings

"I can't see anything," Lowell says once we're inside.

"Kap, is that you? Ouch!" The centaur bumps into someone.

"Quiet," I command as I drop into a crouch. I know—ironic, since I'm often the one running my mouth. Don't think I'm unaware.

We go around a bend, and sitting in front of us is a glowing magenta orb. Just lying there in the red dirt for anyone to grab.

"We may want to rethink our strategy," I whisper to Brutus.

"What for?" he says, voice echoing off the rock.

"Why'd you bring her along, Brutus, if all she's going to do is pick apart the plan and question everyone? If she's so great, she can get the artifact herself," the warlock grumps. I'm ready to pummel him, but I don't think I'll need to. As he steps up to the glowing orb and reaches for it, light flickers to life around the cavern.

Torches, their ends sparkling with flame. Not concerning on its own, but I don't like what's carrying them. All manner of winged magicals, several species represented, are clinging to the walls. Like bats in the night, although I note I don't actually see any of those.

For a few moments, everyone is silent, then one of the creatures screeches.

"Retrieve the artifact!" Brutus yells, pointing to the glowing magenta orb sitting in the dirt. One of the feline shifters dives for it, just before dozens of winged creatures descend.

I want to be clear here: I don't mind violence. I prefer it when justice can incorporate a good ass-whooping. That being said, I don't feel the need to regale you with tales of gore. So I'll leave it at this. The screams you hear in television dramas? Nothing compared to the real thing when someone is being ripped apart by claws, beaks, and talons. And while I'm as up for a good haunted house as the rest of us, I can assure you that real body parts and viscera being slung around have a distinctive smell you won't ever forget.

With the loss of the feline, we're down an enforcer. Our attackers turn from what remains of their prey and move for the rest of us. I catch a glimpse of the orb, the glow dulled by a thin layer of slime and blood. Brutus tucks and rolls under fluttering wings and claws. He comes up running, and he sprints to the orb, still in his skin. He manages to pull off a slide tackle that knocks out some bird shifter and snatches the artifact. In the background, the other feline and the drake are roaring and yowling as they battle our assailants.

"Never," Ever murmurs. I look down and she's in her fur, claws out and ready. She may not like fighting, but she's more than capable.

"Stay with me. Back to back," I instruct her, keeping my voice low as I edge around the side of the melee, keeping to the wall. It's only luck that has kept us out of the fight so far. Amun's priority may be that orb, but I'm watching Ever first and retrieving his knickknacks later.

Across the cavern, a peryton slams into Brutus as he attempts to flee with the orb.

What do you need to know about perytons? Basically a deer-eagle hybrid. Deer antlers and body, massive feathered wings.

Sometimes four hooved legs, sometimes four talons. Sometimes fifty-fifty. This one has eagle talons for back feet and hooves on the front. Lucky for Brutus. Because the thing starts stomping and trampling with a fury, and I just know that's going to hurt tomorrow. If not Brutus's fast-healing body, then his pride.

I charge towards him, but the centaur in our group beats me to it, kicking out at the peryton with her hind legs and sending it spiraling. No sooner has she reached down to pull our fearless leader off the ground and harpies descend, yanking at her hair.

The orb is rolling, and Brutus just manages to throw himself on the ground and close his fingertips around it as something yanks him backward. He'd be able to fight better as a wolf, but unlike Weres, that would leave him without the benefit of hands and opposable thumbs.

"Never!" he screams, tossing it my direction. I launch myself, twisting in the air and managing to catch the orb and tuck it to my chest. I land on my back, rolling and running in one move.

"Ever!" I scream, and turn frantically until I see her keeping pace at my side. Her fear is heightened, but so is her ferocity. She swipes out at an incoming harpy, sending it spiraling into the cavern wall. Proof that you don't have to enjoy a hobby to be good at it. She isn't having any fun at all.

I, on the other hand, grin wide as I fling my free arm out and slam it into the chest of an incoming bird. It hits the wall with enough force to send a fissure up the rock.

"And the crowd goes wild!" I yell, pumping my fist in the air and hooting.

We're almost out. A line of bird shifters flutters in front of us, but I'll just barrel through them.

At least that's what I think, until they start crackling. My fur stands on end as blue light appears between the birds, forming a barrier at the exit.

"Lightning birds!" I yell at Ever and feel confusion in return. "Climb the wall. Go over their heads!" I instruct.

She scrambles up the rock and dirt, pulling at roots for handholds. I make for the other side of the exit, and I see several of the birds breaking off her direction. I twist my neck, looking back to see if we can retreat. But there's chaos behind us. I've lost track of the others. As far as I'm concerned, we've got one shot here; we have to get clear of this cavern.

"Hey! It's over here, you bird-brains!" I screech at the top of my lungs, waving the orb and forgoing the wall-climbing to sprint straight for the exit. The lightning birds descend, and I can tell I'm not going to make it through. But between their feathers I can see that Ever is clear. Good.

I clutch the orb close to my chest and tuck my head down, like I'm some sort of rugby or football player.

My last thought before I hit the wall of crackling, electrical feathers? *This is going to hurt.*

Every piece of fur stands on end as the electricity slams into me. My teeth clatter and I bite into my tongue. I try to scream, but my muscles are all contracted, and I can't get in the necessary air. My stomach roils as the smell of burning fur and flesh hits me. My body slams into the dirt and I black out for a second or two.

My field of vision is still a black wall when I come to, and I can't hear a soul. For a moment, panic threatens to set in as I worry I've gone blind and deaf, but echoing sounds start to funnel in. Welcome, and at the same time jarringly loud. My name, being screamed by at least two people.

First I see light, then blurry figures and shadows, and finally specific species and individuals start to take shape. I shake my head, and burnt bits of ashy fur float off me to the ground. No one hand me a mirror right now—I'm not sure I could take it.

Thank the moon, Weres are tough. But even so, I'll admit I wasn't entirely certain I was going to survive that particular stunt. Moon's damned lightning birds.

When my vision comes into full focus, I can see Ever leaping onto one of them, ripping into a wing with a ferocity I wouldn't have credited her with having. Ji-hwan spins, slamming another into the dirt as it screeches at him. A few more figures flee the cave: Brutus, our warlock, a drake, the teen wolf shifter trainee, and one feline.

"We have to go! Now!" Brutus yells, relief slamming into me from his direction when he locks eyes with me and I hold up the orb.

"What about the others?" Ji-hwan yells back. I can feel Brutus's answer before he shakes his head.

Shit. That's a third of our group gone.

I don't know where the head enforcer expects us to go. Like hell am I getting into a shiny metal tube in the sky with lightning birds around, so the plane is out.

The flying magicals dive and swoop as we claw and swipe. The warlock is shooting colored jets of magic into the sky, but he's beginning to lag. If magic sensing is his key, then this is costing him. I will stand by my resolute refusal to get into the plane, but we're nearing the landing strip, aka the long stretch of flat nothing where we landed that resembles all the other spaces of flat nothing in this area, when that opinion becomes moot.

A shrill screech echoes across the sky. Part roar, part rooster, and all horrible.

The sound is distinct, and I know what it is before it comes into view.

"Prepare for a snallygaster," I warn the others as I continue to lash out at the swooping magicals. A peryton manages to slice my arm with an antler, and I hiss but hold onto the orb as I grab the magical with my free hand and haul it down to the dirt by the offending antler.

"What's a snally—" Ji-hwan gasps as his question is answered.

The snallygaster lands hard on our means of transport, and the top of the plane caves in on itself where the creature's talons squeeze the metal.

Snallygasters aren't actually natural magicals. They were created through some sort of magic-meets-science genetic voodoo. Well, not actual voodoo, but witch and warlock interference. Such experimentation is strictly banned, but the snallygaster is proof that some magicals just don't listen.

The beast in front of us is a good half the size of the jet. Some people say they're like dragons crossed with eagles, but I think that's giving them *way* too much credit in the looks department. Snallygasters have large back legs like a rooster, and no front arms per se. They've got massive scaled wings, and there are talons at the end, so when they walk they hunch down like a wyvern. Their necks are long and scaled as well, and their faces end in a long, alligator-shaped beak. When the snallygaster opens its mouth, I see the rows of crooked, shark-like teeth.

"Hell's moon," Brutus curses as the creature lets out its cock-a-doodle roar. The front of its face is one massive eye, and you'd be forgiven for thinking that's all it has, but it has a smaller one on each side of its face as well. Its large tail whips around, the end feathered but durable as it shatters a window on the plane.

"Flames help us," the drake whispers, awestruck as we get to my least favorite part of a snallygaster.

Its beak stays open, and tentacles roll out from its mouth. They're whipping and striking at the plane. The creature climbs down the aircraft, and the ground shakes as it stops in front of us.

I can't say the fear coming at me from my companions is doing anything to bolster my own confidence, but my intuition has one perk. It lets me feel the confidence and loyalty coming my direction from Ever, Brutus, Lowell, and Ji-hwan.

"Never," Brutus asks, voice even as our group backs away, "how do we kill it?"

At least we won't have to contend with any other enemies right now. The rest of the winged magicals have backed away, forming a circle around us and giving the snallygaster a wide berth. An excellent idea. Snallygasters aren't exactly known for their intelligence, and they're not really capable of having things like alliances and loyalties.

I give Brutus the only answer that's ever worked for me.

"We rip it apart."

Since no one else is volunteering, I lead the charge. As much as I love and adore my own beautiful Were form, this is one of the few times I'd prefer a physical weapon. A nice long sword or something.

The bigger and thicker the better.

Really? *Now* you want to make puns? Come on, people, this is serious. We've got time for dick jokes later.

Because claws and teeth mean getting close to an enemy. And a snallygaster is not something you want to get close to. I leap on top of one tentacle, clawing and slicing with all my might. The others are right behind me, following suit. The distinct smell of sulphur hits my nose. I gag, remembering a part of the snallygaster that's only mildly preferable to the tentacles.

"Watch out for the flames!" I yell at the others.

"Flames? It breathes fire?" Ji-hwan shouts back, ducking under a swiping tentacle just in time to miss the fiery jetstream that sears the air where his head was moments before.

"You all take the limbs; I'll go for the kill!" I scream as a tentacle suctions itself to my torso.

Snallygasters aren't that tough to kill, if you can get under their neck or belly. *That* is the hard part. Who's going to get close when you have to pass flames, talons, wings, a whipping tail, and tentacles to do so?

Me. I must be as insane as I'm constantly accused of being.

"Take the tail!" I instruct Ji-hwan as I dodge another tentacle. Without a word, he's on it, running a circle around the creature to get behind it.

"Brutus, the eyes!"

Brutus clambers over the tentacles and heads to its face.

The others do their best to handle the suction-cupped tentacles. I roll in the dirt, just missing a talon that closes overhead.

Almost. There.

I feel agony hit my intuition and hear the sound of crunching bones. The snallygaster's got our wolf trainee pinned, and a tentacle is crushing one of his legs. Lowell yelps and squirms, but it's no use.

"You like dishing out pain? Let's see how you do on the receiving end," I growl at the snallygaster from under its belly, then jump. The snallygaster lets out another rooster-roar as I sink my claws in. I slice and shred, climbing up the belly and then to its swinging neck. Sticky, wet substances ooze over me from the cuts I'm making, and I do my best not to retch.

The wolf shifter howls, the sound hoarse and strained.

"Just. One. More. Good. Hit." I slam my claws into the neck again and swing myself over it, looping a circle of cuts. The snallygaster flails, its head whipping and sending me tumbling.

I land underneath it just before it falls.

18
A Long Way Down

Shoving against the dead weight, I heave the creature off of me. My beautiful claws are shorn down, broken off in the beast's neck. No matter; they'll grow back soon enough. I swallow down a wave of nausea that comes along with the pain, and have a horrifying thought.

Nahum.

Right about now his dragon talons will be glowing purple and shooting fiery pain up his fingers and into his hands. I'm hurting the dragon when I hurt myself. And I *know* he'll have felt my stunt with the lightning birds. He probably lit up like a glow-stick when that happened. Aw, hell. Now I feel doubly bad. For hurting him, and for worrying him. Not to mention putting him in an awkward position if he's around Amun or the others. And there's nothing I can do about it.

Way to go, Never.

I stumble over a tentacle as the snallygaster lets out a last, whooshing breath, smoke billowing from its ruined beak.

I can't whistle in this form, so I let out a low, one-note howl.

"You guys did a number on it. Excellent job. Now then, may I assume our valiant feat has scared off our enemies?"

Brutus and the drake haul the wolf shifter from the snallygaster's talon. He's wincing and yelping, but he's alive.

Around our group I hear the sound of beating wings.

"No? Too soon for celebration?" I manage a wry smile. Brutus rolls his eyes at me, and Ji-hwan even lets out a chuckle.

"But do we have the orb?" the warlock snaps, shoving past the feline shifter and marching straight up to me. "If you didn't keep it safe while you were busy showboating—"

He's prodding me in the chest with an accusatory finger.

"Showboating? Showboating! I just killed a creature that would have barbecued you, you egotistical parlor-trick magician!"

His cheeks turn a deep red that begins to slide into purple territory. He huffs and puffs, sputtering at the insult. It may not seem like much. After all—magic? Magical? But *magician* is near-unforgivably rude when applied to a witch or warlock. Indicates they have no real magic. Just tricks. And for someone as inflated with self-importance as this guy, whom I can easily read, it's a difficult term to bear.

"Ever! The orb?" She steps up, holding the item out in front of her. Relief washes over me from the direction of Brutus and Kap.

Brutus steps around the warlock. Ever moves to hand him the orb, but he shakes his head.

"No. I trust you with it. Now, we just need to—"

A feathered form swoops in between us, wrapping its arms around Ever before I can react. The creature moves so quickly it's hard to catch what it even is, but it hauls Ever into the sky.

The Wereling shrieks and kicks as the winged creature pulls her higher. Are those wings on its ankles? A wind elf?

First, Calder tries to take over the casino. Is there any chance this is Sky? Another one of Amun's representatives gone rogue? If it is, her reasons don't matter to me for the moment. The only thing I care about is keeping Ever safe.

"Don't struggle! Hold onto it!" I scream at her, hoping she can hear.

"I'm trying. But it's ... it's slipping!" she screeches back.

"Not the orb! Hold onto the magical carrying you!" I yell in desperation. I don't care if that thing shatters as long as Ever's all right.

"Are you completely insane? The head representative told us to bring that orb back," the drake reminds me. "She can't drop it!"

Overhead, I hear another shriek.

"*Diosa Luna! ¡Ayúdame!*" I'm not waiting for a moon goddess to do something. I do the only thing I can: keep pace underneath Ever and her captor as they swoop overhead. But as the possible wind elf ascends into cloud cover, it's impossible. Around me, the others are back to fighting.

"The orb!" the drake shouts as the sphere falls through the cloud cover, magenta light flashing. Brutus dives, just managing to get to the artifact before it hits the ground.

"We have to get them down!" I yell, at no one in particular. Magicals are tough. Weres are tougher than most, but I'm under no illusions that a fall from such a height won't cause serious damage. It could even kill Ever, depending on the speed she hits the ground. And even if she heals ... well. Let's just say I have experience from my life as an enforcer and time on the Isle, waiting for my enhanced healing to handle what would be a human life–ending wound, and it's not an experience you forget. Your body heals, but your mind doesn't. I don't want that for her.

I'm scanning the crowd for a magical large enough that I could use to go up after her. I can't even tell you what I'm planning. To try to ride a bird shifter up there like it's a bucking bull? No idea. But I have to do something.

There's more yelling overhead. Ever's and someone else's. Is she fighting?

For a moment, there's silence, and then a piercing scream. Singular and ear-splitting. And terror. So strong it forces me to my knees for a moment.

Ever is falling.

"Moon help her," I whisper, even though I don't expect the moon to answer. "Do something!" I scream as I run under her, willing to let her crush me if it breaks her fall. Ever comes hurtling through the clouds overhead and into sight. A fully furred Were speeding to the ground like a missile.

And then, she's not. She begins to slow. I look over and see our warlock with his arms out. His face is screwed up and the muscles in his arms and neck are tense. His breath is coming in short huffs.

He's saving her.

And he's using up all his magical energy.

He drops to a knee and I run over to him, pushing against him to keep him upright. But I can't do that and catch Ever at the same time.

"I've got her!" Ji-hwan yells as he runs under her. The warlock manages to slow her enough that she drops gently into the older Were's arms.

She's shaking, and her fur is standing on end. Her eyes are wide, the whites showing in her furred form. Her teeth are on display and she's frothing at the mouth. Her terror only unclenches the slightest bit.

Forms swoop overhead.

"Keep it away!" Ever screeches, waving her arms wildly as Ji-hwan stumbles trying to keep ahold of her.

"We're going to lose!" Brutus yells. I can feel what it costs him to admit it. I look at the group. Ever losing her mind in fear, Brutus bruised and defending the orb while fighting in human form, the depleted warlock and the remainder of our ragged crew.

We have no plane, and no other means of escape.

I let out a deep sigh.

"The hell with this," I say out loud.

I reach up and tap on my eyepatch twice.

The result is instantaneous. Black shadows billow around us.

"Never!" I hear the Wereling yell, panic consuming her again. I reach for her, grabbing her hand.

"Hold the orb tight," I instruct Brutus.

As the shadows get thicker, the winged magicals are obscured, but I see one feathered arm reaching through the darkness toward us.

No, not reaching—throwing. A gold dagger slams into the warlock's chest, embedding itself.

I grab Kap under the shoulders as he slumps, and we're carried away.

"That's just as disconcerting as it was before," I murmur as Visitor's silken shadows slide off my arms and release us back into the light. If I had to guess, we're somewhere outside the Magikai's training grounds, back in Arizona. Who knew I could be so relieved to land in this oven of a desert?

"You are welcome," Visitor intones from his place at the group's center.

I look down, already knowing what I'm going to find. Witches and warlocks are more physically fragile than most of us. And Kap had already exhausted himself.

He's dead.

Brutus walks over to me and places his free hand on my shoulder.

"I'll get him back to the grounds. Make arrangements for him and the others we lost. Get started on contacting families." Somber tone, and heavy responsibility. He can feel the weight of this job, and to his credit he takes no joy in this part of it.

"Thank you," I respond, even as I shrug him off. Contacting families. Dear moon, I hadn't even thought of that part. Until recently, there wouldn't have been anyone to contact if I'd been killed.

Brutus hands the orb over to Ji-hwan. The Were has set Ever down, and she's walking on her own, but her steps are shaky as he leads her back. I stare at Brutus as he bends down and picks up the warlock, my thoughts dark.

He saved Ever. I owe him. I owe a debt to a dead warlock I can't pay. I stand by my original opinion. He was pompous, self-important, and rude. Condescending and a Magikai kiss-ass to boot. But that doesn't change what he did. If he'd had a reserve of power, could he have cobbled together a defensive shield? Saved himself?

I shake my head, letting my hair cascade down, and replace my fur as I put on my skin. It doesn't matter what he might have done. It matters what he did. And I'm a Were who pays my debts.

Which means that I'll have to pass on what I owe the warlock to someone else. The benefit of the doubt. And that's something I don't like to go around giving away for free.

Speaking of which.

"What do I owe you?" I'm unsurprised when I look up and Visitor is only a foot or so in front of me. I've noted over our encounters how smooth and silent he is when he moves. His emotions roll over me. The sensation reminds me of someone pressing on a bruise. The sense is already battered from Ever's panic.

He's far too gloaty and satisfied for my liking. But I took the product; I'll pay the price.

"I'll add it to your tab. The Bone Reader can let you know next time you speak." Visitor smiles, a devilish half-grin. I'm once again reminded of a leading man from some sort of period piece. His suit would certainly fit. Well-tailored and striking. The slightest hint of blue on his vest setting off the vibrant shade of his eyes.

"Why do I feel I won't like it when the Bone Reader tells me my total?" I sigh, one hand rubbing my temple and then running through my hair.

Visitor's eyes gleam, which is all the more noticeable now that the sun has set and the sky's dark around us.

"Oh, I don't think you'll be as upset as you anticipate. Who knows? The payment might even be something you enjoy."

I give a barked laugh. I doubt it.

One thing I will acknowledge about the Bone Reader and Visitor—they're not lecherous. Most magical males saying something like that would be oozing ill-intent and devious lust. Not Visitor. And the Bone Reader, as far as I know, has never traded in flesh. Just what's underneath.

"If that's all?" Visitor tilts his head to the side, gaze and emotions questioning.

"Yes. I don't think I could afford more." Exhaustion hits me like a physical weight, and I just want him to leave. It's thankless, but Visitor's not much for inane chit-chat, anyway.

Although ...

"You were right," I admit, "I did end up needing you."

He smiles again, this time revealing perfectly straight white teeth. The canines ever so slightly pointed. Not enough to shout *shifter* or *vampire*.

"I do tend to be right quite a bit of the time. And knowing that, you might want to consider the following: this will not be the last time you reach out to me before this is all over. If you want the Magikai to fall, you'll need the Bone Reader's help."

He dips his head like he's tipping a hat to me, and shadows start to swirl around his shoes.

"I don't even know if I want the Magikai to fall. I'm just suspicious of Amun," I mutter, more to myself than him.

"Keep digging. You'll see." He reaches up a finger and taps next to one eye. Visitor and his shadows disappear with the cryptic statement, leaving me alone in a desert. The stars overhead are bright, but not as much as the moon.

No moon goddess showed up to save us. But someone did. And I'm certain he's an ally I can utilize.

If I'm willing to pay his price and play his game.

19
Heavy Lies the Crown

Ever drops her duffel by a waiting vamp without protest. Sometimes she balks at them going through her things, but not today.

"Where's the witchling?" I ask the nearest vampire as I walk into my Vegas mansion. She has waist-length mahogany hair and prominent cheekbones. She sashays in my direction.

"With the bears. In your absence, she is assisting the bear king."

I run a hand over my forehead and squeeze my temples. I've been on Rex's payroll for a while. Volunteering my services as an intuitive in exchange for some help he provided me a while back. I gave him some information about himself and his brother's relationship. And he hinted they had a supernatural in custody that he wanted me to meet. Surely he's not going to put Aggie in with anyone dangerous? Not that the stripper can't handle herself. She could suck the magic and ability to shift out of any opponent with ease. Still, I've got one shaky Were with me already; the last thing I need is for them to upset Aggie.

One problem at a time.

It feels like that's become my mantra lately; I say it as often as I curse. Between you and me, I'd rather curse.

"Lady Never."

"Hell's moon!" See? "Don't sneak up on me like that!" I snap, turning to see a repentant Hugh. Being a Were suits him. Even in his skin he looks better, which is saying something, since vampires are made to be attractive and enticing. His deep green eyes fit his face better than the red ones did, although he still gets red vampire eyes when he shifts to Were.

He clears his throat.

"Aggie isn't here. But Chrys has been staying at the mansion." Do I detect a faint blush on my second-in-command's cheeks? "She can check in with Ever. She'll make sure she's all right. I promise."

Chrys's version of love is a bit spiky. It involves insults and screaming. As a form of therapy. Then again, it worked for me. I nod.

"You're early," he observes.

I give a short laugh.

"Yeah. Ever needed the break, and Amun's already got more than his money's worth out of me this week. As soon as we had the orb returned, I marched into his office and told him I was taking a long weekend."

"And how did the head representative respond?" Hugh asks, a smile threatening to spread across his face. I grin, the happy memory warming me.

"He threw a fit. Ranted and raved at me about knowing my place and doing my job. Nonsense like that. He threw a few things from his desk to the floor when I left anyway. It made my day."

"I'd tell you to watch your back with him. But you already know that."

I do. In fact, that's probably mostly what set Amun off. I'd turned my back to him pointedly in his office before striding out of it. A clear sign that I didn't consider him threatening. But I can't linger on the memory for long. Hugh is antsy.

"All right." I wait for a few seconds. "Hugh, I can feel your anticipation and stress. Out with it. May as well."

He wrings his hands.

"It's the vampires, Lady Never. They're becoming restless." I let his emotions hit me. He's not panicking, but he is concerned. And he is focused. This is important to him. I walk down the hall and into the office of the previous vampire lord, which Hugh has been refurbishing for me. The Were follows in my wake.

I let out a whistle when I see the renovation results. Gone is the ostentatious chandelier over the desk with enough heft to decapitate a troll. Gone are the gems, jewels, and goblets for blood and wine. The office is sleek. Midnight blue walls and black shelves holding books, some artifacts Hugh dug up from the last vampire lord's stash, and admittedly still some drinkware. I'm about to ask Hugh to expand on his worries when something catches my eye.

"Hugh. What is this?" I grab the item off the shelf. An orb. With glowing smoke inside. Amun's was magenta, but this one gleams an icy arctic blue inside. A shade or two more muted than the one blue eye I've got left.

He reaches his hands out and I give it over. He places it back on its holder with care.

"It's a somson orb. We picked it up on the Isle, remember?"

Vaguely. We'd been on the hunt for a way to turn him into a Were at the time. So I could pay back the Bone Reader. So I could defeat Damien and the Claw. I'd been a bit preoccupied. Not to mention, the Isle was the place of my worst memories, and the item Chrys had found after the orb had been a weapon that had brought them all back. Now that Hugh mentions it, I do recall him tucking the orb into his pack at the time, but I'd never thought to ask more about it.

"It wasn't this bright then," I manage.

Excitement and eagerness. I've distracted him, but he's always up for a discussion of magical facts and history.

"No. It wasn't. They glow like this to predict and signify times of great upheaval in the magical world, or so go the legends. They're intensely powerful objects."

"Oh, and what do they do?"

He's perplexed. Stumped. Flummoxed.

"Well," he starts, tapping a finger on his chin, "it's hard to say. They're ancient items. No texts even agree on how many there are. Some say they're containers for great and powerful elemental spells. Some say they're actually prisons for magical beings so old we've long forgotten them. And still others say they're some sort of wish granter. Like a djinn without the restrictions or the backfiring properties of making fairy deals. Each orb capable of granting any request, just one, to whoever can activate it. Fascinating theories, hmm?"

He's grinning now, eyes fixed on the orb as he chatters on about it. I mumble an affirmative response. What does Amun want with an object like that? Was it really his? Did we steal it back, or just plain steal it? More and more questions. And every single one is making me more suspicious of Amun.

And great magical upheaval? It's like the orb is accusing me with its glowing; it knows the havoc I might wreak on the Magikai. When Hugh turns his back, I stick my tongue out at the orb.

I know, I know. Maturity. But I'm tired of being under the thumb of Amun. The last thing I need is to be chastised by a glowing ball.

"The vamps," I remind Hugh as I take a seat in my new office chair. It's plush with a high back. Truth be told, it looks more like a throne for a queen, but it's so comfortable I can't complain as I kick a leg over one arm.

"Yes. Restless. It's not that they're going to rebel. They just don't have much to do. And that makes them antsy. Perhaps if you could find a way to connect with them a bit more? Or find a purpose for them, a job for them to do?"

"I was under the impression what vampires did was drink and debauch and amass jewels. And they've got plenty of time to do that. They aren't satisfied?"

He slides into the chair across from me, giving me a frown. The biggest sign of disapproval Hugh normally displays.

"Lady Never. If I may say so, I think you're reading too much into vampire stereotypes. Just because they like pleasure doesn't mean they can't do anything else. And they may have *thought* they wanted a life of leisure, but since when do most magicals know what they want? I think they're finding an eternity of lounging to be less fun than they anticipated."

I rub a hand under my chin. I'd rather put the issue off, but that's what I've been doing since I won the coven.

Hugh clears his throat.

"I believe they could be more than they currently are, if given the chance to find their footing. They were very effective when Costas had them running his businesses, in fact—"

I sit up straight, snapping my fingers.

"That's it! Businesses! Hugh, my good Were, I own a casino now, don't I?" Costas was running it and using it as a cover for funneling some of his money to the Claw. I've kept it shut down with Under Renovation signs slapped on it since acquiring the coven. Truth be told, it was just one more 'to do' that I was more than happy to leave alone. Now, though.

"We revamp—if you'll pardon my vampire pun—the casino. You and Chrys can supervise. Put the vampires' talent for appearances to good use. Then we'll announce a grand opening the week of the conclave. I can use the offices there as a home base for spying on Amun, and a shiny new interior will hopefully draw in some of the visiting representatives. But we've got to pull out all the stops. Games, drinks, shows, the works."

His indecision tips into support and he begins to nod.

"Yes. This could work. And it'll give them something to do. It's just the thing!"

"And Hugh, put out some sort of survey. Ask the vamps what *they* want to do with their eternity, if not work for me." I've kept them from exposing whatever plans I concoct by having Hugh get them all to sign a magical nondisclosure, but none of them have tried to break it anyway. Perhaps it's time I put a little more trust in the bloodsuckers.

"As you say, Lady Never."

"Just *Never*, Hugh." I don't know why I bother. He just rolls his eyes as though the idea is absurd.

"What's my casino called?" I ask him.

"Blood."

"Blood?" It's edgy, and on the nose. Very vampire. Very Costas.

"We can change it," Hugh offers. "What name would you prefer?"

I shrug.

"I'll trust the vamps with that. They'll think of something."

He dips his chin.

"As you say."

I push up out of the chair and walk to the door. I need to get ready before my next guest arrives.

"I'm going to go for a nice run under the moon later, but I'm expecting company. When the dragon gets here, please send him to the garden."

Because I *am* falling for the dragon, in spite of myself.

But also because I'm ready to set things in motion.

20

A Dragon So Nice I'd
Date Him Twice

"I'm pleased you invited me here," Nahum states as he walks up beside me. I'm in my fur for the moment, lying in the grass under the stars. "It's an impressive estate."

It was more impressive when it had Elios here to provide custom cocktails, but alas, he's not in residence this go-round.

"Glad you like it. I've got to meet with the others and come up with some good ways to get us all into the conclave. Hugh's at work forging paperwork and invitations. I called Lynx and Todd today. They'll be reaching out to a few of their contacts that actually work the event, to try and get a real invitation. And Chrys has contacted Aggie and asked her to come back to the vamp mansion."

I tally the tasks on my fingers.

"I'm glad you're prepared. But what about our date? What will we be doing for that?"

I flash him a grin.

"I thought we could fight."

He gets serious, a stormy expression settling on his face and emotions.

"Is that really how you want to spend our time? Considering what you've put yourself through recently?"

I wince.

"Oh yeah. Sorry about that, by the way. I hope I didn't put you in a bad position, getting myself electrocuted. Wasn't sure what you'd do if you started glowing purple around the other representatives."

"*That* part is not the concern. I handled it easily." He smiles, and his severe emotions soften as well, giving way to a mischievous feeling I haven't gotten from him before.

"Just what did you do?" He just laughs, and I walk into his arms, poking him in the chest.

"Spill, dragon. I must know."

His smile grows.

"Very well. I lied."

Not very Nahum of him; perhaps I'm rubbing off?

"Lucky for me, you and Ever are the only intuitives the Magikai has. And to be honest it was necessary. I'd forgotten in my isolation both the joys *and* the utter bore it can be to spend time around others. I was stuck in a meeting with Amun and several other representatives who have arrived. Each time a new one gets here, he wants me to meet them. He's trying to network his way into my good graces, and I keep letting him and feeding him small bits of information from my books about things he expresses interest in. Spells, locations of lost magical items and the like."

"Selfish old lion," I grouse.

Nahum nods.

"Indeed. Thinks a lot of himself. But I was sitting through an indescribably dull introduction with ten others that had gotten off-topic and into the weeds. An hour of discussion had already been spent on potential magical wards to keep the Scottish contingent isolated from the rest of the UK until things are settled with them. The conflict intrigues me, but the advantages of invisible defensive barriers vs. enforcers at checkpoints does not."

He's not wrong. Just recalling it is boring him.

"Then my whole body spilled purple light. I must say, I didn't care for the sensation of being charred from the inside out, but once I assured myself our bond was still in place and you weren't dead, I decided to use it to my advantage. I told them that being so far from my hoard was having an impact on my ability to control myself. That if I couldn't leave soon, I might accidentally spill my nightmarish powers over the whole room."

I suck in a breath. It's the type of thing I'd do.

"You didn't."

"I did. And I've never seen such an effective excuse. They escorted me out immediately, and no one's hounded me for my location or another meeting since. Which is good, because I was anxious to get back to you. I know I've promised you your space, Never, but I have to admit I don't care for how often you've been hurt."

Dare I tell the dragon this is nothing? That I get injured all the time as an enforcer? That my time on the Isle almost left me immune to things as ordinary as pain?

"What were you like, before the Isle?" I ask instead.

His concern shifts to surprise, but I also feel willingness. He may be closed off to the world, but not to me. It's humbling, if I were a supernatural who felt such an emotion.

He taps his chin.

"Selfish, I suppose. I would have had a hoard anyway, but I could have used it for the greater good even centuries ago. I didn't. Just kept the knowledge I gathered to myself. There was a time, oh, six hundred years or so back, perhaps, that I made a true connection. To several villagers of a human settlement, as a matter of fact. A girl got lost and wandered up my mountain instead of down. I lumbered out in dragon form, and instead of crying, she approached me. Asked me for help."

He's sentimental as he recalls it.

"And what did you do?"

"Took her home. The villagers were thankful. Not like others, with their pitchforks and swords. It was a good century. But things change; they always do. Over time the ones I'd first met died off, as did the relationship with the village. Religious emissaries arrived. Eventually they convinced the residents that a dragon was too like a devil. I was no longer welcome. I went back to hiding myself in the mountains."

"And the human? The first one who contacted you, what of her?"

He smiles at the memory.

"Gone with the rest. I held her hand as she passed, an old woman by human standards. I enveloped her in thoughts of younger days when her bones didn't ache. Her dream was meeting her family again in a spring meadow, so I gave her that."

I'm not crying! Shut up! And I'm certainly not wiping away a tear. It's all the grass in this darned vamp garden. It gets to my sinuses. Which is why I'm sniffling.

"I forget sometimes that your abilities let you show good dreams instead of just bad. That was a kind thing for you to do. I'm sorry you didn't have others you were close to." And I mean it. I know what it's like to be alone.

We're both lying in the grass at this point, and I've put my skin back on. He rolls to his side, his eyes meeting mine.

"I had some acquaintances. Magicals I traded with for books. And some of them were all right. And I've had the pixies since fleeing the Isle. Of course, I didn't have you. I didn't have a mate." I'm trying to focus on what he's saying, but I find myself staring at his lips instead.

"Never?"

"Hmm," I swallow, feeling parched all of a sudden.

"You're certain you want to spend our time fighting? Because I can think of much better ways to pass the evening." His eyes glow, and I'm sorely tempted.

A compromise?

"Your idea first. Then mine?"

He laughs, deep and rumbling from his chest.

"It's a deal."

And I don't regret making one, for once.

He positions himself with his forearms on the grass, staring at me from above.

"Nahum? Could you use your dreams to make it feel like we were somewhere else?"

He nods.

"I could. It's dependent on *your* dreams and what you want. Show me where you'd like to go." Mist spills around us, and I'm reminded how realistic his dreams are. Instead of lying in the garden, we're back on his island. I stare out at the waves. His nightmares chill you to the bone, but his dreams have a pleasant warmth. I grab his hand.

"Shall we adjourn to the hot springs?"

His emotions are wicked as he responds.

"Let's."

21

Nightmare to Nowhere

I nap with Nahum under the stars. The "visit" back to his hot springs was wonderful, even if it wasn't real. His dreams are immersive enough that I can't tell the difference. He opens his eyes when I move.

"Morning already?" He smiles down at me before capturing my mouth in his. A gal could get used to this. Then again, I'm no lovesick girl. I'm a full-grown Were with things to do. No matter how tempting the dragon is. It's definitely preferable sleeping in his arms in the grass than sleeping in the Magikai's bunking tent.

"Not quite. Sun isn't over the horizon."

"We can head inside for breakfast."

I smile and roll my eye.

"Nice try. We can get to my side of the bargain. Before breakfast. We fight."

He stands up, brushing a few lingering grass blades off himself.

NEVER EVER155

"All right, although I have to warn you, I'm not sure how helpful I'll be. I don't mind admitting you've got more fighting experience, once you take my abilities out of the equation."

"Out? Oh no, I want them to stay in. Your nightmarish ability is what I'm relying on. I need you to use it on me."

His revulsion hits me as he processes the idea.

"Absolutely not. Never again."

"Never now," I correct, then school my expression. "And I'm serious. Before we fought the Claw, I had Aggie practice her magic-stripping on me. It prepared her and let me know what I was in for if I got in her way during the fight. I needed to be familiar with any potential obstacles."

"We don't even know there's going to be a fight," Nahum tries.

I just roll my eye again.

"Please. I think we're both well aware Amun has something up his sleeve. But nice try. You agreed to my deal."

"I can assure you I have more precision with my skill than Aggie does. No offense to the witchling, but I've had hundreds of years to perfect this burden. And that's what it is. I'm not going to harm my mate."

I step forward, and he takes my hands in his. I stare up into his eyes.

"Nahum, that is incredibly sweet." His eyes drop to my lips as he leans forward. "And incredibly misguided. I'll be in more danger if you don't prepare me. Who knows, Amun could have something that mimics your abilities."

He drops my hands and begins pacing the garden. Murmuring to himself. After a few moments, he walks back over.

"Fine. Fine. But I don't like it. I want that on the record."

"Noted," I respond, although what he intends to do with this objection is beyond me.

"And I will be trying to use our bond to communicate with you during, just to assure myself you're all right. I can at least give you some tips on how to fight back."

I lean in, planting a kiss on his cheek before pulling back.

I've been wanting a rematch with his abilities since I first faced them. I can't stand to lose, and I hate the idea that if the powers somehow were harnessed and utilized by Amun I'd have no way to fight them off.

Nahum frowns, but he takes several paces away and lets me put on my fur as he dons his scales. He turns back and I give the slightest nod of my chin. I'm ready.

I can hear screaming, and the crackling of flames.

"It's not real. It's not real. It's not real," I remind myself before I open my eyes.

Even though I know I'm safe in the garden with Nahum, I can't help feeling my breaths going ragged and rapid. I cough against the billowing smoke the fire causes.

I'm back on the Isle.

"Hello, pet." I shudder as a voice smooth and sharp enough to cut glass reaches me. "Come to see me again?"

A form, only recognizable as a dark outline against the flames, moves closer to me. I bite back a scream. I know that form. I know that voice. There were many villains on the Isle, but I had one tormentor in particular.

"It's not real. It's not real."

"Look at me." A finger reaches under my chin, tipping my face up. I can't escape it now. I open my eyes, and in Nahum's nightmare I do have them both. Because I did at the time? For once, I wish I didn't. I can see with utter clarity the grey elf in front of me. Pale flowing hair. Sharp cheekbones. Eyes lacking all warmth. A beautiful I hiding the blackest of hearts, if he ever even had one.

"I threw you into the sea," I manage, my voice croaking and hoarse. He pulls the finger from my chin and waves it at me.

"Uh, uh, uh. Let's not talk of such unsavory things. Now then, pet, follow me."

Never.

My name is a mere echo in the back of my mind as Nahum calls out to me, but it's enough.

"No." I plant my feet. "No, Mizor."

His head snaps around, glaring and furious.

"You will address me as Master. And you will heel. Now."

I tense, waiting for the familiar rippling of fur. It doesn't come. My tormentor laughs at me, and I look down to find all-too-familiar shackles around my wrists, a solid chain dangling between them.

"You had to know better than that, pet. I wouldn't let some vile, wild animal loose on my island." The elf always did prefer everyone *civilized*. Wearing their skin.

I keep trying to shift. It should be as easy as breathing.

"Pet. Enough of this. I said no." A familiar whip appears in Mizor's hands, long and embedded with metal. A chill runs through me, but that familiar voice calls me back.

He can't hurt you. I'm here.

Again, just an echo. But enough.

I straighten up.

"Not this time." I managed it before; I can do it in a nightmare. I gather all the strength I have and snap my arms open. The chain breaks, and my fur explodes over me. The grey elf in front of me is wide-eyed.

I take a triumphant step forward. I've overcome my fears. Overcome the past that ate at me for so long. I'm winning.

"Never!" This voice isn't an echo. It's in the nightmare with me.

I turn my head, frantic. Searching for the source.

The barn is on fire. The one where the Collectors used to house some of us. I run to it as Mizor smiles behind me. The elf always was devious.

Aggie is inside one locked and barred stall as the fire licks at the building. She's crying as she tries to reach for the door and burns her hands.

"Hold on, I've got it!" I promise as someone yells in the next stall over. I run through the barn. In each new stall waits a new horror. Hugh, Chrys, Todd, Lynx, and Ever. All trapped.

"It's all right. I'll get you out!" I yell, but a rope catches my leg as I step forward. I fall to the ground as I'm hauled back out of the barn doors by the Collectors. I kick and struggle, but they tie me down.

In front of me, the barn collapses.

"No, no!" I scream.

Never. It isn't real. They're all safe.

But the echoing voice can't help me now. I turn to see the Collectors. My grey elf among them.

"Look who else we have." He grins, stepping aside to reveal a cage. A gorgeous black dragon with purple-decorated wings is inside. They haul him out, magical ropes preventing him from fighting back.

"More trouble than he's worth. He'll be more profitable in pieces," one of the nameless Collectors states, raising a spelled ax and swinging it at Nahum's neck.

My heart shatters.

"Never! Snap out of it, Never!"

I gasp, shivering as someone douses me with a bucket of ice-cold water. My teeth are chattering, and that does nothing to help.

Worry and concern hit me in waves, making me nauseous.

"What happened to her?" Aggie demands, running over to me. "Let me see if I can help. He was using magic against you—maybe I can strip it." The witchling made good time. Did she travel overnight?

Aggie waits at my side, hands hovering. If she strips me, it'll take away my ability to shift for a bit, but anything to get the images out of my head. I give a shaky nod and the witchling gets to work. I let out a sigh, breath relaxing as she manages to pull away the worst of the nightmarish chill.

"Why would you do this?" Hugh questions, rounding on Nahum.

"What were you thinking?" Todd rages, piling on. Did he bring Aggie, then?

I stand, leaning on Aggie for support.

"Why is everyone out here?" I demand, although I don't sound too commanding with a hoarse voice. Nor do I assume I look it, shaking, naked, and being supported by the witchling.

"You were screaming," Aggie informs me. I grimace. Just great.

"Why would you do that to her?" Aggie snaps at Nahum, her voice venomous compared to the sugary-sweet quality it often has. She even has a few of Nahum's pixies buzzing around her head in agitation. Unsure whose side to take.

"I did it. I asked him to," I volunteer.

"What in hell's moon for?" Todd demands, copying one of my favorite curses.

"Because. I wanted to be prepared. We may very well be facing off against the most powerful leaders of the magical world. Politically powerful, anyway. Who knows when was the last time they were in a physical fight. But you can bet they've got spells and tricks up their sleeves. And I thought if I could take on my past, take on dragon magic—"

"That would mean you're enough of a badass to defeat the Magikai all on your own," Todd finishes, reading me like a book. He's got a knack for it.

"Something like that." I shake off the witchling and stumble a few steps before falling to my knees in the grass. Nahum rushes forward, but Todd beats him to it and offers me a hand to haul me up.

He cares a great deal about you, the dragon observes, and I'm relieved when I don't feel any jealousy. That, I couldn't abide.

Todd and I do respect each other. As different as our approaches to enforcing and life may sometimes be, I offer.

I gain strength with each step back to the house. Aggie's stripping may have taken my Were form, 'ut it's balanced by how much better I feel without the residual effects of Nahum's abilities.

Hugh leads everyone into the dining hall. He goes into the kitchen to check on the vamps, and Todd goes along. Likely to oversee the cooking. Beings who drink only blood don't always do the best with other food. Aggie brings me something to wear since her stripping has robbed me of my usual outfit. Once that's taken care of she excuses herself upstairs to go see Chrys and Ever.

I sit down next to Nahum.

"I feel ridiculous," I admit.

"You shouldn't. I don't know how to say this without sounding full of myself, but I'm very good."

"Yes, you are." I put a lilt into my voice, trying to seduce my way out of the subject.

"I didn't want to harm you. I was about to pull you out of the nightmare, but I got distracted near the end. I've never seen *myself* in a nightmare like that."

I stare up at him when I realize that he's both disconcerted and cheerful.

He smirks.

"Sadistic dragon," I tease, nudging him.

He scowls, taking my hands in his.

"It tears me apart to see your fears." Then he smirks again. "But I'll admit I was rather pleased that you hold me in such high esteem. You cared so much about the Collectors killing me."

"Is that your way of saying, 'Admit it, you like me'?"

"Perhaps. And admit it. You do like me. I'm winning you over."

"Perhaps." I throw his own answer back at him. "I'm not ready to move in and have dragonlings together. But I think I could agree to more than our contractual number of dates."

He growls, his lips capturing mine in a breath-stealing kiss.

Really, you all, get yourself a dragon. They're great for all sorts of things.

"I don't know why I was so worried. I know you can't be killed," I mutter as he stares down at me, purple eyes shining.

"I can be killed," he responds, straight-faced and serious. I can feel the genuineness of his response.

"But. When we first met. In your cave on the island. Wasn't there something along the lines of 'no living being' or 'no one on earth' could kill you? That you were indestructible. You told the truth. I could feel it. How did you get around my abilities?" I'm suspicious, and I push away from him a bit. Paranoid that if he got around my intuition he could be hiding all sorts of things.

"You're jaded, Never. But I understand why. I was being honest, at the time. I just didn't realize what I do now. That I have a mate. And *that* could hurt me. You could hurt me. You're the only one who can. It's part of the mate deal. Whatever the powers that be are—a moon goddess, mythical, deity-istic flames—they must believe in balance. Because you would be able to kill me. You, and no other."

"Huh." I let the thought sink in. On the one hand, it's too much responsibility. On the other hand, I could kill him. I could fight back. Even against an indestructible dragon. The thought is empowering.

"It's a lot to take in, isn't it? Just promise me not to abuse the ability." He nudges me, smirking.

"All right. As long as you promise not to piss me off. Or it's curtains for you, my scaled friend."

"Pancakes!" Todd announces as he sweeps into the room.

22
Benefit of the Doubt

A long weekend back at the mansion has invigorated me. And more than that, it's furthered my plans. The vamps were just as eager for something to do as Hugh indicated they would be, and I've got a whole contingent of them clearing up the casino under Hugh and Chrys's supervision.

"Just know I'm adding all this work onto your bill, old woman," Chrys had teased, "and I'm very expensive." I don't doubt it. Probably a good idea I'm getting the casino back up and running, if only to pay her and Hugh for all the work they've been putting in during my absence.

Lynx and Todd have reached out to our usual allies to come stay at the vamp resort and casino during the conclave, in case backup is needed. Which means the bears, a few trusted enforcer friends of the duo, and Elios's staff will show up. Elios even volunteered to come run our bar. If you consider heavy bribery, nagging, cajoling, and buttering up to count as volunteerism. Whatever. At least I'll have a delicious cocktail while I scan the casino floor for any dubious conclave activities.

The vamps are all over that as well. They're going all around Vegas, including Lusca Palms, handing out invitations to the exclusive reopening of Vicious, as they've decided to call my own casino. A tribute to the nickname I was given when I ousted the previous vampire lord.

All that's left is for me to go back to Arizona and put on a well-behaved enforcer front until Nahum contacts me. The dragon left yesterday to meet with Amun. I was shocked to hear he'll be back in Arizona as well, and not in Vegas. There's something Amun wants him to see. I have my suspicions that the lion knows how valuable Nahum is. Not just for his nightmarish abilities, but his physical endurance. Moon knows he's pulling out all the stops to win the dragon over.

I can't wait to see the look on the head representative's face when he realizes that won't be happening.

"Ever, grab your bags!" I yell up the stairs. She's a lot calmer, but she's been reclusive all weekend. As she walks down the staircase, she keeps one hand on the bag and one hand clinging to the railing, as if she'll go flying off into the sky without it. I don't fault her. This may be her first near-death experience that's truly hit home. It'll take time. After the conclave, I plan to give her as much as she needs.

I turn and nearly bump into a vamp. Silent little bloodsuckers.

"Hell's bells!" I yell, and just manage to keep myself from jumping back. It wouldn't do to behave like prey around the coven I'm supposed to be ruling.

The vamp bows at the waist, black hair slicked down so it doesn't even fall over his forehead.

"My apologies, Lady Vicious, but you have a visitor."

"Who?"

"He says his name is Unkai, ma'am."

The raiju is my most-liked representative out of a host of bad options, but what's he doing at my mansion? Somebody had to let him past Chrys's defensive spell at the perimeter of the grounds, so he's convinced either my vamps or Hugh that he's got a good reason to be here.

"Unkai. To what do I owe the pleasure?" I stop short when I see him in the entrance hall. The representative stays in raiju form almost exclusively. A massive, long-furred weasel-wolf-seal creature. And yes, that's the best description I've got, kids. Today he's made the rare choice to wear his skin. Sort of. He's clearly out of practice. He's upright and human-shaped, but he's got wolfish ears and furred appendages, along with fangs protruding from his upper lip.

"We need to talk." Solemn. Conflicted. Constrained. Panicked. Whatever this is, it's not good.

I lead him out to the gardens. I'm learning to trust my vamps, but I'd still prefer the sunlit grass, where we'll be away from prying ears.

"Spill." It's the nicest I get when engaging with the representatives.

"It's not that simple. I want to. I just—" He gestures at his form.

"A guessing game, hmm? You don't want to say, or you can't say?"

He locks a stare on me, unblinking.

"All right. Magically prevented from talking?"

He reaches up a finger and taps his nose, but I can tell it takes effort. Whatever magical vow he's working against, it's a doozy.

I place my finger on the bridge of my nose.

Think, Never. He's a representative. It's likely this is related to the Magikai.

"Is it a personal matter?" I ask.

His head jerks, but doesn't shake or nod. All right, so that question's out, then.

I'm thinking of my next question when he speaks again, voice grating and neck muscles tense. He's walking the line on his vow's guidelines.

"I know you don't care for the head representative."

"Duh," I respond, barking out a laugh. Hardly professional or adult, but that's not news. I only agreed to put on a front when Amun's around. But Unkai has known me for years. Found me after I'd escaped the Collectors and recruited me to this job in the first place. Just after I'd boxed the grey elf that had held me captive into the sea.

"Wish I could box Amun sometimes," I mutter.

Unkai grows excited, nodding and tapping his nose again.

Really? Boxing? Even if he also disliked Amun, Unkai's not exactly the violent type. Not that I've seen.

"You can't really be asking me to box him."

"Water," he blurts out, "Weres and water."

Ah, yes, that old adage. From ye olde pirate times. Weres and water don't mix. Because no magical being does well boxed into the ocean and regenerating for centuries. A slow death. A torturous one.

"Wait a minute. Is Amun planning to box me?" I'm furious and horrified all at once. In my opinion, it's one of the worst ways to go.

"Swim," Unkai grunts out, then takes a few shuddering breaths. "When you get back to the training headquarters, why don't you go for a swim? Maybe you'll feel differently about the water this time."

His whole body is vibrating. I don't know what I can say. Could my response get him in trouble as well? He's desperate and worried. Because he needs my help? Or because he's trying to trick me and afraid I'll find out?

"I think you'd better go, Unkai." His despair rushes over me.

Dare I trust him? He's a representative. And while he's been the one I've taken the least issue with, I've never seen him break a rule. Except perhaps when he recruited me. He'd promised me my former freelance status before clearing it with the head representative. Boy, I bet that stuck in Amun's craw.

"Never, please." His eyes catch mine again. Beseeching.

I let out a sigh. I don't know if it's wise, but it's too much of a coincidence. I owe a debt, and here's a chance to pay it. I decide to give Unkai the benefit of the doubt.

"I'll bring a bathing suit," I promise. Relief washes over him. Without another word, he transforms back to his real form, shooting into the clouds.

Well, looks like I know what I'm doing when I get back to Arizona. But I'm not stupid enough to go poking around alone.

My choices are a bit limited. I've spread our group thin. And I'm already feeling guilty asking Ever for more, but I'll find a way to make it up to her.

"Ever!" I yell as I enter the mansion's entrance. "Witchling! Slight change of plans!"

23

Weres & Waterfalls

"What are we supposed to be looking for?" Aggie calls out, cursing as she trips over a rock.

If you consider 'Oh, puddlesticks' a curse. I don't.

"The raiju wasn't specific. Stick close to Ever; she can see well in the dark," I instruct as we scan the ground.

I brought the Wereling and witchling back with me to Arizona. Went ahead and dropped by the tent to check in with Brutus when we got here and then high-tailed it right back out to the grou"ds.

"Go for a swim," Unkai said. There's only one place to do that here. The waterfall and pond that sits past the training circles. At least the representative was able to narrow it down. Even so, I'm hoping to avoid actually going in the water. We're searching every square inch of space around the shore and in the rocks first.

"Hide!" I hiss at the girls when my ears pick up on the clacking of skittering rocks. I scan the night, claws out and snarling as I see two figures racing towards us. The one in back comes to a halt, his palms up in the air.

"Woah! It's just us, Never!" Ji-hwan doesn't relax until I lower my claws.

"What are you doing here?"

Brutus rolls his eyes in a 'really?' gesture. I can feel the skepticism hit me.

"You're up to something. And I want to know what," he says.

"And how would you feel if I said it's a need-to-know assignment," I shoot back, crossing furred arms.

He laughs, folding his own arms over his muscled chest.

"I'd say bullshit. No way a representative gave you some kind of secret mission here. Amun's had a bull's-eye on your butt since day one. He was mad enough I took you to retrieve that artifact."

Somson orb. But I haven't told anyone else that just yet.

I weigh my options. Go back with them, and leave the girls to face a potentially dangerous situation alone? Yeah, scratch that one immediately. Take all of us back, and answer some awkward questions regarding Aggie's presence? I don't think so. Or, bring them in on the plan. At least a little bit.

Who was it that said, 'In for a penny, in for a pound'? I personally think that individual was an idiot. Why dig yourself a deeper hole? It just makes it harder to climb out. And yet, here I am. The next time Elios tells me I've lost my mind, I'm going to tell him he's right.

"We're snooping," I confess. "I can't reveal my source, but I have it on good authority there's something significant around here."

"Like what?" Ji-hwan is all curiosity and interest. Brutus is some interest, and a lot of suspicion.

"From who?" he demands.

"I'm not at liberty to say." I don't want to risk Unkai's safety.

"Then what are we looking for?" Brutus questions, trying a different angle.

I sigh, running my claws over the fur on the back of my head.

"I can't say that, either. But there is something here. In this area. And if you're willing to help us, I could use a couple more sets of eyes to figure out what."

"Sure!" Ji-hwan volunteers at the same time that Brutus says, "*More* eyes. Who else is here?"

"Come on out, ladies!" I yell. Ever and Aggie step out from the rocks.

I introduce the witchling to the males, but I don't mention her key. Doesn't seem like it matters; Brutus is overcome with tension and unease. He probably saw her in action when we all fought the Claw.

"The stripper witch?" Ji-hwan asks, leaning in close to observe her, as though the power's going to come pouring out of her.

Well, that answers that.

"Seems someone can't keep their wolf trap shut!" I growl at Brutus. He shrugs.

"It wasn't me. A stripper bringing down powerful magicals? You had to know that was going to get out." At this point I'm sure we're all becoming a bit infamous, and if things escalate with Amun we might become even more so.

We spend another hour or so canvassing the rocky outcroppings from the ground all the way up to the falls, but find nothing.

"Should we head back to the tents?" Ji-hwan asks. He put on his fur for this trek, and the white parts are streaked with dust and debris.

I sigh.

"No. There's one more spot to check. In the water itself. Don't suppose we've got any volunteers for a deep dive?" I gesture to the murky water, soft waves lapping at the shore.

"I can do it!" Ji-hwan volunteers eagerly. "Swimming is one of the things I have perfected. It's an excellent full-body workout.

Particularly when you're being asked not to spar with people, to preserve your good looks." He flashes a smile and wink at everyone.

"I'll need some light, though," he adds. Aggie raises a hand in the air.

"I should be able to take care of that. And fashion us a bubble breather spell. But it'll take a lot out of me. Illumination and oxygen aren't exactly related to my key."

I don't like it. She pays more for regular magic anyway, given she's a light witch. But there's four of us to guard her if she depletes herself, and we've got squat to go on at this point anyway.

I nod.

"All right. Let's do it."

Once Aggie fashions them both what actually does look like a large bubble enveloping her nose and mouth, and Ji-hwan's muzzle, they dive into the water. After that, it's just a matter of waiting.

"Patience not one of your many virtues?" Brutus questions as I pace in front of him for the hundred and seventh time. I know; I've been keeping count. His eyes sparkle with humor as I scoff.

"You know it isn't. Any number of things could have gone wrong down there. Are we certain there aren't creatures in that lake? What if they—"

Brutus shoves himself off the rock and transforms into a giant grey wolf. I'm already in my fur, but I spin and bring up my claws as the waterfall erupts outward and water sprays all the way to the edges of the lake.

Aggie emerges from behind the falls, doggy paddling, with Ji-hwan swimming a smooth freestyle behind her.

"It's just us!" she assures everyone. "We found something you're going to want to see."

"There's some kind of gathering going on underground. Or deep in the rocks. They've hollowed out a location. There's an entrance under the water, behind the waterfall," Ji-hwan explains as I walk toward the edge of the lapping waves. I dip in one furred toe.

"Hell's bells and moon's hell and hell's moon all at once," I murmur, "of course this would involve a trip to the watery deep." Because the universe seems intent lately on making me do things I don't want to do. Facing Damien, going to the Isle, diving. But also opening up my heart and making friends. I'd give the universe's judgment fifty-fifty.

"Can you do the charm on all of us?" I ask Aggie without looking up. I want to feel her response. It's assured but edgy. Hesitant but agreeable.

"You can. But it's going to leave you vulnerable. Right?" I turn my head and catch her emerald eyes flickering with witchy magic as she accounts how much power that will take.

"Yes. I can get us all down there, but light-magic witches have less energy than dark magic most of the time anyway. And I'm no exception. Elemental spells like air are tricky for me. Maybe because my key has to do with magic directly, and elements are such a concrete thing. But I trust you all to have my back."

She means it. With no reluctance, she'll make herself a potential target and exhaust her defenses. The pompous warlock comes to my mind for a moment, but I banish the thought. Not this time. Not with Aggie.

"Then let's do it."

Aggie grins, clapping her hands together.

"Okay, guys, it looks like it's time to get wet!" She takes one determined step forward before her cheeks go as red as her hair. She holds a hand up.

"I heard it, I heard it. No need to comment."

"Wasn't going to say anything." I grin as Ji-hwan guffaws behind me.

I was. I absolutely was.

Once the charms are in place, we make our way underwater. Ji-hwan swims out in front. He motions everyone through an ominously dark tunnel under the water's surface that goes on far too long for my liking. We emerge on the other end into a small cavern, and I throw my head out of the water.

"You don't have to gasp like that; you've been able to breathe this whole time," Aggie reminds me.

"I know that," I snap, "but my lungs don't."

We start walking through a small tunnel that's an offshoot of the cavern.

There are some twists and turns, along with some narrow areas, but after a few minutes I hear voices echoing ahead of us. I turn and hold a finger up to my mouth. The others nod. Thank the moon, shifters know how to be quiet when they're stalking prey. Aggie's the loudest, but we position her with Ji-hwan in front to guide her steps, and Brutus in the rear for protection.

It gets lighter as we get close, and before we hit an opening I hear a familiar voice.

"Welcome, esteemed representatives, and those here representing themselves or their factions. I am honored to host this prestigious group and hope you're all looking forward to the upcoming conclave."

Amun? It's not like I wasn't hoping to catch him doing something, but he's not one for roughing it. Just forcing others to. So what's he doing in some far-flung cave in the desert? There's got to be another way in, because I can't imagine him putting in the effort of the swim and trek we've just done.

The tunnel grows wider, and I drop to my belly, crawling toward the opening in front of us. I can see the top of a cavern come into view, and by the size of the vaulted ceiling it's got to be massive. I'm at the edge of a cliff when I reach the tunnel exit, with only a narrow landing to look down from. The voices are below us.

I see rows of stone bench seating. Combined with the echoing acoustics and large ceiling, it reminds me of a theater or a sanctuary.

I scan the crowd, hoping that if someone looks up, they can't spot us. The others squeeze into place beside me. We're all flat on our bellies, peering over the edge. I'm prepared for a lot of things: for us to get found out and have to make a run for it; for some gathering of representatives, with bribes being passed around. What I'm not prepared for, what I never in my wildest thoughts considered, is what faces us as we crouch at the rim of the meeting.

24
Trust Me

"Great Moon," Ever hisses beside me, and I can feel she's come to the same conclusion as me. Shock.

I dip my chin. I sniffed out the same thing.

"Exactly. A good third of those individuals are human. And look at their attire. Suits? Sunglasses in the dark? Skin me and stuff me for a taxidermy project if they're not from some sort of alphabet soup entity."

"Alphabet soup? *No les entiendo nada.*"

"Government," I clarify. "Secretive and dangerous. By human standards, at least."

"I can't hear what they're saying," Aggie grouches from where she lies on her belly.

"Lucky you," I whisper back. I can hear them. I can also hear every little clink and clank in the tunnel around us. Is it just a falling pebble, or the tunnel about to collapse? Who knows?

I've put on my skin, to make more room for the others. But I left my ears furred. All the better to hear you with, my sneaky shady representatives.

"We all know why we're here," Amun states, throwing a sweeping gesture around the gathered crowd. "To discuss some moves forward that have been in the works a long time. Moves that will benefit us all. Some can be brought to light at the conclave, but as we're all well aware, some are best kept in the dark."

A human clears his throat. One of the geniuses wearing dark sunglasses even at night, inside a cave. To avoid being recognized? Someone should tell him shifters can sniff him out regardless.

"I must admit, Amun, those of us from the human side of things were worried when all this Claw business reared its ugly head. After all, there's only so much magical activity we can help you sweep under the rug. If things had gotten too out of control—"

"But they didn't," Amun cuts him off, voice smooth and calm. You're not fooling me, feline. I can feel the anger as the human questions him. And what did he mean? Half the point of the Magikai is preventing humans from finding out about us. For their own good, and ours. Just how open is this secret?

"Even so." Another human picks up the conversation. This one has hair that's beginning to gray. A strong jawline that's beginning to soften. All the marks of an active human faced with inevitable aging. "Next time, we'd like to be kept in the loop on things from the get-go. By your own accounts, it was primarily one of your enforcers who solved the whole thing, correct?"

Amun huffs as another representative steps up to speak. Some burly shifter with a beard whom I don't know.

"She took out the leader of the Claw. Not nearly as hard of a feat as it sounds when you learn he was infatuated with her and they were sleeping together."

"That was *one* time, months ago," I argue under my breath. Judgmental sewing circle. Who are they to comment on my life? Ever elbows me.

"Pay attention!" she chastises me in a whisper. I bite back a retort and turn my attention to the meeting once more. The shifter representative still has the floor.

"*We're* the ones who rounded up the rest of the Claw members. To all our benefit, I might remind you. I wouldn't worry about the enforcer in question. We have her well in hand. And we have our own plans on what to do with her."

I scramble on the cliff edge, fist raised.

"That slimy lion," I seethe.

Ever snags my elbow, whispering frantically.

"*No sea boba.* We can't be seen!"

She's right, of course. Sometimes I have control over my temper. And sometimes I just think I do ... right up until that point that it runs away with me.

"Speaking of splitting things up, perhaps this will ease some of the tension," Amun states from below us. He stands up and claps his hands twice. The sound of stone scraping against stone echoes as an arched door set into the rock, which I didn't notice before, creaks open from behind the head representative. Magicals come out, pulling long ropes. Behind them is a train of cages. Wooden frames, long vertical bars. They look like aged circus crates. Old-fashioned ones. The kind that used to haul wild animals around for the entertainment of humans.

"Aggie," I whisper, "can you feel anything from the cages?"

She holds up a hand that shakes, and she flinches as her eyes flicker. The hand drops, limp.

"Magic. Lots of it. Containing whatever's within."

As I suspected. But I'd wanted to hold out hope it wasn't the case.

Amun dips his chin to one of the magicals in the audience.

"If you please, Sellius."

The magical claps his hands together and extends them toward the circus cages, and light shines forth. Some sort of warlock, then.

"Hell's bells," I breathe. And it's the last breath I can take for the next minute.

"Never," Ever hisses, "Never." She's shaking my arm as I snap back to the present.

There are supernaturals in each of the caravan cars, visible now that the warlock has removed whatever cloaking was in effect. The first contains a longma—a gorgeous scaled but horse-like creature with antlers. The second holds a wolf shifter. A massive one. He throws himself up against the bars in his fur, and they sizzle as he's thrown back onto the wooden floor planks. The last caravan contains a chamrosh. The absolute mother of all guard dogs. The canine has wings and naturally protects birds. But if it could be forced to turn its protective instincts to anything else? Well, it would make one hell of a bodyguard. I've even heard of the chamrosh and birds sharing their sight with one another. If that's true, you could use it as a scout as well.

Below us, Amun's guests are whispering to one another. There are too many overlapping voices for me to catch more than snaps.

"—bring it back to the prince."

"—we'd be the strongest coven in South America."

"—could use it to hunt down—"

Amun holds up his palms, and the audience quiets. The creatures behind him continue to snarl and snap.

"May I assume we are all feeling a bit less animosity toward the Magikai now? We are generous hosts. Each faction will leave the conclave with just such a prize. And tonight, we will hold a drawing for these three specimens. Just a taste of what is to come. I am not a stingy gift-giver. If you are lucky enough to win this evening, your new charges will also come with caretakers."

Amun snaps his fingers, and a bear shifter walks out, tugging ropes along behind him.

As the end of the ropes come into light, I see and smell the humans on the other end. Two of them look similar to one another, both with strawberry-blond hair. The third is a short man with brown curly locks. My hands dig into the stone, claws ripping loose and scoring cracks into the earth.

"No!" I bite out.

Ever slaps her hand over my mouth as the sound echoes. I feel her alarm wash over me. She stares, wide-eyed, as we flatten ourselves. From this distance, it's all jumbled together, but I can feel the concern. The suspicion. The focus as they all go on high alert.

Shit.

Me and my massive mouth.

Dammit, Never.

We scramble down on our backs, not standing upright until we hit the larger tunnel further down.

Do I even need to ask whether it's you sneaking around up there?

I jump a good few feet off the ground as Nahum's voice echoes in my head.

"You all right?" Ji-hwan asks, putting one hand on my shoulder. I give a shaky nod.

You have got to stop doing that! I chide the dragon.

As soon as you stop putting yourself in situations like these. I feel the humor through the statement, as if he is well aware that won't be happening any time soon. Or ever.

If he's in the cavern ...

You can stop them! Throw all those bastards into a nightmare from which there is no waking. Save those magicals! I insist. There's a long pause. *Nahum?*

I'm sorry, mate, I won't do that.

Who even knows what he's feeling now? All I can register is my own disappointment. I feel sick. He doesn't even bother saying he *can't*. He goes straight to *won't*, acknowledging that it's a choice.

How can that be your decision? After what was done to both of us—

That is precisely why I can't. I know it's difficult, but think of the bigger picture here. He said this is a small taste. The real show will be at the conclave. If I stop them now, whoever or whatever is being held for that event may disappear forever. If I go along with him, I can find out how far this goes. We can stop all of it, once and for all. If we're willing to wait a matter of days.

I let the words echo and linger. Can I really let the ends justify the means? Allow these magicals and humans to get bartered off tonight to go after a larger target? And what if, once this is all said and done, I can't find *these* victims?

If it takes another thousand years, I will make sure we catch every last individual responsible. We will get all these innocents back. I promise you, Never.

I know he's said he can't exactly read my mind, but this has me doubting. It's what I needed to hear.

I let you go with them ... and just hope that you're telling the truth? That you're really on my side?

Yes. If you trust me. Do you trust me?

The whole scene reeks of déjà vu, and I don't like it.

I once had an ex whom I trusted, and he got me hunted down by the Collectors and abandoned me. I also once dated a guy who insisted he was a double agent for the Claw, but he was really on my side. Right before he blamed the murder of the group's leader on me. And then I once had an ex who had promised to love and protect me forever, but instead he hunted me across the globe and forced me into a bloody showdown that ended up with him getting sent to the Underworld.

Oh, wait. That was all the same ex.

See? I have terrible taste!

And yet, this time I've been let in on the ground floor. Nahum is letting me know his motivations and his goals. And he's right. I don't see any other way we can find this new stronghold of creatures. A magical on the inside is our only way.

I will find them. I won't rest. Not until I've saved every last one, I vow.

Is that a yes? Nahum clarifies.

Yes. Go with them. But I want to know who takes the magicals and humans tonight. Because someday soon, they're going to be introduced to my most violent side. And it will be the last thing they'll ever see.

They should be so lucky, he responds, and if I weren't filled with so much fury at Amun that I could burst, I'd be touched.

I've chosen trust.

I just hope the others don't have to pay the price if I'm wrong.

25

No More Mrs. Nice
Were

Nahum's voice echoes in my mind again.

Your outburst has drawn his attention. Amun's called in a few enforcers to patrol the cave while this deal is done. You'd better get moving.

I shake my thoughts loose, then look around at the others. They're all quiet. Waiting. Aggie and Ever are curious. They've met Nahum, but they've never experienced the in-brain dragon speak. Ji-hwan and Brutus are looking at me like I'm crazy. And I can feel their concern that I might actually be.

"All right. We need to get going. Now."

The Wereling and witchling launch into action, making their way back to the water, where we came in. Ji-hwan follows suit. Brutus casts a glance over his shoulder.

"How could he?" The head enforcer lets the question hang, but I get the gist well enough.

I clap him on the shoulder.

"Them's the breaks, huh? Doesn't it just ruin your day when the ruler you've given your life to support has been breaking his own laws behind your back? And using his position to abuse not only the magical world's finances, but also the lives of those he's supposed to be looking out for?"

Brutus stares at me, jaw hanging open.

"Yeah. It does ruin my day, actually," he croaks out. I reach down and grab him by the wrist, tugging him along.

"Come on, bud. This will all look better after a quick escape, followed by a long drink. Water for you, if you insist."

"I might just be willing to join you for a beer after all this," he mutters. But he starts moving. Thank the moon. We're getting close to the water when I hear footsteps behind us, and the sound of pebbles clattering and echoing. Ever is still a bit jumpy, and her terror shoots up.

"Sorry," she mutters when I cringe next to her.

"'S fine," I assure her, doing all I can to temper my emotions so I don't make myself a liar in front of the only other intuitive on the planet.

We dive into the water. I kick furiously, tugging Aggie along with me. The witch is spent. Brutus reaches out underwater and grabs hold of the witchling, helping me out. I suck in air when we break the surface.

"The only swimming I want to do after this is in my own bathtub. With bubbles. And perhaps a scented bath oil," I murmur as we make our way out of the water.

"Come on!" Ji-hwan urges everyone.

"Wait! Over here!" Brutus motions us all to the edge of the falls, and we step behind them just as several enforcers surface. We're at the very edge of the falls, just the rock wall behind us. With any luck, this will hide our scents and prevent us from being seen.

I peek around the cloud of mist that the falling water creates, spying on the others as they reach the edges of the pond and fan out, sniffing and searching the desert. Ever tilts her head at me, staring. I just shake my head.

Not yet.

We wait until they fade from sight and smell. A few of them circle back and dive into the waters. My knees are sore from standing up straight, plastering my back against the rock shelf. I kick them up as we exit, stretching out my legs.

"Where do you think the rest are going?" Aggie asks, leaning heavily against Brutus.

"The compound, most likely. Moon knows how we'll beat them back. It'll certainly be noticed if we're unaccounted for," he responds.

"Brutus, can you carry the witchling? Everyone else, shift. Run as silently as you can and skirt the edges of the compound. Keep your nose to the air and avoid any other scents out in the open. They'll be slowed down by their search. If we hurry, we can beat them. And we'll figure out something for Aggie," I instruct.

When Brutus shifts and kneels to let me place Aggie on his back, I realize how far he's come. Mr. "I'm in charge here" from the battle with the Claw would never have allowed some witch to use him as transportation.

By the grace of the moon or whatever is actually out there, and by the skin of our teeth, we make it back to the tent. The only good thing I can say about the Arizona heat? It's dry. If it weren't for that we'd all be suspiciously dripping and damp, but as it stands we're dry and dusty as we enter the sleeping quarters. I shift and scramble into a bunk, and so do the others, just moments before the flap swings open and a flashlight shines in our faces.

The wolf shifter trainees grumble and cover their eyes.

"Hey! What's the big idea?" I demand. "Some of us are trying to sleep in here, asshole!" I toss a pillow at the offending enforcer.

The individual ducks, and when they stand back up I can see and smell they're a reptile shifter of some sort. Not one of those who have joined our group training sessions.

"Geez, we're here under orders! No need to get testy," he snaps as another figure steps up behind him. A warlock, and, given his professional state of dress, one of the representatives.

"Trainees. Line up," he instructs. The young wolf shifters jump to attention, lining up in front of their bunks. Ever, Ji-hwan, Brutus and I join them. Brutus is standing with all his muscle-y bulk shielding the red-headed lump under his covers.

The warlock and reptile shifter make their way down the aisle between the bunks, making shifty glances between us all.

"You!" the warlock snaps at the first wolf shifter he comes across. "Has everyone in this bunk been accounted for the entire evening?"

The wolf shifter gazes around at everyone, and I can feel his guilt and how uncomfortable he is. We are so royally screwed.

"Yes sir," he answers. I'm ... shocked speechless. And that doesn't happen to me too often.

"And you? What do you have to say about it?" the warlock asks the next shifter in line. It's Lowell, fully healed after his snallygaster incident. He glances at me across the aisle.

"Of course, sir. It's been a regular evening here, with the exception of you two waking us up in the middle of the night." He smirks, and I could just hug him.

"No need to get cute with me, trainee! Just answer the questions." The warlock glowers. One by one the wolf shifters lie for us. I'm so touched I could cry, if I went in for that sort of emotional display, that is.

After he finishes the trainees, he rounds on Brutus. I notice he doesn't ask any of the Weres present.

"And you? Head enforcer? You haven't noticed anything out of the ordinary?"

"No sir." Brutus's voice is quick, clear, and professional. No surprise there.

The reptile looks behind him, where Aggie's hair is spilling onto his pillow.

"What about this? You of all people should know we aren't supposed to fraternize with other enforcers, *sir*." The reptile sneers as he drops the last word. It's obvious not everyone likes a wolf in charge.

"He's right," the warlock clarifies. "She'll have to go."

We are in deep trouble. If gossip about the stripper has been going around, it's fully possible they'll recognize her.

"Yeah, Brutus, get your booty-call out of the barracks." The reptile gives a wheezy laugh.

The change in Brutus is instantaneous. His eyes go dark as he advances on the reptile and the warlock, fangs growing.

"She's not a fellow enforcer and she's not a booty-call. That is my mate. And I'll rip anyone to pieces who says a bad thing against her. So, consider your next words, lest they be your last."

He looks feral, practically foaming at the mouth.

The reptile holds up his hands in surrender.

"Woah, I was just kidding, wolf. No need to go all mate-mad on me. Besides, how was I supposed to know? I didn't even realize you *had* a mate!"

The warlock is still giving the Aggie-shaped lump of covers a suspicious stare. Brutus steps between them.

"I have kept it close to the chest. You make a lot of enemies in this profession. I don't want any of the magicals I've hunted down coming after her in revenge. I would appreciate you keeping this to yourselves. Or do I need to convince you?"

The reptile backs all the way to the door.

"No, nope. We're all good here!"

The warlock is more reluctant, but he, too, backs away and leaves after lingering for another moment.

"Way to go, Brutus!" Ji-hwan says, walking over and clapping the wolf shifter on his back. Brutus's eyes go back to their normal blue and his fangs retract.

I storm over to him, ready to thank him and punch him at the same time.

"Over my dead and rotting corpse are you going to claim that witchling. Now you listen to me, and you listen good, wolf. Just because your species has a mating instinct does not mean you can—"

He grabs me by the arms and starts laughing, which just makes me fume more.

"Never. Never, relax. I was lying. You know, like you do every time you pretend to approve of Amun?"

"What!" I sputter, utterly gobsmacked. "That—Brutus, you may have missed your calling. That was some of the best acting I've ever seen. You lie with flair! With panache! With commitment and style!"

He nods.

"Yes, true. Too true. And you are a terrible liar."

"Only when I'm having to make nice to people who piss me off, but thanks."

Aggie's poking her head out of the covers while the wolf trainees all introduce themselves to Brutus's "mate."

"Brutus." A smile spreads across my face. "You're going to lie some more. I need you to find us a mission. Any mission, and make it believable. Something urgent. Something that requires we leave right away."

"Yes ma'am!" He throws me a mock salute. "You know, you could have been a good head enforcer."

It's my turn to laugh.

"I'd rather swim the English Channel."

"I know you would."

He heads out, instructing a couple of the other wolves to go with him. The rest of the teens get back to bed. Aggie settles into Brutus's bunk, asleep in minutes in spite of the noise. Sleep won't add much to her magical stores, but it'll help the basic exhaustion.

I make my way over to my own bunk, where a conflicted Were is waiting for me.

"We need to talk," Ever says, nervous but decided. I follow her outside and into the desert until we're far enough out to avoid being overheard.

"What was that, back at the cavern? You blew our cover. You could have gotten us killed!" Ever accuses, bristling and pissed off, now that we're out of immediate danger. I don't blame her.

"It was the caretakers. Two of those humans they brought out."

Surprise hits me from her direction.

"You risked our lives just because you saw humans? There were tons of them down there!"

"Yes, but these two are special. The caretakers for the captured magicals, the ones with the strawberry-blonde hair. Their names are Meeri and Ardus. They were looking after the Isle, last time I saw them." Nahum had checked in on them for me, delivered my gift. Which means … "Amun must have gotten to them just after Nahum. But why? Did he figure out my connection with them? Is this a taunt at me?"

I nearly run into a cactus, too caught up in my thoughts to watch where I'm going. Ever armbars me in the chest to stop me.

"Right. Surroundings," I mutter.

She rolls her eyes.

"Remind me again how you managed to become some fearsome enforcer for all these years when you can't multi-task?" she demands.

"Reflexes. Stubbornness. The fact that Weres are very hard to hurt and heal quickly compared to many other magicals." May as well be honest. The latter details have helped me just as much as the former. I'm good, but I've bested better. Sometimes with my mind, but sometimes just by out-enduring people in a fight. "And because I make it my personal mission to live up to the term 'refuse to lose.'"

She sighs, some of the anger dropping away.

"Look, I'm not happy that you put us at risk. That being said, you're family. And I would have had the same reaction if I'd seen you down there. I get it."

She holds out a hand and I grab it, pulling her into a hug. She relaxes, and in spite of my former hug-aversion I've got to admit I like this sisterly bonding thing. Perhaps I'll even wear my 'hugs' shirt. In the vamp mansion. Where no one else can see it.

"So, what now?" Ever asks as she pulls away.

"Now, we wait for Brutus. As soon as he's ready, we grab him, Ji-hwan, and the witchling and head back to the vamp mansion. Round everyone up and head to Vegas for the conclave. No more playing nice or trailing after Amun. This time, we're getting in on the action right from the start."

26
The New Crew

We're gone well before sunrise, in a panel van Brutus commandeered. The back has a couple of futon-like seats along the side walls. Aggie is snoozing on one, and Ji-hwan and Ever sit on the other. I'm up front with Brutus, separated from the others by spelled bars.

"We normally use it to transport back dangerous magicals, but I thought it would add some legitimacy to this 'mission' I was supposed to say we were on."

"Good thinking," I acknowledge, even as I dig a moldy fast-food container out from under my seat. Whoever had this vehicle before us was no stickler for cleanliness. "A van, though? Puts me one step closer to soccer mom."

Brutus laughs.

"Never, I don't think you have to worry about anyone taking you for anything other than a calculating and conniving ass-kicker."

"Brutus! I didn't know you were capable of such compliments. Be still my heart," I gush, fluttering my eyelashes at him. His grin grows wider, and his emotions wash over me. Relieved and relaxed, even with all we're driving into.

"You know, I never really had friends like this," he acknowledges. "There were some other trainees when I started with the Magikai, but they've all since moved to other areas. And with my position, I don't really get the chance to get close to people."

"Your condescending and chauvinistic attitude may also have had something to do with it," I muse.

He tenses for a moment, then laughs again.

"Yeah, maybe. Believe it or not, I've always just wanted to do good. Provide a real service to the magical world. And this may be the first time I truly feel like I'm doing that."

His mood dims.

"But I don't know what we'll do if we manage to stop Amun and the others. It's a disaster beyond comprehension. How do we even fix something like this?"

I give his muscled bicep a pat.

"One problem at a time, my friend." And I mean it. The *friend* bit. If you'd have told me a few months ago I'd be adding this brute to my close-knit circle, I'd have laughed you out of the vamp mansion, but the world is full of surprises.

I called the others the minute we hit the road, and everyone's waiting eagerly at the gates of the vamp grounds when we pull in. I roll through introductions as we walk into the great hall.

"Ah yes, Brutus. That enforcer who was such a jackass to you the first time we all met." Lynx smiles, holding out his hand for the wolf shifter to shake.

"I think I'll reserve judgment, if it's all the same to you," Hugh states, keeping his distance. I don't blame him. Hugh's feeling protective, and as he glances over at Chrys there's no question as to the cause of his feelings. Brutus may have helped protect Chrys when we fought the Claw, but she was only in danger because he bull-headedly followed a Claw member into a trap he should have seen coming.

The witch in question marches straight up to Brutus. They're standing chest to chest. Well, head to chest. Brutus is notably taller. Chrys looks up at him.

"So. This is the one whose ass I saved after he ran headfirst into a Claw ambush?" she demands.

Brutus blushes.

"Then again, you also stuck around to defend me when I was unconscious afterwards. Which is more than I can say for the rest of those enforcers. So, what do you say, even?" She holds out her hand, and a bewildered Brutus takes it and shakes.

Ji-hwan's introduction goes much smoother. After all, *I'm* the only one who wanted to throttle him. I explain our first meeting and Ji-hwan's set of skills.

"Wait. This is some sort of magically based ability? Like Never's intuition?" Todd questions. The bear is even taller than Brutus, and that leaves him towering over Ji-hwan. I can tell the Were is intimidated. Which is silly, since technically a Were is a lot more durable than a bear shifter, not that I'll be reminding Todd of any such thing.

"It's magic. But maybe not as powerful as Never's ability. I draw people to me and influence them, but I can't *make* anyone do anything. It's not mind control."

Todd looks unconvinced, and suspicion leaks from Lynx in spite of his earlier welcoming statements. I sigh.

"Look, I'm not one to force someone to use their abilities. I certainly didn't like the Claw trying to hunt me and Ever down over our intuition. That being said, we really don't have time for this. And if we're going into that casino together, we've got to have a certain amount of trust. Ji-hwan, would you be opposed to demonstrating?"

We've drawn a crowd. A good dozen or so of my vamps are hovering on the stairs and in the wings.

"All right. But during the conclave I'd prefer to use my fighting skills and not my seduction, unless it's absolutely necessary," he shares. I don't blame him. Who knows how Amun took advantage of it.

There's no visible change to Ji-hwan, but there's a definite change to almost everyone else. I don't get a good chance to see how my crew responds, because they're all bowled over by a crowd of vampires pushing and shoving to get to the Were.

"So handsome," croons one of the vamp males, reaching up to run a finger along Ji-hwan's jawline.

"Come to my room with me; I can take care of you better than these others," one of the ladies whispers in his ear, twirling a piece of his hair around her finger.

"All right! That's enough! That is enough!" I yell, pushing past my own vamps and hauling them off. Ji-hwan must have dropped whatever he was doing, because as a group they all freeze and then back away. Bewildered and with a lingering feeling of arousal.

"That was a bit more intense a reaction than I anticipated," Ji-hwan admits.

Hugh shrugs.

"What'd you expect? You let loose a seduction ability in a lobby full of lusty vampires."

Okay, perhaps the Were hasn't quite let things go with Ji-hwan. They can fight it out another time.

"Petty squabbles later. Important discussions now," I instruct, leading everyone into the dining hall.

"Wait a minute. Are you saying the Magikai have been carrying on some version of the Collectors all this time, or are they just using the fall of the Claw and your visit to the Isle to make an example?" Todd questions, fingers flexing and claws going out and in as his hands change from furred to skin and back again. Agitated. And I wouldn't need my intuition to see it. He normally picks a form and sticks to it.

"I don't know. Thanks to my mouth, we had to leave before we could get clarification on that," I admit.

"Whether they're running a continued operation like the Collectors, or using the fall of the Claw to distribute the losing magicals out like prizes, either is despicable," Hugh declares. I notice his fangs lengthen. They're first to go when he shifts. His eyes flash red.

I'm torn on his proclamation. I detested the Collectors. Still despise everything they stood for. And yet. When we fought the Claw I would have killed any of them that stood in my way. Decimated their ranks, if that was the only way. But I take issue with their being in cages?

Then again, who knows how many innocent supernaturals are captive as well.

"What do we do with them once we free them?" Aggie pipes up across the room. She's tucked on some ornate fainting couch, sipping a hot chocolate with a blanket wrapped around her. She winces and adjusts her seat. The vamps cared more for aesthetics than comfort when picking the decor here.

"We can't let them go," Lynx argues before Aggie can make whatever compassionate suggestion she'd been on the verge of, "if the magicals being traded off are Claw remnants, then they may be captives, but they're also villains."

I tap my chin.

"Maybe yes, and maybe no."

"What do you mean?" Todd asks.

"Some of these individuals might be Claw members. But I'm leaning toward that not being all. The Scots' representative led a rebellion, and he was looking for someone. Maybe Amun has her as well? And he sent us after an orb that was guarded by flying magicals. I could swear I saw Sky, another representative, guarding it. It's possible he's just taking people and objects from a wide variety of entities. And as much as I'm for hunting down the bad guys, this is bigger than us. Bigger than one enforcer mission," I reason, letting my thoughts form as I'm saying them.

"Just what are you suggesting we do, Lady Never?" Hugh questions, steepling his hands under his chin. Chrys nods next to him.

"Brace yourselves, kiddies. I'm going to suggest we use those potential alliances. The ones we already have, like Elios's guys and the bears, and the ones we suspect. Approach any other Scottish shifters or the winged magicals in Oklahoma. Work together. And I vote we make the focus on stopping Amun and any other representatives, magicals or humans involved in the illegal trade of people and artifacts. Once we've procured said magicals, we hand them over to their respective species and groups. Their covens, sleuths, packs or whatnot can decide how to handle them."

Todd whistles as I finish.

"You're handing over authority to someone else? When you could just take someone out yourself? *And* you're suggesting more allies? It's a viable plan. One that might not end with all of us killed or maimed. Pinch me, I must be dreaming."

I let out a mirthless laugh.

"Not possible. Nahum's not here to put you in one." That sours me. What is the dragon up to? Is he safe?

Across the room, only one individual is feeling upset about this whole thing.

"Those winged magicals killed our enforcers. They tried to kill me. And we're just going to offer them our help? To ask for theirs? *Esto me huele mal ... no se si es una buena idea.* They should pay for what they did."

What a time for Ever to take after me. I look at her, knowing she'll feel the sincerity of my words.

"You're not wrong. If this is what we think it is, this will be the largest coup ever attempted in the magical community. We *need* help. And I don't say that lightly. We will find out who was responsible for those deaths, and you being dropped from the sky. And we can make those people pay. But first, can we set it aside? Not forget it, just table it for a bit? Use whatever advantages we can get to win this? Because if Amun's stockpiling wealth, magicals, and spells, we can bet he'll have something up his sleeve."

Ever stares back at me, brown eyes burning into my blue. She's scowling. I can't even blame her. I know what it's like, to take attempts on my life personally. And she has to know I'm feeling like a giant hypocrite. I wouldn't align myself with someone who dropped me like a rock.

She gives one curt nod, a better person than I am.

"Fine. For now. But I'm not letting this go." She sweeps her gaze around the group, as if anyone of us objected. Then she slides her chair back from the table.

"I'm going to get something to eat. You can let me know the plan when it's settled."

It's easy to forget the Were is still so young. I've asked a lot of her, and I keep asking more.

I lay out my plan for the others. Using the casino to draw in conclave members and spy for information, hoping Nahum or one of them can get us into the actual conclave meeting. Gathering our allies to bust up said meeting and detain all in attendance, while freeing any captive magicals and liberating any stolen goods.

"Then all that's left is to hold trials, mete out justice, return any stolen items or freed magicals, do damage control based on how much the humans know, and rebuild a government for the entire magical community. Thank goodness it's nothing difficult." Lynx rolls his eyes.

"Please." I wave a hand as if it's nothing. "Hand the government stuff over to Hugh and he'll have it back up and running in a week."

Hugh's pride hits me as he receives the compliment. And what's more, I believe it. Might even suggest it if we manage to win. Although that would add "put out a job notice for a vampire mansion manager" to my growing list of to-dos.

"That's it, then. The conclave officially starts later this week. I'll let my brother know the plan," Todd states.

"I'll inform Elios and the few enforcers we trust up here," Lynx adds.

"And we'll go back to the casino and ensure everything is ready," Chrys says, linking arms with Hugh. "We can take along your two friends, get them up to speed." She nods at Ji-hwan and Brutus.

"What about you? What will you be doing?" Todd asks, brown eyes boring into me with curiosity and anticipation.

"Something vital," I say, keeping this bit to myself for now, "but I'd like to keep Aggie with me."

She agrees, and the rest of them leave.

"So, what are we doing?" the witchling questions when everyone else is gone.

"Hedging our bets," I reply.

I read emotions, not the future, but I'm overcome with apprehension at what I'm about to do. I feel like I'm taking my furthest step yet down a road with no turning back. But I'll be damned if I place myself over the entire magical world.

I'm vain. I'm prickly. I'm sarcastic. I'm bull-headed. But I'm not *that* selfish.

I reach up with a finger and tap twice.

27

The Last Puzzle Piece

"I'm beginning to wonder if you think I'm a djinn, to be summoned for wishes," Visitor states, wiping imaginary dust off one sleeve of his suit. That thing is immaculately clean, so I'm not buying it for a second. Nor am I buying his mood. He's pleased. Entirely *too* pleased that I've reached out again. Which makes me even more uneasy.

"Save the dishonesty, Visitor." He quirks his head to the side at the nickname I've given him. Not like I have anything else to call him. He's thoughtful, and I imagine him rolling the name over in his mind. Deciding if it works. Trying it on like a shirt at the store to decide if he can't live without it.

In the end he doesn't acknowledge it, but he doesn't correct me.

"Very well, honesty it is, then," is all he says.

"Good. I've already got a few small debts going with the Bone Reader, and I sure as the moon don't want to make any more deals."

"Then why am I here?"

"Because I'm going to make one anyway. I need you to get your boss down here. Posthaste."

He raises his upper lip, all distaste and disbelief.

"The Bone Reader does not like to make house calls. The customer making the effort to go to him is part of the process. I am only here because of the Bone Reader's interest in you and an overly magnanimous mood he's been in lately."

I nod along, ignoring him entirely while pretending to listen.

"Yeah, sure. I hear you. Be that as it may. I do not have that option. Things are kind of coming to a head down here, and if I visit him I'll miss the whole party. So, what do you say? Are you going to help a gal out or not?" I stamp a foot down, drawing myself up to my full height.

Visitor looks down his chiseled nose at me.

"You don't really want his help. But you desperately need it. And you won't go to him, but you expect him to drop everything and come to you. And here I am, giving in to this ludicrous request because he likes backing your little schemes. The Bone Reader must be going mad."

The shadows swallow him before I can blink. Now we wait. I'm not sure how the Bone Reader will make an entrance. Shadows of his own? A private jet?

Within moments the floor starts to shake. Cracks form on the hardwoods. The chairs around the dining room table topple and fall. I clutch Aggie, putting my fur on and holding her close to keep us both upright as she squeals. Adding a few windows to this mansion is one of the few updates I have gotten around to, so I can see out the ones in here and onto the grounds. Everything seems still, not even a breeze blowing in the trees.

What? Okay, all right, okay fine. *Hugh* made sure the windows got installed. Not really the time for splitting hairs, is it?

Now, where was I?

Ah, yes. Dining room coming apart. Now that I'm certain it's no earthquake ...

"You can come out now! Point made! Grand entrance achieved!" I yell over the din as a large mirror falls off the wall and shatters.

"You can also take that seven years of bad luck. That's not on me!" I shout into the air. Over the dining room table, the chandelier chimes and clanks as the glass beading is tossed together. The metal portion screwed into the ceiling starts to creak, and the whole thing comes crashing down. It shatters all over the dining table, glass flying everywhere. The metal embeds itself into the tabletop.

I throw my arms around Aggie's face and throat and in the process take glass shards to the forearms, face, and neck. Small injuries for a Were, but enough to make me livid.

"You owe me for all this damage!" I scream into the storm that my dining hall has become.

The wind stills.

In front of me stands the Bone Reader himself, his form cycling through features like a slot machine.

"Funny you should mention 'owe.' You realize you're running up a pretty steep pile of debts with me? And here I thought you'd sworn off such things." Amusement. I'm pretty sure this is why the Bone Reader likes me so much. I'm the only Were whose decision-making process is half-assed enough that she keeps repeating the same mistake over and over. I wonder if I'm his only frequent customer? I've got to be his most entertaining.

"You can step away from the witchling. While it's valiant of you to defend her, I have no intent to cause either of you physical harm."

What about emotional? Mental? Financial?

I keep those thoughts to myself as I take a step back.

"As it so happens, she's perfectly capable of defending herself," I say instead.

"I'm a stripper," Aggie pipes up from behind me. The Bone Reader is all interest and intrigue, moving around me and facing her instead.

"Ah, yes. I recall Never bringing you to my home once before. How fascinating. Not very common at all. And light magic." He takes a long inhale. "How positively refreshing. Oh yes, we must chat about that. I'm most intrigued to hear how your coven reacted to your stripping key. And other magicals? I know strippers aren't wildly popular, but that's only because ignorant individuals fear how powerful they can be."

Aggie is fiddling with her hands under the Bone Reader's scrutiny. I, already being in deep, decide to try for some free information.

"Could she strip *you?*"

The Bone Reader sneers with thin lips, pouts with full ones, scowls and shows short fangs.

"It would be unwise in the extreme for her to attempt it," he says, tone ominous.

I cross my furred arms over my chest.

"Meaning?"

"It would result in rather unpleasant consequences. Permanently altering ones."

I tilt my head to the side, whispering out the side of my mouth toward Aggie.

"Ix-nay on the ip-stray witchling. Or he's liable to go all homicidal on your bespelling behind."

The Bone Reader laughs. For once, a singular sound. Metallic, cold, and hollow. It chills me to the point I rub my arms for warmth.

"As if I would mete out a punishment as dull as death. Think again, little Were."

If I weren't terrified at the possibilities, I'd take offense at 'little,' but as it stands ...

I give a curt nod as Aggie tugs on my arm.

"Very well, then, no stripping. At least not the magical kind."

"We have a deal." The Bone Reader smiles, sharp fangs and dull teeth as he holds out a hand. I roll my eyes, but I know he's serious, so I take it regardless. "Now then, you're the one who requested my presence. I do hope if I've come all this way it's because you're ready to make a true deal."

I steel myself before giving a swift nod.

"I am." The answer escapes through gritted teeth, tension in every muscle as my body rebels against what I'm doing. I know better. And yet I keep on making these blasted deals. I'm more addicted to poor choices than caffeine.

"Very well. Do you know what you need, or would you like me to tell you? The second option would, of course, be more expensive."

"Thank you, but I believe I know what we need."

We need a whole lot of supernaturals who aren't familiar with each other to work together as a unit. We need a better understanding of which individuals are on the opposing side. We need to know where the captives are being kept, and what defenses we might have to break through. We need to know what to do with any humans afterward, and how to fix the mess of a broken magical government. If we even should fix it. *We* need all that, and *I* need a cup of coffee followed by a stiff drink at the Lusty Lute and a nap.

"We need targeted enhancement," I say instead.

I relay my plan to the Bone Reader. I'm well aware that you can't just create true magic from nowhere. Spells and curses are nice and all, but they're no substitute for the real deal.

"Let me get this straight. You want your own abilities strengthened? Only the ones you already have, so they're innate to each of you. And you want it to last longer than your average spell, and you want it to have a blanket effect on your allies, but you can't specify exactly who's included in that particular group?"

"Not all of them," I clarify.

He gives that same chilling laugh as his features slide from spotless porcelain to freckled and sunkissed and back again. He rubs his hands together, and I can feel his excitement increasing.

"Wonderful. A true challenge. It's been a while since I've had one of those. Very well. When do you expect this beyond-magical magic to take effect?"

"The conclave meeting itself isn't until this weekend, but those attending are already descending on Vegas. So, as quick as you can manage it."

"Have you considered that having your intuition enhanced might be a bit overwhelming to your senses?" He reaches one hand out, as if he's trying to caress my mind. Or remove it. Honestly, with the Bone Reader it could be either. At the last moment, he curls his fingers back, their length shortening.

"I have. But it's one of the best ways for us to separate friend from foe. When we bust up whatever illicit affairs Amun has going, I'll catalog who reacts how."

"And your protégé? Can she handle it?" His eyes flash blue, then green, then silver. In spite of Were superstition, I'm drawn to the silver ones.

"I have faith in her."

"You know how this works. I guarantee my product. Let's shake. And then I'll tell you what you owe." His eyes are gleaming again, and he's so satisfied with himself and this deal that I consider canceling the whole thing for a good half a second before I shove my arm forward.

He holds his palm up in the air.

"One last thing. The witch." He looks around me at Aggie. She's running her hands through her wine-red hair and chewing her lip.

"Why bring her?" I ask. He nods. "Because I was hoping you could give us a sample of whatever enhancement you plan to use.

And her ability puts the rest of us to shame." I'm a big enough Were to admit it. She's outclassed only by Nahum, and he's not here. Although, if all goes according to plan, he'll be reaping the benefits of this deal along with the rest of us.

"Don't worry, I'll have her practice on me," I specify. At those words, the Bone Reader puts his hand back out. Before he can change his mind, I clench my fingers around his and give a swift shake.

"Wonderful," he croons, his voice almost musical. He glances at the witch. "Go ahead, light witch. Try it out."

She moves her hand. Barely the twitch of her pinky finger in my direction. I drop to my knees, gasping and clawing at my throat. I feel like I've just run a marathon ... as a human. Which I essentially am until this wears off.

"Well, that was certainly effective," I grit out through my teeth as Aggie slaps her hands over her mouth in alarm. She bends down to help, but I wave her off. "It's all right, witchling. The floor's more comfortable than you'd think. I'll get up soon enough." As soon as my legs stop shaking.

"All right, Bone Reader. You've shown you can hold up your end." And if it was this easy for him, he'd better be giving me a discount.

He dips his chin. Squared, rounded, pointed and sharp.

"Let's see. What could I ask of you? You're already agreed to loan me that ride on Halloween. And you owe me for sending Visitor to rescue you from the winged supernaturals. Perhaps a package deal. I'll make this one simple. On Halloween when you pick me up, I am going to be giving you a gift. You will accept it. And you will follow through with all the consequences that transpire because of it. Until such time as you are able to return the gift. No refusals."

"What a thoughtful gesture. A present I don't want, and which I don't get to keep." I snarl. His eyes flash for a moment and I clamp my mouth shut. It's unwise to lose one's temper with the Bone Reader, but I'm less than kind when I'm feeling this rotten.

"It is, actually. But that will all come to light soon enough. I will be seeing you again, Never. Big things are about to happen, and it may come as no surprise that you'll be right in the middle."

In the middle?

Hell, I plan to be leading the charge.

28

Escapes and Innocence

"How are we looking?" I ask Todd as I pass him on the casino floor. He's back in his fitted, black-on-black suit and shirt ensemble. He's even got in an earpiece and microphone attached to his cufflink so he can communicate with everyone.

"Same old, same old," he responds.

My plan with the vamps worked wonders. The casino floor of Vicious has been packed since our arrival. My vampires are having tons of fun, and their moods have significantly improved. My own is growing worse with each passing minute. We've heard plenty of juicy gossip from the representatives who have graced our casino with their presence. Cheating scandals, embezzlement of their own region's funds, hating their mothers-in-law. But nothing about Amun or the wealth held here. Nothing about the humans who know about us or the captive magicals. A few have seemed like they're getting close to the topic, but they always start speaking of something else or trail off altogether.

If I were a smart Were, and I am, my money would be on some sort of magically binding NDA. I asked Hugh the same thing yesterday.

"Oh yes, a binding non-disclosure agreement isn't just possible, I'd say it's highly likely. We'll just have to pay extra-close attention to what they're discussing just before they lose hold of the conversation. See if that can give us some clues," he'd said.

I've been itching to just barge back into Lusca Palms and take our chances.

The dragon's been silent in my head for days. And after Aggie's brief display of power, no one is acting supercharged on our side, either. Todd reached out to the winged magicals in Oklahoma, but they all claimed not to know Sky. And even Hugh couldn't come up with a good way for us to try and reach out to the Scottish magicals in advance.

The short and sweet of it? This situation stinks. The only positive is that if our powers don't get a major boost soon, I'll have one debt from the Bone Reader forgiven. But if he fails for the first time ever and we don't get what was promised, I doubt I'll be alive and free long enough to celebrate.

"Chrys, Ever, Aggie? Everything okay in the cage?" I speak into my own hand-dandy wristlet microphone. Mine's contained in a bracelet. I've kept a low profile the last few days, since I'm supposed to be on a mission, but now that it's Friday I'd say I'm safe to show myself. It's almost show time. One way or another, I have no plans to go back to the enforcer training ground charade.

I've donned a form-hugging, sparkling sapphire gown for the occasion. My bracelet, necklace, and of course eyepatch are silver. Even my heels are silver. When I go in, I go all in.

"Doing good!" Aggie squeaks over the mic. "No! That's too big! Stop trying to shove it in, it's never going to fit!" She argues with someone on the other line. Laughter echoes—Chrys's, I'm pretty sure.

"Did you pick up on that, Never? Seems my light-magic counterpart thinks we'll need a larger container for the massive ruby someone put up as collateral for their chips."

I roll my eyes, homing in on Aggie's embarrassment from across the playing floor and the crowd.

Wait a minute.

I really *am* picking up on her emotions.

And that's the last realization I get before I clutch my head at the roaring, screaming monsoon of emotions pummeling me. I drop to one knee, clutching at a bewildered Todd for support.

"I think I'm going to be sick," I moan.

"Never? Are you—" He starts to bend down and offer me a hand, but then tenses. His facial features pull into a grimace. He clenches his teeth as they start to extend, and the hand he holds out grows fur and claws.

"Steady, Todd," I caution him. Not that shifters in their fur are any problem in a magically warded casino. But if he shreds this suit and mauls the guests? I'm thinking they'd notice that.

After a good full minute, he pulls his bearish features back in, presenting me with a fang-less smile and flawless, deep brown skin instead of fur.

"I'll take that hand now," I mutter, grabbing it and hauling myself up. "The Bone Reader kept his word after all."

"*¡Caray!*" Ever yells into the mic.

"Anyone mind telling me what that was? I felt like shit for all of a minute, and now I feel like I could put a defensive spell over all of Vegas and have plenty of power left over," Chrys chimes in. She's thrilled at the prospect. I hear Aggie murmuring in the background, no doubt reminding them of my Bone Reader deal.

"Well, whatever you paid him, I'm going to say he gave you the bargain price," Chrys states, "because this shit rocks. Check it out!"

I look over toward the cage, but I don't see anything.

"Um, Chrys?"

"Oh yeah, forgot it's invisible if I'm not weaving the magic with an element. But trust that I've just locked down this cage harder than Fort Knox. No one's getting in here without my express permission." She's thriving on the increased power.

"Just don't ward out our guests for now," I remind her.

Lynx walks up, rubbing his head.

"Anyone else just go full fur by accident? I haven't done that since I first started shifting," he whines.

Brutus and Ji-hwan flank him. I'm turning to ask them how they're faring. And to ask Ji-hwan whether he's got a hold of his seductive abilities. I don't want the whole casino after him.

Brutus lifts an arm, pointing a single finger to the front doors. I look where he's indicating and spot a disheveled shifter running through the doors and into my casino. She's wearing a magenta evening gown, and her auburn hair is falling out of its updo. She had heels at one point, but the back's broken off one of them. Her other foot is bare. Her face is dirty with streaked mascara, and I can feel from here she's frantic. I begin to make my way down to her and her eyes lock onto mine. She sprints through the crowd directly at me.

If I thought I could feel desperation and despair before, it's nothing to what I can pick up on now. Whatever the Bone Reader did, he didn't do it halfway. Swirling tendrils of hope mix with fading horror. And it's as if *this* hope is special. It's the feeling of *last* hope. And she's directing it right at me as she barrels into me and clutches at my arms.

"Are you Never?" she demands, shaking me and herself as she begins to sob. "Please tell me you're Never. He said, he said to come to you and you'd help me. He said—"

People are beginning to turn and stare, and Todd steps in front of us, blocking us off from the crowd. Brutus and Lynx flank me as I lead the sobbing shifter off the floor and over to the staff elevators.

"Nothing to see here, folks! Just a bad run at the roulette table. Who hasn't been there, eh?" Ji-hwan states behind us. I feel the tension ebb as whatever else he does begins to work. The woman with us is quieting down, growing calmer, until the elevator door dings open and I shuffle her inside.

"No! I won't! No boxes, no cages! No!" She starts lashing out and kicking for all she's worth.

It goes against every reaction I'd normally have when someone's trying to punch me in my only good eye, but I don't fight back. I stand in front of her, then drop to a crouch in an attempt to appear less menacing. I hold my palms up and out, and keep my skin on.

"It's all right. If you don't want to go, you don't have to go. I have an office down here. Right this way." I take a step back out of the elevator and gesture down the hall. She grows quiet, and then takes an uneven step after me. Todd shadows her as we walk, but she doesn't try to bolt again. When we get to the office, I leave the door ajar but speak into my wrist.

"Chrys. I'm going to need you to come do me a solid here in the office."

I think about it another moment and speak again.

"Better yet, bring Ever and Aggie. Ask the vamps to take over for you in the cage," I instruct.

I can see a red mark around my guest's throat that's not quite healed. That has to mean magic. A collar? I give a subtle sniff. Is she some sort of bird shifter? I'm absolutely getting feathers, but something else distinct as well. Whatever was done to her is throwing me off.

"Can you shift?" I ask her. She tenses her muscles for a second, fists clenched, then shakes her head.

NEVER EVER211

"No. The—" And that's the end of that statement, but she points at her throat as she continues mouthing words.

"Here!" Chrys yells as she barrels into the room, white spiral-curls swinging. Hugh's with her as well. Thank goodness, I was about to need to make another call on the mic.

"Ward the room. Make us invisible and silent." It's done within moments.

"Aggie, I think our guest here is suffering the lingering effects of a magic dampening collar. I know you can't add magic in, but let's see if we can't pull some out. I suspect something's been put in place to prevent her from talking?"

Aggie frowns.

"But if she signed a magical contract like the representatives, can I work around that?"

I stare at Hugh. He takes the hint, clearing his throat.

"Well, since we're all extra-powerful at the moment, this is your best shot. And the following is just a theory, but I think it will apply. Magically binding contracts require willing participants. If she was forced to sign, I think you'll more easily be able to untangle that magic from her."

Aggie gets to work. I sit back, prepared for a long evening, but it takes only minutes.

"Done," the witchling announces as she drops one arm and wipes her other across her forehead. It's beaded in sweat. "It didn't take much power, just finesse to untangle that magic without hindering her ability to shift further."

"You can separate it like that?" I question.

She shrugs.

"For now. The Bone Reader is keeping his word."

The shifter in front of her is panting; sharp, shallow breaths. Sweat glistens on her brow, but she doesn't bother wiping it off.

Her cerulean eyes roll like that of a frightened horse, and she gulps, swallowing air a few times.

"All right," she says, voice shaky, "I think I can tell you now."

Her story is both terrible and familiar. Hunted down in her home, and a shift-preventing and magically dampening collar thrown on her. Transported not to the Isle, since it's no longer running, but to some underground location stacked wall to wall with crates and cages containing other magical species. A warehouse of enslaved supernaturals.

Amun really has brought back his own version of the Collectors. If they were ever really disbanded in the first place.

"I felt like someone had thrown me into a zoo. But the worst part was when they started pulling us out and making us up like this." She gestures to the tattered evening gown and broken heels. "We were warned a very important event was coming up, and we'd be sold or gifted off to new owners."

My reaction in a similar situation on the Isle was to get fire-spitting mad and put up a fight; hers is to start crying. Neither is wrong. After hiccupping tears for a bit, she composes herself and wipes her eyes. It streaks even more mascara across her cheeks.

"I'm sorry. The whole thing felt unreal. And it seemed hopeless. They had some really strong creatures there. I didn't think I stood a chance of escape. Not with the collar. And then, today, someone rescued me. He was there looking for someone, but they caught him too. They were collaring him while I ran. I would have helped, but he told me ... he told me to leave him." She devolves into tears again, hiccupping. Ever passes her a cup of water, and she takes the cup and sips on it.

"Thank you."

Ever nods.

"The male who let you out. What did he look like? Was he a dragon?" I keep reassuring myself Nahum hasn't turned on me, and this would explain why he hasn't reached out. If he found the captive magicals on his own, maybe he thought he could handle it himself.

She shakes her head, more hair pulling loose from her updo.

"No. He said he was a representative. He was a raiju."

Dammit. Unkai. I guess that's one thing settled. He's on our side if he's being taken prisoner. And now he's one more person to save.

"Why you?" I ask, and she flinches. I rephrase. "If he was there for someone else, why let you and only you out?" I'm confident in her answers so far. I could sense dishonesty a mile away with the Bone Reader's boost.

"He was frantic, checking the cages. I happened to be nearer the entrance. He heard someone coming, and I guess he realized he wasn't going to get who he was looking for. He was saying something about 'need to warn them. They have to be able to find it.' He asked the male in the cage next to me what he was. He said drake, and the raiju moved on. The female above him refused to answer. Then he got to me. I told him I was a unicorn, and he let me out of my cage and collar. Then he told me to run. Over here. To you. He said to tell you where I'd come from and you'd know what to do. The guards were busy with him while I slipped out."

Once she gets going, the words come in a rush. She stares at her hands through most of it, but up at me when she gets to the part where Unkai told her where to go.

"Hell's bells," I whisper, awed, "a unicorn?"

"They *really* did this to a unicorn?" Lynx asks from behind me, equally shocked. I'm reading similar reactions from most of the others. Those who are in the know, anyway. Ever's perplexed, but she's run into less of a variety of magical species.

In case you're like Ever, let me break it down for you. Unicorns are saints. Pure kindness and light. I've been around a few, and per my intuition, I can agree that I've never met one with the slightest ill intent. Only an absolute asshole would hurt a unicorn. Their horns *are* very valuable for spells, but a unicorn sheds its horn a couple of times a year. There's no need to hurt one. They can also bless you with luck or health. You're better off staying in one's good graces.

"Can you tell us where it is? It's very important we find out where they're keeping the others." I do everything I can to not let my intense desire for the information leak into my tone. I don't want to scare her.

Her voice wavers.

"I'm sorry, but I'm terrible at giving directions."

My heart sinks.

"But, I think I could take you there."

29
Don't Bet

"This building here! I went through the alley next to it." Sasha waits for Todd to check the alley before heading in and looking for the next landmark she recognizes.

When the unicorn gave me her name, I wasn't surprised. It can mean *defender* or *helper*. Perfect for a pure-hearted being of healing and luck. My fists clench. All these years. I've been working under the Magikai, thinking I was doing good. Thinking I was helping the organization that had hunted down all the Collectors I didn't get when I destroyed the Isle.

And she's confirmed what I strongly suspected. They never shut anything down. They just stole the idea and perfected it. I'm confident the individuals I've gone after as an enforcer have been bad news. At least my intuition told me that much. I won't lie about my statistics. I tend to kill a lot more than I bring in alive. But of those who are taken prisoner, how many are sold? And what about the other enforcers? The ones who wouldn't know if the supernatural they've tracked down for the representatives really is evil, or just a being they wanted for their collection?

It's sickening. And I'm somehow managing to be angrier about this than I was about my own captivity, if such a thing is possible.

At least we lucked out with the unicorn. She was right, she's not good at giving start to finish directions, but through trial and error she's found familiar landmarks that are taking us in the direction of Lusca Palms.

We only go another block or two before Sasha stops us again. We're in an empty lot behind Amun's casino property. The security lights are broken and shattered. There's a few cars scattered around that are complete junkers, rusted and missing parts. What are they doing with this property?

At the back of the lot is a metal building.

"Through there," Sasha whispers, pointing at the building. "There's a stairwell inside that leads underneath the lot. They've carved the whole thing out into a massive cave to hold the cages."

"That's not structurally sound," Hugh observes.

But who cares about structural soundness when you've got witches?

"Do you have any idea where they were going to take you during the conclave? The event where you were told you'd be sold off?"

Sasha shakes her head.

"No, but other than the staircase there's only one way out. A large tunnel. The raiju said it led into a secret underground level of the casino."

"Then that's where we're going. Sasha, thank you for your help." I had a few vamps join us, and I wave them over.

"Can you escort her back to our resort? Put her up in the nicest room we have. Room service, extra blankets, the works. Whatever spa treatments she needs. All on my tab," I tell them.

One of my vamps, a leggy and curvy woman with long hair the color of a neon carrot, licks her lips and looks over at Sasha.

"Absolutely, Lady Vicious."

I'm about to intervene when Sasha walks straight over to her, allowing the vampire to offer her an arm. They walk off with the other vamps trailing them.

"I thought you said unicorns were super pure, innocent beings?" Ever whispers as the vampire leans into Sasha's ear and whispers something, planting a soft kiss on her cheek. Sasha giggles.

I roll my eyes.

"That has nothing to do with sex," I clarify. "Unicorns are good-hearted. Kind and compassionate to a fault. All right, team, we're going in. Chrys, can you put up a defensive spell to shield us? Aggie, I know you mostly pull magic out of living beings, but do you think if the door's spelled you can get us in?"

The two witches look at each other, then to me with a nod.

"Never," Todd's deep voice rumbles, "I'm going to say this and you're not going to like it. I'm not sure we should go in now."

My head whips around.

"What?" I snarl.

He sighs.

"Told you that you wouldn't like it. We have no idea what's going on right now. If the representatives are even down there with the captives. It may be whatever Amun has planned doesn't take place until later this weekend. If we go now and miss the representatives-"

"We risk letting the guilty parties walk while we help the captives escape," I finish for him.

He nods his head.

"Yes, and if they escape you can bet they'll be gunning for all of us. It's your call."

He waits for my response. I know Todd and the others will back me up no matter what I choose. But it'll be my choice, and the consequences will be on my shoulders.

We're running into danger, but that doesn't bother me. It's been the waiting that was killing me.

"We go now." I sweep my eye over the group, and can feel their support. "Chrys provides the defensive spell. Aggie pulls the magic out of any locks or 'stay out' perimeter spells. Hugh and I will protect the witches. Lynx is our eyes. Todd is our ears. Brutus, bulldoze anyone who gets in our way. Ji-hwan—"

"Will flirt anyone around into a veritable stupor while the rest of you sneak by if needed. I know what I said, but if it's to help people ... I'll do it. But I'm not sleeping with anyone!"

"Wouldn't ask you to," I clarify, thankful that we have one more Bone Reader–enhanced ability in our back pocket. "I'll reach out to the vamps at Vicious and tell them to be ready to secure the perimeter once we're in."

I get ahold of the vamps and tell them to plant themselves around the parking lot and casino exits and to help any captives that come out to the safety of our casino. And *only* our casino. If any bad guys slip out alongside the prisoners, I want them where I can find them.

"After we've sorted out who's who, and given any medical attention needed, we can reunite people with their families, packs, covens, or whatever they have," I finish.

"And what do we do with the representatives and any humans who are here to buy or take other supernaturals?" Hugh questions.

"That's where Ever and I come in. There's still the slimmest possibility some of those in attendance at this event are in for a big surprise when Amun wheels out captive magicals and illegally obtained artifacts. She and I will watch for those. We let them haul out the first item or supernatural, and we monitor the reactions of the crowd. Anyone who's shocked and horrified gets a pass. Everyone else ... is an enemy."

"*Estos hijueputas,*" Ever agrees. Violent spirit or no, she's just as on board with this plan as the rest of us.

"And what do we do with the bad ones?" a vampire in the mix asks.

"They don't leave that property alive." Not if I have anything to do with it. "If you can, find the Scottish magicals, or Sky and her flying group in the mix of cages. Look for Unkai. Anyone that can lend their forces and help us out. If they're really on our side, then per my Bone Reader deal, they'll also have extra power. We can use that to our advantage."

I plan to flag down Nahum at the earliest opportunity. Doubt tugs at the back of my mind, but I ignore it. Nahum isn't Damien. He'll be more powerful than ever right now. I'm depending on him being able to subdue a lot of the crowd while we take them out.

We run to the metal building under Chrys's cover.

"Not getting tired?" I check. I'm a little terrified that the Bone Reader's magic could wear off in the middle of this whole to-do, and that would put us in a bit of a bind. A complete clusterfuck, actually.

"I could do this all night." She smirks, flexing her arms.

I hold my breath when we get inside and Aggie works on the door to the stairwell. Sasha was lucky it was open when she escaped. This thing reeks of some serious magic.

"Almost, got it," Aggie grunts. "I'm not used to working on inanimate things, but I think I can. Yes, that's the spot. Right there!" She gasps and falls back as the door opens. I catch her and look down into her face.

"Witchling, someday we have *got* to have a talk about your filthy mind." She sputters as I help her back to her feet.

"Well, that's a fine thank you!" she manages as I'm walking past her.

"Would you all shut it!" Lynx hisses from the front of the group. I zip it. Just because Chrys is covering us doesn't mean I should be any more reckless than normal.

We're as silent as the grave as we descend the rest of the way. There's another magically sealed door at the bottom. Aggie makes quick work of it, and we're in.

The moment the door creaks open, the silence is done. There are metal cages, circus cars with bars like what I saw back in Arizona, crates and even a few fenced paddock areas. They've got species stacked several containers high in places. Dozens and dozens of captive magicals in here. And in a far corner, locked in with iron bars, I can smell humans across the room. Meeri and Ardus among them.

It's an assault to the senses. Sweat, dirt, and dried urine pummel my nose, while despair, confusion, loneliness, hopelessness, and anxiety threaten to drown my enhanced intuition under their weight. I shove my arms out, physically pushing against a sixth sense that isn't really tangible. But I've got to do something. Ever's on her knees, hands over her ears. I've always thought of intuition as being like water, or a breeze. Something tactile. Maybe to her it's a sound. I hook one hand under her elbow and haul her up.

"We can do it," I insist. At the other end of the cavernous space, I see the tunnel Sasha mentioned. Milling about between us and it are a good two dozen magicals or more. Either enforcers under Amun's thumb or employed by him in some way, I'd wager. And they're all staring at us.

A few freeze, their hands on the ropes they're using to lead a captive centaur into the tunnel. The rest make a run at us.

"Aggi—" I don't even have her name out before the witch moves forward, blasting them with a yell. Lucky for us, there's enough mewling, yowling, sobbing, and yelping in here that I doubt she can be heard down the tunnel. She keeps screaming with each individual she throws her stripping ability at. It's satisfying to watch them fall.

She starts with the shifters, taking down two bears, a feline and a wolf with ease. While they're distracted, Brutus and Todd rush past them in fur at some of the others.

Hugh snarls, eyes flashing red against his russet fur as he relieves a vampire of his head. Chrys is next to him, grinning like a madwoman as she throws a bolt of colored light into someone else.

"Not very defensive-spell of you!" I yell over the noise as I kick a warlock square in the jaw. I relish the cracking sound that follows.

"I'm in more of an offensive mood," she shouts back. The anger runs deep through her as she battles next to Hugh on one side and Ji-hwan on the other. I notice my newest Were pal is also choosing to let violence reign on this occasion. He's pummeling a naga that keeps trying to use its snake tail to squeeze the life out of him.

"Witchling! Start on the cages!" I scream at Aggie. She gives a swift nod and gets to work, her brow knitted in concentration as she starts pulling the magic out of the lock on the closest crate. It contains a cluster of glowing purple pixies.

Why do I feel like they might end up at the vamp mansion? Nahum's got his own posse of pixies. Blue ones. And they took to Aggie immediately. Something about nature-loving pixies liking light-magic witches.

I'm prevented from further contemplation when I hear my name. I follow the sound and come face to face with Unkai across the melee. He's locked inside two circus caravans soldered together in the center.

"Are there keys?" I ask him. He waves behind me.

"Search the jailers!" Ever calls, picking up on the raiju's message. It's slow going. Amun's no idiot. They don't all have the same keys. It's likely that some open the containers and some the actual collars, cuffs, shackles, and whatever other lovely accessories they've got the various magicals wearing.

Another enforcer comes through the tunnel entrance. I'm running for him, but Ji-hwan beats me to it, snapping the elf's neck. He falls to the dirt, and I finish separating head from body.

I wave Ever over to me.

"Now or never," I tell her. We need to get down that tunnel and figure out what we're dealing with, before someone raises a real alarm.

"I was kind of hoping it could be now *and* Never would be involved," Ever jokes, giving half a smile.

I put a hand on her shoulder.

"Wereling. You are like family to me. Truly. But leave those jokes to me, hmm?" She just laughs, and I can feel underneath it that the humor is a defensive mechanism. She hates this whole thing.

Me, too.

"Todd?" I call behind us.

"We're all good here," he responds as he knocks out the last enforcer standing. "I already reached out to Elios's bouncers and the bears to meet us over here. We'll follow you when we can."

That's a relief. Between the bears, the bouncers, my vamps and the rest of our motley crew, we might just be able to free all these beings *and* help their captors swap places with them. Maybe. If I am extremely lucky and the moon smiles on me, even though I refuse to acknowledge her.

The tunnel is longer than I expected. All the better to not hear your screaming captives, my dear. At least that's what I suppose the reasoning was. Unlike what happened in Arizona with my slip-up, I keep my mouth clamped shut as we reach the end. We're in a dark area, and looking ahead it appears we've come out behind a stage. I can see the back side of curtains and the wooden framing. Lights pointed outward to an audience we can't yet see. There are only a couple workers back here, and we reach both before they've noticed us.

I'm coming for you, I promise to myself as Amun's voice booms from the front of the stage.

"... has been a very productive day thus far. And as we all know, the festivities are just beginning. In fact, I daresay many consider this the best part of conclave, eh?" A few snickers and titters from the audience. I want to know who's laughing, and I want to squeeze the life out of them until the smile falls off their faces.

This might be the moment where my brain would normally give me some sort of chastisement: *Not so violent, Never.* Or: *Mustn't murder the employer, Never.* Not today. Amun continues pandering to the gathered magical elite.

"... and then artifacts will be auctioned tomorrow evening before we leave. This will give everyone a day or so to figure out how you'd prefer to transport your live product back. Now I know at a lot of auctions they start with the small stuff and work their way up to the big finale. Not here! We're all in this together, and I aim to please. In that spirit, I think we'll start with what I consider to be our most valuable prize of all. And I warn you, I'm liable to place a hefty bid on it myself." Amun chuckles.

I chance the smallest peek from behind the curtain as he steps away from a podium, and a warlock with a gavel walks up. I focus on the audience. My anger and disgust reaches new heights when I can't feel a single individual who's disgusted. A single individual who's surprised by Amun offering to sell them other supernaturals. I don't think this audience hold all the representatives. But the ones who are here? They're all complicit in this. And there's plenty of humans in the seats as well, just like Arizona.

From the other side of the stage comes a creaking noise, and a circus caravan comes rolling out. Inside is a beast, fully transformed despite its collar. Roaring in fury at the crowd.

Amun puts his hands around his mouth as he yells to the audience.

"Ladies and gentlemen! I give you, the nightmare dragon!"

30

What You Can't Afford to Lose

Nahum bellows again, wings spread as far as they can in the confines of his cage. But no smoke billows out. No one starts screaming, taken over by a nightmare. The glowing obsidian collar on his neck probably explains why.

A terrifying thought hits.

Does that mean he's more vulnerable as well?

"The hell with waiting. I'm going in," I mutter.

Ever grabs my wrist, hauling me back.

"*¡Está loca! Ese no era el plan.* We were supposed to check the crowd. We did that. And spoiler alert, they're all rotten to the core. All the simpler for us. *When* help gets here. But you can't go in there now. They'll rip you apart." Ever scowls at me, keeping her hand wrapped around my wrist.

I tug it away.

"Don't worry. Go back to the others. I can handle this. I've been on my own before."

"¿*Que la pasa?* I may disagree, but you're not alone. If you insist on this insanity, I'm going with you."

"Do I hear a million?" the auctioneer out front asks, his voice amplified with magic instead of a microphone.

It takes everything in me to stay where I'm at while the bidding continues.

"Anyone over six million? Do I hear six and a half? Six and a half? Six and a quarter? Anyone? Anyone? Sold! For six and a quarter million to bidder twenty-nine!" A gavel bangs on the podium. Amun moves back up to it as the auctioneer steps away. Two other magicals come from the other side of the stage to start wheeling Nahum offstage, in our direction.

"Hell's bells and moon be damned, where *are* they?" I curse, readying myself to defend Ever, rescue Nahum, and take on the auction attendants alone.

"Right here, you daft Were." A grizzled voice next to me makes me jump. I was too focused on what was in front of me, and not behind. Rookie mistake.

"Elios?" I'm confused as I turn around. "We asked for your bouncers, not you! You're supposed to be back at Vicious, serving drinks."

"Thankless wolf," he jabs, "as if I'd keep out of something this important. You might be surprised what I can get up to." He pats his stomach. There's an apron around it with the pockets stuffed full of small vials and an assortment of odds and ends.

"Um, all right, then." I have no idea what the old goat's up to, but I've every confidence in him, and we're out of time. I'm just relieved to have backup.

The bouncers Elios brought along fan out behind him. A rough-looking group made up entirely of large shifters. Haggard and weathered, but that's kind of Elios's crowd.

Behind them I see a welcome sight.

"Todd! Rex!" The bears put a hand up in acknowledgement, and the bear king points behind me as he begins to shift.

I roll my neck, cracking it and letting out a long sigh.

"Now we get to the fun part."

Nahum's cage is almost to our curtain now, but we're hidden in the shadows. I can still hear the chatter from the crowd about what a good catch he is. The uses for him.

I may have seemed wishy-washy on wanting to date the dragon. I'll tell you the truth; in spite of my confidence, at times he seemed almost too good for me. His relaxed spirit and his books. His cute pixies and his planning of garden getaways. But I like him. And not just because of what he can do during recreational activities, if you get my drift. He's principled and kind, even after what he suffered through on the Isle. An experience we both have in common. Which means I can relate to all the emotions that crash into me from where he sits in the cage, roaring. His only real fault was not being involved enough. And he agreed to help us easily. Put his life on the line for a mission I couldn't even tell him the end result of. And this is what he gets for it.

My decent, devoted dragon.

My dragon.

Todd and Elios jump the individuals pushing Nahum's cage. The dragon keeps right on roaring, and I'm not even sure he notices me as I walk past him.

One thing I do trust? My friends. They'll get him out.

"The next item up for bid is a set of identical wolf shifter twins, each gifted with an elemental magic. Further proof that I only stock the absolute best. Now then, who would like to start the bidding?" Amun calls out from the podium.

"I'll take them." I stride out onto the stage. Gasps sound from the audience. Surprise, curiosity, affrontedness, and worry all mixing as they reach me.

Amun's eyes go wide for a moment, and as he turns to me he takes a single step back into the podium. Like scared prey. I stalk closer as he regains his decorum.

"Never! What are you—"

"I'm sorry. I thought this was an auction. So I'll say it again. I'll take them."

The wolf twins in the cage are in their skin. They look like they're barely teenagers, which means their age is accurate. Our aging slows somewhere in adulthood. Selling kids? Really? The lion is beyond redemption.

"I'll be retrieving my wolf shifters now. The only thing is, I don't intend to pay. But I'll make sure the rest of you do."

I can feel the presence of the others behind me as I lunge forward. Amun tenses, and I ready myself for impact. He turns and leaps off the stage into the audience.

"Get the wolves!" I shout, pointing back at the shifters in the cage as I dive off the stage after him.

Amun disappears into the crowd, but it doesn't matter. I know I'll catch him. I can always sniff out a rat. I move through the crowd indiscriminately, taking out any supernatural in my path. And a handful of humans.

It might be smarter to leave at least a few alive, so we can figure out how this happened, but that's not my priority right now.

The others wade into the crowd after me.

I'm about halfway up the row of seats when I spot Amun again. The cowardly lion has buried himself in a crowd of feline shifters. As if that could hide him from me. We lock eyes.

"You're mine," I mouth at him, a grin spreading across my face as his goes pale.

"Never," a crackly voice breaks through the chaos. I may be as insane as they say, because I spin in a circle looking for the source before checking my own wrist.

Hugh's idea. Make the casino mics expandable so we can keep them when we shift. A smart move on his part.

"Never! We've almost cleared out the containment area. They're taking everyone back to the vamp resort. But you need to get down here! There's enforcers trying to run off with some of the captives. And a couple of them have Nahum!"

I snarl into the mic.

"You go; I'll try to grab the head representative," Unkai yells, freed and flying past me. Thunder echoes in his wake.

I'm torn on what to do for only a moment.

I give Amun one last glare, then turn and run.

I move faster than I ever have. I hit the other end of the tunnel and exit into the containment room just in time to see Chrys clambering up Nahum's back. Her posture is awkward as she leans over his shoulder, a key in her hand.

There are several enforcers trying to push the dragon back into a cage, and Hugh is swiping at them.

"Almost, got it," the witch grunts. From across the room I hear a click, and Nahum's collar drops.

He roars, tail whipping around the cavernous space. Several of the enforcers surge forward. Nahum roars again, and this time fog spills from his open mouth. It builds until it engulfs the group. It only takes a few moments before I hear the screams.

Truly terrifying. And worse, I can feel the abject horror that slams into me from each and every supernatural Nahum's using his power against. I stagger back, winded by the onslaught of emotions that batter my intuition.

"Never!" Chrys yells, running over to prop me up.

"Just need to catch my breath," I wheeze, staggering as I pull on her arm and right myself.

That packs a punch! I shout mentally to Nahum.

They've got some truly terrible nightmares. Villains often do. The ones with any shred of soul left always fear retribution from their victims.

And these? I ask.

Would you like to see? I think I might be able to show you. Push images instead of just words. Since you're my mate.

And yet you never call, I tease.

His voice in my head gets serious. Rumbling in anger even in my mind.

I am sorry, Never. Amun showed me where he kept the artifacts. He never showed me this area, but I decided to go looking. I got caught. A foolish error, and it could have put you in jeopardy.

This isn't your fault. It's theirs.

I'm livid he'd even suggest such a thing. As if he asked to be captured. As if he's responsible.

Show me, I insist, determined to take his mind off his ordeal. He dips his scaled and horned head, and smoke engulfs me.

I'm standing inside the nightmare of a reptilian shifter. I can see him in front of me, but when I reach out, my own form is translucent. I'm just a bystander here. And thank goodness, because I don't want any part of what's coming for him. Several large creatures made of mud; golems maybe? Bubbling and oozing. The ground underneath the reptile is quicksand, holding him in place while the creatures drag him down.

And that plays on loop?

Unless I remove the nightmare, Nahum clarifies.

Good.

The fog recedes and I'm back with the others.

"No one else, right?" I ask Hugh. He shakes his head, some spittle flying off his fangs. He licks one.

"Apologies, Lady Never." I wave him off.

"You and Chrys get back up to the empty lot over us. Make sure no one got lost on their way to Vicious. And Chrys, put up the biggest and strongest defensive spell on our casino you can."

She nods. The two of them start for the stairwell door when something comes clattering down the steps. It rolls onto the floor.

"Is that a human grenad—" I manage before I'm blown backwards. My head slams into the concrete floor.

"Nahum!" I yell as I sit up, rubbing my sore skull.

"Right here." He's kneeling over me, wings spread out behind him to shield us.

"Chrys? Hugh?"

"We're here, but the stairs aren't," Chrys gripes. "Looks like we're all going back through the auction room together."

Just as well. I have unfinished business there.

31

Nowhere to Run

We make it back down the tunnel. A good portion of our group are still fighting, and the moans and yells tell me several of the auction's attendees are still with us.

"Anyone get away?" I ask Todd as he lumbers up. His fur is streaked with red. I wrinkle my nose. "You, sir, are going to need a bath."

He growls at me, and I reach out and tap him on the nose.

"Boop!"

I scan the wounded representatives and other attendees. "Any of ours hurt? And where's the lion I'm hunting down?"

"A few made it past us. And some injuries, but no fatalities on our end so far. I'm told we have you to thank for that. Due to a certain deal with a certain Bone Reader," Rex answers, standing in his skin next to his brother, extending me a hand to shake. I grin at the bear king.

"Yeah, don't mention it. As I recall, I'm still available to you for intuitive readings as part of another deal I made."

Rex laughs, the sound at odds with the carnage around us.

"True. Although the witchling has helped us quite a bit in your absence. You'll have to ask her about it sometime." He's hiding something. Which he knows I can sense. "I see you got the dragon back."

Nahum nods at the shifter.

Speaking of dragons. Think you can help us subdue the remaining auction guests?

Say no more.

Nahum walks to the center of the room and fog billows around him, rising into tall waves that flood the auditorium. He was right. He does have more precision than Aggie. The mist flows over and around us, but only the individuals who attended the auction are affected.

Rex whistles.

"Impressive. Why don't you let the bears and me get things cleaned up in here? You head back to Vicious, and when we wrap things up we'll head down the tunnel and meet you."

I frown.

"That's a no-go, bear boy. The other side of that tunnel ends in a collapsed staircase."

"Really? Shit," Ji-hwan states as he joins our little group, "because someone barricaded the doors to the auditorium not long after Amun got out."

"Shit indeed," I mutter, rubbing my claws over my furred forehead. "And with all this extra power from the Bone Reader, no one's been able to bust us out?"

Ever and Brutus join the group. The wolf shifter is back in his skin but has some open cuts. They'll heal soon enough. Ever's sporting her brown fur.

"We didn't think we needed to. There was plenty of action inside, and we figured we'd go back out the way we came," Brutus says by way of explanation.

"Moon save me from other shifters," I murmur. "If they're blocking all the exits, that is a bad sign. Everyone, grab a set of double doors and start pushing. We've got to get back to our own casino and catch up with Amun and whoever else made it past us."

Brutus, Ever and I head to one of the doors. Brutus reaches it first, shoving his full weight against it, but it doesn't budge.

"Let me," I insist, coming up beside him. He steps aside without a single snark or disagreement. Progress. I'm so proud I could cry. Maybe later. Standing next to each other, we give the door another shove, but it won't open.

"Hell's ..." I grunt and shove my shoulder against it again. "... bells."

"Looks like Amun had more up his sleeve than we thought," Ever observes from behind us.

"Allow. Me." I turn to see Unkai weaving his way around the seats with his long body. He's wounded. Blood dripping along his sides.

"Glad we were able to bust you out," I state.

"Glad my gamble with the unicorn worked," he responds.

"Who were you really after?"

"My niece. Amun has to have lost his mind, to go after our families. He's got a sister of Calder, which is what upset the Scots. And an aunt of Sky's, the wind elf you met in Arizona."

The whole statement is sincere.

"And the other captives. Did you know about them?" I press. I'm almost afraid of the answer. Unkai is the one representative I know whom I haven't added to my naughty list.

"No."

I breathe a sigh of relief as the words ring true.

"But I suspected something was wrong. The closer this conclave got, the worse it became. Particularly after your showdown with the Claw. I think you scared him, threw him off his game. If you could sniff out the Claw and unravel their operation, what could you do to his? I think it's why he insisted on keeping such a close eye on you."

"Keep your friends close—"

"And your enemies closer. Yes, that was the gist of it."

I step aside and allow the raiju to pass. He grunts, sucking in small breaths. I frown but usher the others around him out of the way. He's in no state to do this, but we're in no position to argue.

Unkai makes a run at the door, and several sounds hit at once. The crack of what might be his injured horn snapping, the screech of a door sliding loose, and booming thunder. I lean over Brutus and look out the exit. Unkai shakes his head, dazed, and the tip of one horn clatters to the ground. It should grow back. He stumbles forward, and as soon as he's through the doorframe, we follow. We're in some sort of lobby.

Priorities? Nahum asks.

Our casino first. Amun and his posse later. Before we go after him, I want to make sure none of his group slipped in with our captured and wounded.

The last thing I want is a bloodbath under my own roof.

Nahum nods beside me.

"Walking back, are we? Leave it to you to make a poor old man hike instead of having a car service waiting." Elios's gruff voice is a welcome sound as he joins us. I could almost hug him. Almost. If I didn't know how befuddled he'd get about it. Maybe I *should* hug him.

"I notice you don't have even a scratch," I observe.

"I've got my ways."

"Never! Never!" A voice calls out from behind me, and as I turn I see two individuals running up to us. Calder, the each-uisge I haven't

seen since his attempt to take over Amun's casino, and Sky, the wind
elf representative.

"You!"

"You?"

"You."

"You!"

The lobby becomes an echo chamber as Ever sprints past me
toward the wind elf, claws out and a snarl on her face. Nahum stands
at my back with his wings spread over us as Elios goes barreling past,
face red and furious as he charges Calder.

For several moments, the scene is all chaos and flying fists. Sky
screeches as Ever pulls at her hair and her forearm feathers.

"I'm going to rip these out!" Ever promises.

*Guess that answers our question of who dropped my mentee from
the sky.*

Do we separate them? Nahum asks.

I let out a sigh. I'm tempted to let Ever pummel a Sky-shaped
hole into the floor, no matter whose side the wind elf is on. But not
until *after* we're safely off the premises.

I think we'd better. You take care of Ever and Sky? I'll get Elios.

I'm not putting myself on Ever's bad side. She's got a right to her
feelings.

I step in between Elios and Calder. The each-uisge is in terrifying
horse form, fangs showing and talons raised. Elios moves to smash
a glowing orange vial onto Calder's head. I duck just in time to
miss the full force of the blow, but a few droplets spatter on me. It's
something acidic, and it hisses as it starts melting away fur.

I grimace as my forearm becomes a bloody mess, but stick a hand
out toward each of them anyway, separating them. Calder snorts in
my face as he tries to get around me to the cursed satyr.

"Do you mind!" I demand. "Look, I don't know what sort of
beef you two have with one another, but—"

"This double-crossing, no-good kelpie knock-off got me cursed!" Elios yells, one fist still raised.

"I thought you'd gotten my sister killed!" Calder yells back, but he puts his skin on.

"It was an accident! I never meant t—. Wait. *Thought*? She's not dead?"

Okay, things are starting to come together a bit here. I'd asked Elios once about how he ended up cursed to look like an old human. Back in his younger years, a thieving Elios had been in a heist gone wrong. He'd accidentally gotten a family member of one of his accomplices killed. Now, in fairness, she'd also been trying to steal what they were after, but he got cursed nonetheless.

"I'll let you both go if you promise to play nice while we get out of here. Then you can beat each other senseless in the parking lot. Deal?" I take a few steps back as they both nod.

"I did think she was dead. Turns out she survived, and Amun took her," Calder mutters behind me.

Beside me, Nahum's got Sky and Ever separated as well. The Wereling is scowling and casting dirty glances in the wind elf's direction, but she's letting Todd guide her to an exit regardless. Sky runs to catch up to me.

"You have to understand. The way you were acting, I thought you were working with Amun. When he sent you all after the somson orb, naturally I assumed you were against us."

I round on her.

"And your solution was to try and murder a teenager? Why not take your problem up with me directly, if you were so upset about it? I was the one Amun was using. And I'd be more than happy to take you on."

Her feathers flutter.

"You weren't the one holding the orb," she simpers.

I huff, putting my arm around Ever as we walk on ahead of her.

Eventually we find a set of stairs that lead us back to street level. As we step outside, I try to orient myself, but something's wrong. There's smoke billowing around us.

"It's magical. It doesn't smell like fire," Chrys observes.

The smoke rises, enveloping us. I try to look through it and see a flash of silver.

Is that? No. A gun? Why would any magical be carrying a—

A shot rings out, and whatever the chamber was loaded with, it glows green as it barrels in our direction. Before anyone can so much as scream, the glowing bullet slams into Brutus's forehead and he falls.

I drop next to Brutus as more shots ring out.

"Chrys!"

"Already on it!" She starts waving her hands, and the smoke clears. She's weaving pure air into her defense shield. The rain of bullets continues, but they bounce off the translucent dome she's encased us in.

"He'll be up soon, right?" Ever whispers beside me.

I throw a hand over his nose. Nothing. Dammit. I press my ear to his chest, but it's still. Double damn.

"Brutus!" I slap the enforcer across the face, beginning to panic.

"What happened!" Ji-hwan drops to his knees next to me.

"Can we move in this dome?" I ask Chrys.

"Yes!"

I haul the wolf shifter into my arms.

We make our way several blocks over. More attacks hit the shield, but none get through. I can't see who's after us, but I'd bet my life to the Bone Reader that it's Amun and whatever forces he has left. When we get to the vamp casino, we crowd through the front doors as Chrys stays to touch up its defenses.

"Never ... I think that boost is beginning to wear off," she warns me. "I can manage this, but I'm running out of juice." Hugh reaches down and grabs her hand. All pride and support.

"Never?" Aggie runs over to us.

"Stripper!" I yell, an idea coming to mind. "Can you tell if he's alive? Sense any shifter magic?"

She scrunches up her nose, holding her arms out over Brutus.

"No good. I can only feel the magic of whatever they shot him with. He could be dead, or it could just be a side effect of whatever they hit him with."

"I'm going to dig the bullet out. Anyone with a weak constitution, turn away." I give a half-second's warning before I shove a claw into the wound . It's messy, it's bloody, and it's worrisome that Brutus doesn't so much as groan when I dig the projectile out, but I manage it. I drop the offensive item on the floor, the glow on it beginning to dull.

Brutus does groan now, and a laugh escapes me, hysterical.

"He's alive!" Ji-hwan yells.

"Aggie! Where's Todd? Where is that b—"

A hand whaps me on the shoulder.

"Right here! Sometimes you are the *most* unobservant enforcer." I turn to see him standing behind me, gone a bit green. "That was disgusting. But effective. Let me guess? Bear transport time?"

I give a swift nod.

"You've got it exactly right, Todd my friend. Get him and that bullet upstairs. There's got to be a magical we've rescued somewhere in this blasted building who can find out what they shot him with. Check with the unicorn! Maybe she'll heal him." Sasha does owe us, but it's not a given. Unlike the Bone Reader, you don't barter with unicorns. They either bestow or they do not bestow. But she may be his only shot, because even though he's breathing, the wound isn't closing.

32

Nowhere to Hide

Aggie's chattering away next to me, but I'm struggling to focus.

"Never, we found the Scottish magicals and the winged contingent while we were clearing out the cages. They were behind a separate door and ... Never?"

The lobby of this casino is filled to the brim with freed supernaturals. All their emotions are dizzying.

"Yes. Rescued representatives. We caught up with a few of them," I murmur.

Perhaps we rest a bit, then go after Amun and the others? I won't let you lose their trail. Nahum suggests.

I don't want to stop. But my casino and hotel turned refugee building is teeming with injured and despondent supernaturals. The vamps are moving double time giving out blankets, assigning rooms, and carrying trays of food.

Is the lobby spinning, or is it just me? I'm beginning to remember why I like to work alone. Being responsible for this many people is dizzying.

I've got you. Arms wrap around me from behind, and I lean back into Nahum's chest. I'm able to breathe again.

"All right," I say after a few moments, "we take a tally of any wounded. Determine any supplies we need and don't have. Make sure everyone's fed and has somewhere to sleep tonight. We'll get around to contacting families, covens, and so on tomorrow. If we run out of regular rooms, ask the shifters who are comfortable in fur to curl up on the floor."

Hugh starts taking notes, and who even knows where he got a clipboard. Maybe he's able to summon one from thin air. At least I'd think so if he were a warlock. A key for organization. That would be Hugh.

"Who has energy left to go after Amun?" Several hands raise. None of my friends deny me. I get choked up for all of a second, then clear my throat. "In that case. Those of us going after the remaining representatives, grab something to eat quickly. Now that the Bone Reader's help is waning, we need to make sure to stay at the top of our game. And then meet back down here. We can—"

I'm thrown to the ground as the room really does seem to spin. An echoing boom sounds somewhere around me, but I can't pinpoint the source of the noise. Several smaller explosions come after, and bits of the ceiling rain down on us.

They're bombing my casino.

"We're under attack! Everyone out the front!" Rex yells, waving at everyone in the lobby. At the bear king's side, the others try to calm the panic as a wave of magicals makes a stampede for the doors.

"Get everyone down from the other floors!" I yell at no one in particular. Anyone really. The alarms in the building kick in and start blaring.

I have to get upstairs.

"Never!" Nahum yells, wrapping his arms around me and launching us both into the air with his wings as a hunk of concrete lands where I'd been standing. I stare, open-mouthed. He keeps flying for the doors.

"No, we need to go back! I just sent Todd and Brutus up there!" I insist as another explosion rocks the hotel and the ceiling starts to cave in.

Nahum lands outside. Hugh still has hold of his clipboard, and he's waving down any witches and warlocks in the crowd to help Chrys come up with some defenses. The street out front looks much the same as before, with a single, notable difference. My destroyed and flaming casino. Partially destroyed. Half is still standing.

Ever and Aggie are directing various magicals. Lynx trudges by, the arm of an injured warlock thrown over his shoulder.

"What in all hells happened here?" I demand, scanning the wreckage. But I know. Amun. Somehow, that lion got to us. Got his revenge. I sniff, trying to separate the scent of death from that of injury. It's not hard to find.

Chrys marches over. The witch often maintains a pretty steady emotional rhythm. It's part of her draw. She never punches my intuition with emotions. Almost never. She's a mess now. Determination, regret, guilt, and even anger are vying for the top spot in a pile of feelings.

"It was my fault—" she starts.

"Our fault," Hugh interjects. His speech is gravelly, and Chrys searches the area, running over to a first-aid kit someone's thought to bring out. She returns and hands him a pair of pants. He's already half back in his skin. And if you're thinking, *pants*? Yes. Shifters keep spare clothes everywhere. Including and absolutely in a first-aid kit.

"We made the mistake of thinking we were safe. We *wrongly* thought a bunch of escapees would be low on Amun's list, with his life on the line. But he found a way. How did I not see this coming? I should have come up with better defenses. If I had—"

Chrys lets the sentence hang.

Hugh finishes tugging on a pair of pants; shifting still takes him some time. It's an art form, as much as anything, and he hasn't had time to master it.

"There's nothing else she could have done. Chrys was brilliant," he defends now that he's got his lips again. "As soon as she realized what was happening, she threw up defenses around her and myself. She cleared an exit for as many of us as she could. Even with how exhausted she is."

He's defensive and riled up. She looks dead on her feet.

"Chrys, thank you for having our backs. Go find somewhere to lie down."

Some of Hugh's tension falls away when he realizes that Chrys is the only one blaming herself. I'm planning to heap all the guilt on my own shoulders.

They wander off, and I look at the piles of rubble. She'll have a hard time locating anything comfortable.

"Did everyone make it out?" Ever asks, making her way to my side along with Aggie.

"Make it out? Half the building is down!" Lynx yells as he runs over. He's streaked with soot and dirt.

"We need to take a head count," I answer, "once we get everyone else accounted for we'll—"

A hand clamps around my shoulder, and I look up to see Todd. He's got a gash across his temple and a bloody lip. I throw my arms around him without a second thought.

"Thank goodness! I was afraid yo— "

"We lost Brutus. I tried to keep a hold of him when the wall caved in, but he slipped. One of the rescued shifters pulled him out of the rubble."

I look at Ever first, because I know she'll be reading me. Getting the same uncomfortable sensation I do when someone sends off too many emotions at once. I try to hold them back, but I'm struggling. I give her shoulder a squeeze. I want to say something comforting, but I can't quite manage. I walk past her instead.

"I'll get him," I say, voice dull. The least I can do is get the wolf taken care of properly in death. It doesn't take me long to find him in the rubble. Someone's laid him atop a pile of concrete. There's dust and insulation on his face, covering the freckles. I haul him up. He isn't even that heavy. Not with my fur on. I take him to the side of the building that isn't collapsed and sit him against the wall.

Hugh follows me.

"He's a wolf shifter. He has to be buried at night, where he can see the moon." At least that shouldn't be difficult. I'll find him somewhere nice, with a clear view of the sky. "I should have told him."

"Told him what?" Nahum asks, walking up behind me.

"That what Amun did wasn't his fault. That he had a spot with us. In this family." There's plenty more to say, but I won't get the chance.

I go back to Chrys, who's returned to task delegation instead of lying down like I asked her to.

"As long as you're up, stack all the med supplies near whatever's left of the kitchen. See if we have a working mini fridge somewhere in this mess, from one of the rooms. Some of the medication might need to stay cool," I tell her. Chrys turns to a group of passing witches who were among the ones we rescued and starts handing out my instructions.

"Who did this?" I demand.

"Never. We know who did this. The representatives. Amun," Ever reminds me as if I've gone mad. I likely look it. I'm covered in dirt, and as I look down I see crimson swiped across my fur from carrying Brutus out.

"Yes, but who did he send to do his dirty work?"

"Sylphs," Calder answers, joining our group. The Scot's green eyes glint. I cast a frantic glance over his shoulder, and I see Elios lumbering around the rubble. Thank the moon. Both that he survived and that he's let the fight between the two of them go, for now.

"Stinking Sylphs?" Air spirits. Soulless. Not particularly dangerous. But near-transparent. They'd have been impossible for us to see and stop in time.

"The seahorse wannabe is right," Elios admits grudgingly as he joins us. I pull him into a hug.

"Stop that this instant!" he insists as he pries me off, but I can feel how touched he is.

The first thing I'm doing when we get back to the vamp mansion after all this is throwing on that shirt Aggie gave me.

"Amun will bear the consequences of this," I declare.

And thanks to his behavior, I think I know just where to find him.

"We're going back to Lusca Palms? Why?" Aggie asks, jogging to keep up with me as I storm down the street toward Amun's casino.

"That bastard of a lion bombed my safehouse. That's a shifter with firing power. And a shifter who's willing to destroy his inventory. Amun wouldn't do that. He wouldn't leave himself with nothing. But magicals weren't the only valuable items he had, were they?"

"The artifacts," Nahum supplies from beside me.

I tap the end of my nose. "Exactly. Dollars to donuts that mangy feline is stuffing his pockets with the most valuable items he has before he disappears. But he'd never leave his seat of power peacefully. So he bombs us with some of what he has stockpiled away. He gets his revenge, and prevents us from saving the captured magicals. Dead or in cages, either way we've failed them."

The lobby of Lusca Palms is deserted. All the workers and customers, gone.

"I can get us to the room with the artifacts," Nahum states. "Amun keeps them in his personal rooms."

The other supernaturals were kept far below ground. But this time? We go up. We all shove into a couple of elevators and Nahum presses the button for the top floor. The penthouse. At first, the button glows red, the screen asking for a keycard.

"Aggie? Chrys? Could one of you—"

Elios leans forward, his fist smashing the panel. It flickers green.

"There," he says, pleased with himself as he leans back, "sometimes you don't need magic. Just the right touch."

We shoot up. The elevator slows as we near the top floor. The door pings as it opens.

In front of us is a sprawling penthouse. Floor-to-ceiling windows and massive, stately pieces of furniture. The size a lion could lounge on.

Speak of the devil, here's Amun pulling items off a series of display shelves. He's surrounded by a group of enforcers and the few representatives who got away from us. A couple bolt the moment they register what's coming for them.

"Get them," I snarl. Ji-hwan, Todd, Lynx, Calder and even Elios sprint after the escaping representatives.

"You." Amun seethes, glaring at me from across the room. He holds up some shining, crystal vase glowing with purple light. Like a threat.

"I'll shatter it."

"I don't even know what it is. Go right ahead," I counter. Hugh sucks in a breath behind me. Dismayed. All right. Valuable. And likely historically significant.

"Retrieve the stolen goods," I instruct. Ever, Hugh, and Chrys peel off and make their way around the lion. Nahum and Aggie flank me on either side.

"Want me to strip him?" the witchling offers. Amun is awash with fear at that statement. He may not show his lion, but that doesn't mean he wants it out of his reach. I can tell Aggie's tapped out, but Amun doesn't need to know that.

I shake my head.

"That won't be necessary. Right, Amun? Not if you agree to settle things the old-fashioned way. What do you say? Let the witch suck out all your power just before Nahum throws you into an endless nightmare, or fight me?"

He throws down the vase, but Hugh dives, just managing to catch it before it hits the floor. Amun freezes, and I wonder if he's going to try to make a run for it.

Then he drops to his knees and starts to shift.

33

Long Live the King

His mane is magnificent. Even I can admit that much. A deep brown, the massive and distinguishing feature makes him look twice the size. And in typical shifter fashion, he's already much larger than an actual barbary lion would be.

One disadvantage he'll have right off the bat is that he needs to keep four on the floor, as I like to say. Unlike a Were, many animal shifters lack the ability to stand on two legs. And similarly, magicals like a vamp or a witch certainly couldn't run around on all fours. I can do either.

"Here, kitty kitty." I crook my finger at him, beckoning him closer as I bare my fangs.

I see a tell as he ducks his mane down, tensing. Determination washes over him. He's going to charge. I drop to all fours. Maybe a little ungainly in appearance, but that's the thing about Weres. We're much more than appearances. In spite of the number of times I've declared us breathtakingly beautiful, not all magicals agree. And screw them. I know what I am. A Were isn't just built for beauty.

We're built to be adaptive in combat and hunting. I lope forward on all fours, howling straight into the old lion's face. I see the whites of his eyes as they widen, and he almost trips as his steps stutter. It's clear he's been off the battlefield for some time.

Just as we're about to collide, I pounce, leaping over him. As my front claws land on his shoulders, my back ones manage to kick him in the snout and use it to push off for more momentum. He shakes his head and roars, and it throws me off balance. I'm slung sideways, and I tuck and roll across the floor.

I can see the others move as we trade blows. Nahum is taking on several of the remaining enforcers on his own, and while there's fog spilling from his jaws, no one screams. They're wearing glowing cuffs that must be protecting them. Amun has one as well, and it's shifted to fit his large legs. The head representative has all sorts of fun treasures in here.

The lion roars in my face, and I respond by baring my fangs in a snarl.

I'm not in the habit of letting villains wax poetic when I'm fighting them, but I want to know a few things. And it had better be now, because I don't plan on letting the lion leave this fight alive.

"Why Amun? Why bring me back? Why shove me in the faces of the representatives like Sky and Calder? Why send us after the somson orb?"

He makes a sound that's somewhere between a growl and laughter.

"You still think I answer to you? That I'd deign to give you any explanation?"

Instead of responding, I wait. Tensed, and ready if he charges, but still. An interrogation technique I've used a few times as an enforcer. Whether they think they're clever or sly, most villains will spill information when given the opportunity. He's no exception.

"Several birds. One stone, Never. I needed you where I could keep an eye on your antics. You've been out of control for too long. I've been suspicious of those representatives possibly working behind my back for some time. I used you as a distraction, and a threat. Got you to agree to act like you were on my side. Scare them into submission. I don't think nearly as much of your heroics with the Claw as others, but using you was effective. The other representatives mistrusted you and they got sloppy. Gave me the opening I needed to stop them."

I spare a second to glance behind me at Aggie. Nahum's keeping the enforcers away from the witchling. Hugh, Ever, and Chrys are emptying Amun's shelves of artifacts.

"What did you want with that orb? Calder attacked you, but Sky didn't."

"She would have. It was a matter of time. And if you don't know what they're for, I'm certainly not going to enlighten you. You're not nearly as clever as you think you are Never."

"And you're an evil, foul, waste of magic," I counter.

The lion leaps at me. I manage to get my teeth around Amun's neck as he dives, but he rolls me off. He slams my back onto the floor of his penthouse, but I slice open his paw. We go back and forth, moving through his home and toppling furniture.

"This is your doing you know! Your fault! It was your encounter with the Claw that inspired me to expand my operation. Can you imagine how embarrasing that could have been? The Claw overthrowing us? That couldn't happen. I would have used my inventory and the caged magicals to stop them, of course, but it would have exposed us. I realized I needed more power, more security."

I keep swiping away at him while he huffs and puffs and spills his secrets. Let him get winded. I'll save my breath.

"This conclave's auction was planned as the biggest one yet. I would have solidified my alliances with the human and magical representatives alike. By capturing key relatives of the others I was keeping them in line. I would have gone from a government figurehead to a being with absolute authority. Then you ruined things."

His fury must be motivating, because his next blow is harder. One of his front paws slams into my windpipe and I gag and cough, tripping backward.

"Never!" Aggie starts our direction, but Nahum sweeps out his tail and cuts her off.

Do you need help?

I appreciate the offer, but this lion is mine.

Nahum flashes his fangs.

Give him hell.

"Enough talk lion. You have nothing to say that could change your fate."

I run at him, raining down blows. To Amun's credit, he lasts longer than I would have anticipated. I can feel it when he starts to get weary, and scared. He's losing, and he knows it. The others dive out of our way as I slam into him, and he goes sliding across the hardwoods, leaving gash marks.

He scrambles to his paws and bolts. I chase after him, but he veers left, running away.

No, not away, he's running toward someone.

Amun leaps on Aggie. The witchling screams as his teeth pull her hair, hauling her across the floor. He stands over her, his teeth just above her neck. I can see the reflection of his tail in the windows behind him as it whips back and forth. Agitated. Cornered.

"You take one more step, and I rip out her throat. No matter how talented the stripper is, she's not invincible. She'll die like any other witch if I take her head."

Aggie whimpers under his paws. Chrys and Hugh start to sneak up on his side, but Amun snarls at them.

"You keep doing that and I'll kill her!"

Now's my shot. He's distracted.

I leap forward.

I trust you, I tell the dragon as I collide with Amun and send us both crashing through the penthouse window.

The head representative yowls like a drowned cat as we fall. I'm holding back a scream myself, and I let a growl loose as one of his claws slices into my arm. We're tumbling over one another.

He manages to sink his claws into my back as we hurtle toward the ground. I try to shake him off, but it's no use.

Talons close over my arms. Nahum.

"You save her, and you have to save me too," Amun yells, grip tightening.

Nahum's purple eyes glow, and fog billows out of his jaws.

"Never," he says.

Amun may have the same glowing bracelet his enforcers had on, but as the fog encases us he starts to scream, and he lets go.

The hulking lion slams into the concrete with enough force to crack it. His mane waves in the night breeze just before he shifts back to his skin.

He's dead.

Nahum sets us down, and I walk over to the head representative. I'm sorely tempted to kick him, but I hold myself back. Barely.

"Long live the king," I drawl.

"Thank the flames you're all right," Nahum breathes, his hands roaming over my arms as he feels for injuries.

"The flames?" I tease. "That's a new one."

"Similar to the moon for you Were and wolf shifter types. I just haven't had anything dire enough to spur me back to religion until now."

I blow out a breath and wave a hand.

"As if that burly old windbag could best me."

"He could have. If one thing had gone wrong," Nahum insists.

"How is it you got around that bracelet?"

Nahum shrugs.

"I decided to pull a Never. I relied on sheer willpower. There was no way I was letting him hurt you."

I put my hands on the dragon's chest.

"Thank you, for saving me."

"Thank you for trusting me to do so," he responds.

"Get them! They killed the head representative!"

Over the top of Nahum's wings I spot figures moving as rage and malice hit me. A group of humans and supernaturals alike, running at us from the Lusca Palms fire escape. I see silver flash as they lift guns. Not again.

"Nahum!" I yell, trying to shove him out of the way. Cracks explode and lines of neon light fill the air. Nahum roars, arms and wings wrapping around us, shielding me. I hear the thuds of impact, and a few bullets tear all the way through the edges of his wings, but I'm covered by the bulk of his body, and none hit me.

The same glowing bullets that took down Brutus. I start to move, but Nahum clutches tighter.

"Multiple rounds," he warns me. Another volley echoes, and I endure feeling Nahum tense, his anger building as round after round of bullets slam into him. The cracks echo in my ears. And then, after the eighteenth round, silence. Nahum's hold loosens, and he staggers.

What have they done?

"It'll be all right. I'll get you help," I insist, determined to go after his attackers. There's at least ten, and while a good half are human, the others are a smattering of Magikai magicals.

Nahum wraps an arm around my wrist, and I realize he's been speaking.

"Never. Never!" I blink up at him. "I'll be fine. Remember. Only one can kill me."

And with that he turns away and stalks over to the others. I don't know how he manages. I can feel his disorientation from the poisons coating the bullets. His back and wings are riddled with holes as the bullets dislodge themselves and he starts to heal.

He doesn't so much as break his stride. When he reaches the first male, he grabs his gun, holding tight.

"You will *not* harm my mate."

I go still at the admission. It's the first time he's uttered the words to anyone outside our circle of friends. The humans' emotions don't change, but the magicals? Their fear ramps up to dizzying heights, hitting me like a monsoon. They know what that means. The lengths Nahum will go to.

He whips his tail out, disarming three more of our attackers and sending the guns skittering toward me.

"You will answer my questions," Nahum states. No one's arguing at this point. "What did you intend for the Were? Were you trying to kill her?"

I'm surprised when I feel and hear them decline. Even the ones who don't answer out loud, I can figure out well enough.

"Were you intending to do something worse? Captivity, torture perhaps?" Nahum questions. I feel the blood drain from my face, skin going clammy as affirmation hits me like a solid wall.

Amun, that unforgivable bastard. I wish I could kill him again. I've been a captive once. It's an experience I have no intention of repeating.

Never, never, never.

And it's not even where I got my name.

Nahum's purple eyes gleam as he looks at me, and I realize he's waiting for a response.

"They were going to *collect* me," I confirm.

He dips his chin.

"That's all I needed to know."

He looks back at the group in front of him, and a few are smart enough to be crying by now. Fog billows from Nahum's jaws, surrounding and engulfing the soldiers.

"Suffer," he says around the smoke. As the screams start, he turns, leaving them.

"My lady." He offers me a claw when he reaches me.

"I'm no lady," I remind him, but I take his claw anyway.

34

When Winning Feels
Like Losing

It's been two weeks since the conclave, and I haven't gotten a single good night's sleep. I slam down my third espresso of the morning, but I don't take any joy from the beverage.

"We've got a meeting set up with the European representatives this morning." Hugh peeks his head around the doorframe of the office. "They were insistent about having it somewhere overseas, but I won them over. Then you have lunch with some of the other enforcers. This afternoon, there's a coven of witches on schedule who are coming to try and locate a few of their sisters who went missing in the last few months. They're hopeful that the witches were among the captives we recovered. Also, you should know that we have an unexpected visitor waiting in the lobby."

I slap myself in the forehead several times in a row.

"Coffee. I need more coffee," I mutter, turning to the fancy espresso machine behind the desk. We're back in Arizona for the time being, and I hate it. I've taken up residence in the air-conditioned representative building, but only until I can get this mess sorted out. I haven't seen my own bed in Sacramento in far too long. Hell, I'd pay good money just to get back to the vamp mansion.

After Amun's little stunt, Casino Vicious wasn't an option. The vamps and some volunteers from the rescued supernaturals are working to rebuild it, but some of the projectiles that hit the building were cursed. It's going to take time. Lusca Palms was another option, but I couldn't get over the idea of cages under the floorboards. And I'm *not* letting my mansion be overrun by people I don't know and don't like.

This was the best of our bad options.

"Whoever it is, Hugh, tell them no. They'll have to wait until I've had a good night's sleep. I'm in no mood for surprises."

I am tired. From lack of sleep, and because I've been forced to play the political princess role for the last couple of weeks. Toppling the standing government leaves a pretty large hole to fill. Who knew? Ever and I have spent hours every day meeting with, and using intuition on, all the remaining representatives. Those who pass are given access to any missing magicals from their territory. But after Lusca Palms, plenty of regions are lacking leadership. And there are lots of leaders who didn't realize those under them were going missing in the first place. It's a mess.

I'm even grumpier, given that all this has separated my group. Nahum's been traveling the globe, reaching out to as many supernatural factions as he can to bring people here to retrieve lost loved ones. Chrys, Lynx, and Todd are doing the same. Aggie's been in a cycle of working herself to the bone and then building up magical stores just to do it all over again. She's had to strip a few individuals who were indeed hiding among our rescued magicals. Rex set his bears on the task of helping some enforcers figure out just how many humans were in on Amun's schemes. Calder and Sky are in Arizona with me, helping to ensure I'm taken seriously by the other representatives.

Hugh clears his throat.

"Do you remember your idea to use Amun's bones? Give them out to the various magical leaders?"

"I do."

I laugh, managing the barest feeling of satisfaction. One of my better ideas. I'm done doing all the dirty work for people. I would have preferred a lion skin rug, but that wasn't possible. Still, no reason Amun couldn't be useful. Every magical leader that's shown up here has been given a bone. It's up to them to go to the Bone Reader and have them interpreted so they can track down anyone from their coven, thunder, flock, or pack who's still missing or on the run. The lion held all the details to his underground network, so the answers are all in him somewhere.

"Yes, well. I think the influx of customers has caught his attention."

"Caught his—"

"Ah, Lady Never. Two house calls in so many weeks. Who would have thought." The Bone Reader sweeps into the room. The temperature drops by several degrees, and I throw on my fur for warmth.

"My residence in Alaska has seen an uptick in business lately, but you already knew that, didn't you?" He's tall, he's short, he's got chiseled cheeks, then soft cherubic ones. It's too early in the day for his dizzying appearance-shifting. I look at the clock. Eight in the morning. Moon preserve us.

"I'd have thought you'd appreciate the customers. So many deals to be made."

He dips his chin while his hair shifts from deep brown to steely grey.

"I am raking in quite a profit, but that's not why I'm here."

"Did you know?" I demand, putting forth my own topic before he can.

The Bone Reader just smiles at me, disconcertingly. He's got square white teeth; he's got pointed vampire canines; he's got a full row of spiny teeth like a deep sea fish. Maybe all of it's true. Maybe none of it is.

"You act as if it was my idea to send you to the Magikai. I might remind you it was your own. And I'm not just talking about now."

I throw up my arms and pull at my fur.

He's right. The first time I ever met the Bone Reader was not long after I'd escaped the Collectors. I was taking the long road from their Isle to where I settled in Sac. On my journey, I stumbled on the Bone Reader's dwelling. A happy accident, as they say. Although it hasn't always been happy.

Fate. A voice inside teases me, and I become hyper aware of the chill of my eyepatch on my cheek.

"But did you know? All this time. Did you know they were keeping other magicals and continuing where the Collectors left off?"

"My dear." The Bone Reader is mere inches away, having moved so fast I didn't even catch it. He reaches out a hand to caress my cheek. Ivory and long-fingered, twisted knuckles, skeletal bone. I freeze. I don't think he's ever touched me like this before.

"I was aware that something untoward was going on with our magical management system, yes. I wasn't privy to every detail, but you must know you're not the only one I've read bones for. How else would I stay in business? I've collected quite a bit myself over the years. Bits of information, along with payments."

"As if you need the money," I huff, and his lips set into a thin line on several different faces that rotate over one another.

"Gauche. Speaking about another's finances openly like that. Really, Never, you typically have better manners."

I blow out a breath and roll my eye.

"Good point," he acknowledges. "You don't. But I'm afraid there's rather more to it than simple financials."

"Someone's speaking like an old-world gentleman. Just how ancient are you, Bone Reader?"

I'm over the line. I know it. But after everything that's transpired, I'd happily blow the line to smithereens.

He wags a finger at me, tapping me on the end of my nose. If he were anyone else, I'd snap it off. What would the finger look like then? Would it keep changing? The thought sends a shiver down even my spine.

"Do you really want to know that? It would cost you." His eyes twinkle in blue, then purple, then amber. "Who has time to track such things? But for the right price, I'd be happy to do the math."

I shake my head. I already know the answer near enough. Old. Ancient. Possibly younger than dirt, and possibly not.

He taps his chin.

"You've been sending an awful lot of supernaturals my way. And then I send them right back out, hunting. For their stolen loved ones, but also those responsible for their capture. Now, just what *are* we going to do with these naughty magicals and humans? *That's* the question."

"I thought you didn't like to directly involve yourself in petty things like the squabbles of all magic-kind," I retort. He savors the sass. I can feel the same satisfaction coming from him as someone who's just taken a bite of something delicious. And maybe that's how attitudes are for him. A savored snack. There are stranger things.

"I can take an interest. When it suits me. And it so happens this does. After all, I've tempered my base nature for the greater good. As have you. It's only fair that everyone else plays by the rules as well."

I don't for one second believe the Bone Reader plays by anyone's rules but his own. That being said ...

"What do you propose we do? We may have taken down Amun and his auction guests, but if anything that's just created a whole new pile of problems. You know that much. And I hope you know what it costs me to admit this, you being obsessed with prices and all, but I can't handle this on my own. I like to hunt down evil and exact justice, not rebuild and restructure a complex ruling system for all supernatural-kind. I'm not strong enough for that," I admit. I'm loathe to say it aloud, but I suspect the Bone Reader is already aware.

Inspiration wraps around me, soft, twisting breezes that lift my limbs and tickle my nose. His eyes gleam.

"Ah, but what if you could be? What if you're the only magical in the world who could be?"

I roll my eye again, slow and dramatic.

"Seriously B.R.? Are you sure *you* wouldn't like to be that magical? For the greater good and all?"

He chuckles, laughing off my comment.

"You do amuse me, Never. But no. Alas, even I have *some* limitations. However rare and troublesome they may be."

His limitations are a curiosity, but they're not what I need to focus on right now.

"What do you suggest we do? Or what do you suggest *I* do, if that's really the case?"

The Bone Reader turns away from me. I'd be insulted if he weren't obviously more powerful. I'd be a fool not to admit it. He reaches into a cloak he's wearing, that turns to a suit, that turns to shifting shadows. He pulls out something, and I feel relief, as if he's reassured himself it's still there. I catch a glimpse of ivory, but as he faces me again the item is gone.

"Play nice with the other representatives for now. Trust your intuition, and the Wereling's. You'll be able to determine well enough who has good intentions. Who's worthy of leading the supernaturals into a better age."

"And when we find those who aren't? Beings in positions of power who don't want to give them up?"

The Bone Reader shrugs.

"Do what you always do, dear. Eliminate them."

One thing I'll give the Bone Reader: he does nothing by halves. Fully committed, that's him.

"Besides, Never, this shouldn't take much longer."

"What won't?"

"Do you recall that at one point I said you'd be so deep into magic you couldn't even fathom? That it would make your eye seem a small loss in comparison to what could be gained?"

I nod, hesitant.

"That time is coming. And, as intrigued as I am at what you are now, I am going to show you how to be something more. Now then, please do ask the representatives to try and space their visits out by at least a day or so. I don't entertain more than one bargain a day, and I'm beginning to amass quite a crowd outside my home. That's all I came to say."

And then he's gone. No fancy billowing smoke. No sparks and lights. Just gone.

"Hugh!" I yell. He runs back in.

"Yes, Never?"

"Is it possible for Weres to take caffeine intravenously? Because I'm going to need it."

In the end, we manage it. It takes over another month, but we get the job done. At the very least, we've put together the groundwork. No head representative, for one. And no one sneaking their own business under the table. All the representatives from the different species get a say, and they're all on committees. And not ones they chose themselves, full of their friends and closest neighbors. Ones with people who will keep them accountable.

"I still don't like her, but I won't kill her," Ever vows in regards to Sky. My Were protégé has decided that, for the moment, she'd rather work as a representative in training than an enforcer in training. "I don't know if this is what I want, either, but I'd like to be done killing for now. And I can split my time between Arizona and Colombia," she informs us all.

After our weeks of work, it's nice to have everyone back at the vamp mansion for dinner.

"Don't worry, I'll keep an eye on her," Ji-hwan whispers as Ever goes on about her new position to Todd and Lynx. The spotted Were has also chosen to stay on, although he's planning to head up enforcer recruitment.

"A more transparent process. And a focus on real, applicable skills. Not training people to act as unquestioning hitmen for whichever representative snatches them up," he promises.

"Lynx, Todd, what about you two? Going to stop your carefree, freelance ways and sign up full time?" I call across the table. They just burst into laughter, not even entertaining the idea.

"What'd she say this time?" Elios questions as he walks in with a tray of sparkling drinks. Some are silver, some gold, and some the shining white of stars. I'm about to be on my third round, so I already know they're delectable.

"She's trying to recruit us!" Lynx laughs.

"What about you, witch? Are you going with the Were, or with us?" Rex turns to Aggie.

"I think I'd prefer to stay here at the mansion. But I'm more than happy to keep helping with your, um, situation."

I wave a knife at her.

"One day, witchling, you're going to have to let me in on all this work with the bears."

I'm in my office with Hugh after dinner, going over vampire paperwork, when Ever knocks on the door. I set down the stack of papers. Hugh took me seriously, and he did give all my vamps a survey. A surprising number of them are more than happy staying at the casino, now that it's back up and running. We've also acquired Lusca Palms, recently redubbed Revolution. A gift to me from the remaining representatives, for all the trouble Amun put me through. With ownership shares for my friends, of course.

Ever stares at me, then at Hugh, worrying her bottom lip.

"I'll just, um, go check some paperwork," Hugh states as he exits. I wave an arm.

"Come on in. Grab a chair."

Ever paces instead. She's carrying a small bag with her.

"Never. I wanted to thank you. For rescuing me. For teaching me. I hope you know that my choosing not to be an enforcer doesn't mean I disapprove of you. But I want to be my own magical. I don't know how to say this without being rude, but—"

"You don't want to be like me? Hunting people down and ripping their heads off? 'S all right, I kind of figured. No offense taken."

Relief washes over her as she plops into a chair.

"What will you be doing?" she asks.

"Well, on Halloween I've got a date. Before that, I plan to take a nice long vacation back to my own house in Sacramento. And show a certain dragon the very best sights of California. And if we get bored we might even leave the house." I chuckle at my own joke.

"I'm going back to Arizona tomorrow, but I wanted to give you something. For safekeeping, and just to keep in general." Ever reaches into the bag and pulls out the magenta somson orb.

I whistle.

"Do the winged ones know you have that?"

She nods.

"Sky told me to keep it. As an apology for trying to crack my skull open. But I don't want it. I mean, I wanted the apology, and I know the situation was complicated. She thought we were working for Amun. We'd have done the same thing to her if the situations were reversed. I mean, *we* wouldn't have. You know, because our intuition would have told us whose side she was on, but even so. I appreciate it, it's just that ... ugh, I'm messing this up."

I reach a hand out, placing it over hers and the orb.

"You may have accepted the apology, but that doesn't mean you like her. You don't have to. And you took the orb for the sake of being polite, but you don't want it."

"Exactly. I don't want this thing anywhere near me. I almost died to get it, and it's meaningless to me. I know it's supposed to be some hyper-powerful object, but I don't care. I know you've got one in your office, though, and I thought, maybe you'd like it."

She holds the orb out, and I take it. I set it on a shelf next to the blue one Hugh brought back from the Isle. They both glow a bit brighter.

"I'll keep it safe," I promise.

"Thanks, Never. *Tenga cuidado y no se valla a meter en problemas. Me llama si necesita algo.*"

I can't help but laugh at that. Stay out of trouble? I'm pretty sure I'm walking into the middle of a mess, but that's a me-problem.

"I'll reach out if I need anything," I promise.

"And Never?"

"Hmm?"

"I think I'll go back to Nadia now, if it's all the same to you."

"All right, Nadia."

Epilogue
Who Else Indeed

"You're sure you don't want me to go along as backup?" Nahum offers again.

I turn in the dragon's arms, placing my hands on his chest.

"I'll reach out at the first sign of trouble," I promise. "Well. Maybe not the first sign. But I'll contact you if I really need help," I amend. I lean down and nip his bottom lip. "Trust me."

He gives a wicked smile before flipping me under the sheets.

"I do trust you; I just know you have a propensity for danger."

He's not wrong, but I'm not giving in so easily.

"I do not! It's just everyone else around me that insists on causing issues. And the problems I track down. And the situations I involve myself in. And the deals I make."

He laughs at me.

"Mischievous Were."

"I'll show you mischievous."

"Do you have the time?" Nahum asks, looking around for a clock. I just stare at the window, checking the level of the sun. I've got a good few hours before I need to meet the Bone Reader, and the pick-up location he gave me is only a couple of hours out of town.

"The Bone Reader can wait."

A few hours later, not late but barely on time, I'm speeding down a country road in northern California. Through one of those barren, empty areas tourists sometimes forget we have. The moon is full overhead. A perfect Halloween night.

I'm blasting loud music that almost drowns out the sound of the GPS telling me where to go. The Bone Reader had better be okay with a margin of error. After all, this machine is accurate within a few hundred yards, but not to an exact tree.

I slow down as the GPS destination marker gets closer.

"Continue straight for one mile. Continue straight for three-quarters of a mile. Continue straight for—" I shut the voice off and bring the car to a crawl.

I lean forward in the seat, scanning the dark for any sign of the Bone Reader. There's nothing to see but barren stretches of road and trees.

"Oh, good, you managed to be on time."

I jump, my foot slamming the gas pedal and sending the car lurching forward. In the passenger seat of my sports car, the Bone Reader throws out hands to catch himself on the dash. Ivory pale, summer tan.

"Careful!" he hisses at me.

"Wear a seatbelt!" I counter. "And don't sneak up on me like that!"

"It hardly counts as sneaking when you were told to expect me," the Bone Reader argues, straightening the cuffs on a collared shirt, which turns just as quickly into a long robe.

I blow out a breath in exasperation.

"As wonderful as it is to see you, you'll understand that I've been enjoying my time off. Now, I pay what I owe, but I'm a busy Were. So whatever this deal entails, let's get on with it, shall we?"

He smiles at me.

"You couldn't be more right. We've got lots to accomplish. We should get going."

I sit, staring at him as the silence grows.

"Well?"

"Well what?" He blinks his eyes at me, the colors cycling.

"The deal. You told me to pick you up, take you somewhere, accept a gift from you, and et cetera et cetera. I only have the details for step one."

"Ah, yes. Quite. We'll get to all that. But we have to begin at the beginning."

Cryptic, ancient, secret-keeping, deal-making, confusion-causing supernatural.

"Then this whole thing, where do we start?"

He reaches into a pocket and pulls out a thin ivory box. The same one he held in my office back in Arizona. His features shift, but his expression stays the same as he looks at me. A smile, lit by the moon behind him and chilling in the dark.

"We start where all good stories start. With a murder."

Acknowledgements & Upcoming

I want to say a HUGE thank you to all the readers of this series. I love to write, and I especially love writing Never and her friends. It means more than I can say that there are so many people who have joined Never and crew on these adventures. It's been so much fun connecting with people.

If you did enjoy this book, and are able, I would be very grateful if you could leave a review or rating. Each review makes a huge difference to authors, and helps other readers find the same books you loved. I would truly appreciate it, and it helps inspire me to keep writing!

"Never More" will be the next book in the Shifter Vengeance series. You can pre-order it now, or add it to your wish list.

To keep up with updates on Never and be the first to hear about new books you can connect with me here:

Instagram: @reameswrites

Facebook: Silas Reames-Author or Never's specific group "Never's Vengeance Vixens"

Newsletter: nightlochpublishers.com

About the Author

Silas has long been a lover of all things reading. If you lose track of her in a bookstore, you're responsible for the pile of new reads she'll carry out.

When not writing or reading while drinking what might well be considered too much caffeine, she can often be found swimming or spending time with her husband and dogs.

Read more at nightlochpublishers.com/silas-reames.

www.ingramcontent.com/pod-product-compliance
Lightning Source LLC
Chambersburg PA
CBHW021005260626
47169CB00006B/1960